Huda Suroor

AL YAAH

Austin Macauley Publishers™
LONDON * CAMBRIDGE * NEW YORK * SHARJAH

Copyright © Huda Suroor 2023

The right of Huda Suroor to be identified as author of this work has been asserted by the author in accordance with Federal Law No. (7) of UAE, Year 2002, Concerning Copyrights and Neighboring Rights.

All rights reserved. No part of this publication may be reproduced, stored in a retrieval system, or transmitted in any form or by any means, electronic, mechanical, photocopying, recording, or otherwise, without the prior permission of the publishers.

Any person who commits any unauthorized act in relation to this publication may be liable to legal prosecution and civil claim for damages.

This is a work of fiction. Names, characters, businesses, places, events, locales, and incidents are either the products of the author's imagination or used in a fictitious manner. Any resemblance to actual persons, living or dead, or actual events is purely coincidental.

The age group that matches the content of the books has been classified according to the age classification system issued by the Ministry of Culture and Youth.

ISBN – 9789948778226 – (Paperback)
ISBN – 9789948778233 – (E-Book)

Application Number: MC-10-01-9294302
Age Classification: 13+

Printer Name: iPrint Global Ltd
Printer Address: Witchford, England

First Published 2023
AUSTIN MACAULEY PUBLISHERS FZE
Sharjah Publishing City
P.O Box [519201]
Sharjah, UAE
www.austinmacauley.ae
+971 655 95 202

(1)

Mansour married his cousin Meriem, one of the most beautiful girls in the village – almost brown-colored skin, medium height, long black hair with large waves, a round face with soft features, full cheeks adorned with redness, two sparkling eyes with long, thin eyebrows that almost met above the nose, and a small nose drawn with precision. Mansour won her hand in marriage after a long and fierce competition with his other cousin Mutaib who also wished to marry her. Both of them proposed to her father, Hajj Mubarak, who was unable to decide which one to give her to, so he left the decision to his daughter, who chose Mansour as her husband because of the love she had for him in her heart.

Mansour was a young man of eighteen years. Ever since he was a child, he was known for his courage, generosity, and kindness. He learned the Quran from the religious teacher Halima and memorized some parts and interpretations of it. As he grew up, he turned to the sea and worked in fishing, diving for pearls, repairing wooden ships, and sailing for trade, as the sea was the destination for work and the source of livelihood for most men in the Gulf region in the past.

Mansour helped his father provide for the house and his four sisters, as he was the only male son of his family. His income from the sea was abundant, while his father gave up working in the sea due to his old age; he left it for his son and turned to raising and trading livestock. Meriem was the love of Mansour's life and his eternal dream, which followed him since childhood. He married her after his four sisters settled in their husbands' houses, and they consummated their marriage in the house he had built after saving for years from his long work.

Mansour's parents held a celebration of seven nights reveling in chanting, singing, and extended tables, which were only raised when replaced by other full tables. Every day of the seven nights, four sheep were slaughtered at noon. All people ate until they were full, both relatives and strangers. On the first, second, third, and fourth days, a banquet was held for the invitees. The celebration was led by folk bands of Al-Yowla and Al-Ayyala with traditional folk songs and dances.

On the fifth day, Mansour's mother sent "Al-Zahba", the bride's dowry, which was carried on the backs of twenty donkeys in two stages, filled with some boxes of the bride's clothing. The clothing included "Kandoura" and "Jalabiya" which are traditional dresses made of various fabrics, decorated with some embroidery or colorful ribbons known as "Tally". Also included were "Jalbab", a wide cloak worn over the Kandoura and made of a lightweight fabric to cover it, decorated with some embroidery or colorful ribbons on the chest area, "Shayla", a head covering made of black cotton fabric adorned with silver or gold threads, and "Abaya", a silky body cover made of black fabric, interwoven with some "Breesim" threads and silver or gold threads.

She also sent boxes containing incense, sandalwood, oud, concentrated oil perfumes, rose water, musk, amber, shoes, sandals, makeup tools such as "Deeram" (wooden lipstick), "Athmad" (kohl powder), "Sray" (black kohl paste), henna, perfumed Shabba powder, imported body powder, dried seder leaves powder used for hair washing, Nile pellets (a skin cleaning substance), imported soap cubes, jasmine oil for hair, hair combs, hair accessories, boxes of silver and gold jewelry, as well as other boxes containing different pieces of fabric, which are up to the bride to keep for the future or distribute to her relatives and friends.

On the sixth day, the henna day was held, where Al-Zahba, (the bride's dowry) was presented to the bride and the invitees, and the palms of the hands and feet of the bride were dyed with henna.

On the seventh day, the marriage took place and Mansour took his bride to his home.

(2)

Mansour was very happy to have Meriem, so all her demands were answered. He loved her as people do in old tales, he thrived to make her happy at all times, for she was the light that lightened his life and he never loved anyone else, she was the present, past, and future. She was the main reason for his happiness; she also loved him and was faithful to him just as much. She could not stand being away from him and was not happy unless she was with him.

His daily working hours at sea were reduced, and he didn't care about earning money after being granted his wish. Only a little was enough for him and his beloved. They lived happily and spent the first seven months of their marriage in the bliss of love and passion.

One day, Meriem was inflicted with a fever that put her to bed. She was weak and sick, unable to move, and the disease worsened, causing her legs to be paralyzed. It was said that she was inflicted by the evil eye of a neighbor who came to visit and got to know her for the first time. As soon as the neighbor left, Meriem felt a strong headache that spread to her head, and then she was hit by a fever that led to weakness in her body and paralysis in her legs.

Mansour remained by her side, taking care of her, changing her clothes, bathing her, soothing her, combing her hair, trimming her nails, cooking food, and feeding her himself.

He took care of her and nursed her tirelessly and without disgust, treating her like a sick child. Someone told him that Meriem needed treatment, not just medicine, and he didn't waste their advice. He brought healers from all over the country and nearby cities, each of whom diagnosed her with a different illness. They didn't agree on a single opinion, and the many drugs and diverse herbs they prescribed, only made her weaker. One of them suggested that he bring in an ironer to see if she needed ironing or not, so he did.

The ironer examined her and decided that she needed to be ironed at the back of her neck and the top of her head. He ironed her, took his fee, and left. That night, Meriem suffered greatly from both the burning of the ironing and the illness. The next day, her moaning and pain increased. His father suggested to him to perform cupping therapy on her to relieve her body of the pain and toxins so that she might feel better. He did so and sent for the female cupper who performed the cupping therapy for her. Afterward, Meriem felt relieved, slept peacefully, and the headache stopped for a week, but weakness and fatigue remained with her. Nevertheless, she became better and was able to talk to her husband and family, laugh, and participate in their conversations and chats. After a week, the headache returned with intensity, and everyone was at a loss as to what to do about this disease. They tried giving her water from the Quranic recitation which the volunteer Halima had prepared for her, and it eased her pain, but weakness remained with her, and her condition lasted like that for two years.

One morning, Mansour woke up to see that his wife was not next to him. He was surprised as she was unable to move and had been paralyzed for over two years. As soon as he got up from the bed, he was shocked to see her standing on her own two feet in front of him, in complete health, her face radiating with vitality and wellness. His face lit up with joy, and he leaped to her, not believing what he was seeing.

'Mashallah … Mashallah … Are you well, my beloved?'

'Praise be to Allah … Allah has healed me.'

'A thousand thanks and praise to you, my Lord. We will hold a great feast and feed everyone, the poor before the rich, the enemy before the beloved, and I will make everyone pray for your good health and long life.'

'Insha'Allah.'

Mansour's heart was filled with joy, and he could not contain himself from the intensity of his happiness.

'What … what do you want me to do now?'

'Now?'

'Yes, now …'

'I want to get rid of the effects of this sickness that set us apart. I want you to fetch some water from the well for me, and heat it so I can take a shower. I want to shower to pray first …'

'Sure … gladly.'

Mansour ran to the well, drew water, and placed it in the Zeweya (a room for changing clothes and bathing) in a large container on a small gas stove to heat the water. He hung her clothes there and told her that he would go out to inform her family of her recovery and would bring two lambs for them to slaughter as a form of praise to Allah Almighty.

Mansour rushed out of the house to the house of his uncle, Meriem's father, to tell them the good news. Then he went to his father's house to inform his family and take two lambs from his father's pen. He then headed to the market to buy sweets and pastries to distribute to neighbors, family, and children.

He returned to his house, and when he entered the courtyard of the house, he smelled the delicious hot Bajela and Dango (fava beans and chickpeas) that she had just prepared. It came down on him holding the glad tidings of the joy that descended from the sky, in addition to the scent of the baked bread in the oven, and the coffee that Meriem had prepared with saffron.

He was very happy, but he wondered to himself how much time and effort did it take her to prepare all this food as if she was preparing a feast for the family who would now attend?

He searched for her and found her praying in the room, her pleasant fragrance and the scent of incense filled the place. He wanted to hold her in his arms and kiss her, but she was still praying. He missed her so much and longed for her. Two years had passed, but it seemed like she had been gone for twenty years, and now she was in front of him, praying with all her health. She looked beautiful, strong, and full of energy. He noticed the cleanliness, warmth of the place, and the light that invaded it, a feeling of comfort that he had missed and had not felt ever since she got ill and remained in bed.

He went back to the yard and heard a knocking on the door. He stood up and opened the door to find his wife's family, her father, mother, brothers, and sisters. Their faces shone with happiness and their mouths congratulated him as if it were their second wedding. Everyone was happy. They all sat in the courtyard on the ground around the circular table prepared for eating, waiting for Meriem to finish her prayers so they could greet her and Praise be to Allah for the blessings he bestowed upon her.

Hajj Mubarak, Meriem's father, asked: 'Mansour, did you bring those two sheep?'

'Yes, I brought them to sacrifice them in thanks to Allah for his blessings.'

'May Allah bless you, my son. When will you slaughter them?'

'Right now. I also need your help.'

'Sure, no problem, but Meriem must see them and touch their backs with her hands.'

'As soon as she finishes her prayers, we will sacrifice them.'

'We want to enjoy this delicious breakfast. Did you buy it from the baker, my son?'

'No, uncle. I found it like this when I returned home. She had prepared it herself.'

'Masha'Allah, Masha'Allah.'

'Please, come and have some food.'

'Yes, please, go ahead and eat. I will go and bring my beloved daughter. She has been delayed, as always, because of her long prayers.'

Merah, Meriem's younger sister, interrupted her mother's sentence and said: 'No, we will not eat until Meriem comes.'

'Okay, I will go and hurry her up.'

'But I am hungry, my daughter.'

'Wait, Father, wait a little bit. You never have patience when it comes to food.'

'Can you hear the sounds of my stomach growling from hunger?'

'Wait a little bit, Father!'

'Just one bite to silence my hunger.'

'Not even a bite, Father!'

Suddenly, everyone was startled by the sound of the mother's screams: 'Meriem, Meriem, oh my dear!'

Everyone ran into the room to see Meriem laying on her mother's lap … her face was radiant and the blush that had covered her face for the length of the last prayer, her eyes closed as if she was a sleeping bride … but now she had become soulless …

(3)

Mansour suffered greatly from Meriem's illness, and he certainly believed in Allah's decree. She was so sick that he feared this could happen to her at any moment. However, he did not diminish his efforts to treat and nurse her until the end. Because of his great love for her, he continued to pray for her healing and worked toward it with all the resources he had.

Meriem died, the disease disappeared, and the pain went away. The style of his prayers for her changed from asking for her well-being to praying for her mercy. The hope was shattered in moments that proceeded the happy and bright moments, but unfortunately, they were just moments. Her recovery on that day reignited the flame of hope in him, lighting up the temples of love and hope. In those hours of happiness, he had forgotten all the miserable years and nights of sickness, every time he cried in sadness for her, the times he panicked for her, the holidays he isolated himself to stay by her side. He forgot every painful memory, and his memory was only occupied by her face in the morning. On the day of her death, her peaceful expression and liberated voice from the constraints of illness and pain were the false and deceitful awakening, the fake awakening of death.

With her death, his existence was torn apart, and his pieces were lost in the folds of the days of union. His essence vanished, and his body remained as ruins, proving to existence that its owner had a beating heart but no soul. Mansour remained human remains, staying in Meriem's room, embracing her clothes. If he went out, he would go to her grave to seek solace in her proximity and complain about his condition after her. It was said that he was seen digging her grave more than three times, trying to extract her "just to see her", this is what he told people who prevented him and expelled him from the cemetery, leaving him outside and closing the gate before his face. He would cry and call her name as if she could hear him and answer his call until everyone agreed that he had gone crazy, as he lost his mind after her death.

When the elders of his tribe and family gathered to advise him, his response to them was: 'My beloved recovered completely from the chronic illness and was very happy, then she died in moments, I am certain that my joy killed her.'

He became known as the madman, walking the streets with his long-disheveled beard, messy hair, and tattered dirty clothes. Young children ran after him, calling him crazy as his condition worsened. He abandoned his work and activities and didn't care about his food and drink.

He would lie on the clean warm scented bed, waiting for her to come to him and lie next to him, as if it were their wedding night. She would approach him, lay her head on his chest, and he would embrace her, shivering at the moisture of her breath, and then they would sink into a deep sleep. He would wake up afterward to find himself alone in that cold dirty bed.

He would sit near the well, waiting for her to finish filling the water jug so he could help her carry it back to the house. He drew lines and circles in the sand and wandered in his thoughts, jumping up with excitement when she called him to help her, carrying the water and running to the corner to put it in its place … but it was only the remains of that old love in his hands.

He would wake up hungry, and she would come to him with a hot plate of "Arasiyah" (rice paste boiled with light chicken slices), and he would take a big hot bite, and scream as the heat burned his tongue, while she laughed with a burst of joyous laughter that made him happy … and then he would suddenly find himself holding an old empty plate covered in rust and dust.

He remained in that state for a whole year, and when the blessed month of Ramadan arrived, the people of the village spread out a mat made of palm fronds in the inner courtyard of the village and arranged pillows and blankets on its sides, and covered it with a roof made of palm fronds and reeds. This Ramadan gathering was set up every year, where the people of the village would gather and sometimes have their iftar and suhoor meals, which the women would prepare. Each woman would send her husband or son's share of food, which would be collected and served on a large extended table. Mansour's father was one of the most important men in the village, and his presence was essential, but due to his son's poor condition and his mental deterioration, he did not attend the Ramadan gathering that year.

During one of the Ramadan evenings, while Mansour's father was present at the gathering and meeting with the villagers, one of the men suggested that Mansour's father take him and travel with him to the Holy Kaaba in Mecca to be treated with prophetic medicine there, and then they would perform the Umrah rituals in Medina, so that his heart would be relieved, and he would return to his senses and become as he was before, the best and most respected of the young men in the village.

The suggestion was welcomed by Mansour's father and the villagers, and after the twentieth night of Ramadan, Mansour, his father, and his brother-in-law traveled by sea to the Kingdom of Saudi Arabia and stayed there until the month of Dhul-Hijjah to perform the Hajj pilgrimage. During that period, his father would take him to preachers and imams who blessed him and prayed for his recovery, treated him with prophetic medicine, recited the Quran to him, and gave him Zamzam water. They also urged him to perform the Tawaf (circumambulation) of the Kaaba, pray on time, maintain cleanliness, and read the Quran until he returned to his senses and was healed. He became convinced and believed that Meriem's death was only by the will of Allah, the Almighty, and that her time had come.

(4)

They brought Mansour back, healed, to his hometown, family, and the house where he grew up. His father asked him to go back to his job and sell the house where he lived with Meriem to cut off painful memories. Following his father's wish, Mansour sold the house and bought a large piece of land for his father. He lived his life as he did four years ago, without a wife, and now without a dream.

He spent his entire day at sea and returned home after dark only to sleep. His family insisted on him getting married, but he refused the matter completely. His mother even planned many tricks that could make Mansour change his mind. She planned for him to have pre-arranged meetings with beautiful girls from the family. For example, a girl would come to visit Mansour's mother, and she would know in advance that he would be at home at that time. When someone knocked on the door, Mansour would go to open it.

Or when he returned from work in the evening, he found the house full of women visiting his mother, along with their beautiful daughters. His mother would call him to greet them; among them would be the girl who could steal his heart.

Sometimes, she would send something with him to one of the family's houses, and one of the marriage candidates would open the door for him.

His poor mother followed all the tricks, plans, and measures on many occasions to make him want to get married again. But he was not affected by any plan or trick. In short, he was not moved by the beauty or grace of the girls. He became like a stone, devoid of feelings. Only Meriem and her memories, he did not want anyone else to share his heart.

After a year, and after connecting all houses and other facilities in the seven emirates to electricity generators, the Dubai government established a special maritime force called the Coast Guard. It requested that young citizens of the country join this force, and a group of young men from the village, including Mansour, applied for these military positions which are characterized by a fixed monthly salary and some benefits for him and his family. Young people were delighted with this news and headed to the command center in Dubai to undergo the necessary medical tests, attend the military training course, and start working. For them, traveling to Dubai was considered a long journey in those days.

The work involved joining a military group consisting of military battalions. Each battalion is composed of a unit, and each unit guards a specific coastal area, with two morning and evening shifts. The young men who traveled to Dubai had to find a housing unit close to their work. Mansour was assigned to guard a remote coastal area with few inhabitants on the southern border of Dubai, where there were only a few scattered houses due to the scarcity of population in that area. He searched for a good house consisting of two rooms, the first being the living room with a bedroom, a showering corner (bathroom), a toilet, and the second building with a kitchen, a small store, a corner, a bathroom, and a large sandy courtyard with a water well and a ladder leading to the roof of the house.

The house that Mansour rented was located at the end of the sandy area and the beginning of the rocky area, meaning that it was a few meters away from the beach. The house bordered the coastal sandy area, as it was located at the end of it and the beginning of the rocky area. It was the last house in this isolated area, and it was said that it was once inhabited by one of the smugglers who used to smuggle jewelry and gold from one shore to another, and his identity or nationality was unknown until he fled one day before being caught.

Originally, Mansour was from the northern areas (Al-Fujairah city), which was far away from his house and workplace, and his current neighbors were his colleagues who came to work with him. Their houses were not attached to his house but rather were scattered and distant from each other. Mansour spent his day starting with his work if his shift as a guard was in the morning, and when he returned home, he would finish his household chores such as cooking, sweeping, laundry, extracting water from the well, and filling the tanks in his house for daily use. As for drinking water, he used to buy it from the water seller (the man who sells drinking water, usually carrying the water in a large circular tank with wheels and a faucet that is pulled by a mule, and he visits the houses, shops, and restaurants in the area until his tank runs out of water. This water seller visits each area once or twice a week to sell water to houses, shops, and restaurants).

If he wanted to invite his friends over for a meal, he would go to the market in the center of the city to buy chicken, vegetables, and meat, while he would get fish from his workplace where the fishermen sell fresh fish at a low price. At other times, he would go out with his friends and they would travel long distances on bicycles or take passing cars to go to the coffee shop in the city center to enjoy some entertaining times with the youth and play games like cards and dominoes, and have some famous foods such as "harris" (mashed wheat), "samosa", fried pastries, boiled grains, hot drinks like tea, coffee, thyme syrup, milk with saffron, and milk with ginger, and cold drinks like soda, "falooda", and "sherbet".

During the monthly vacations, which are ten days after every twenty days of work, they would travel to their homes and families by public transport. Mansour would give his entire monthly salary to his father who would save it for him, and he would also give him a quarter to cover his expenses on food, drink, travel, and rent for the rented house and his daily life in Dubai.

Every time Mansour visited his family, his mother would bring up the topic of marriage and continuously insist, saying:

'My dear, isn't it time to get married? I want to see your children before I die.'

'Don't say that, may Allah protect and care for you, Mom.'

'And how do you know? Life isn't what it used to be … Your sisters, Allah bless them, got married and are enjoying happiness and stability with their families, their children are growing up, and you are still as you are.'

'Praise be to Allah; you and Dad have grandchildren that you cherish and enjoy.'

Then the father intervened saying: 'What's this talk, my son? You are the origin, your offspring who will carry my name.'

'Insha'Allah, Father, may Allah bring forth what is good.'

The mother sensed a softness in Mansour's words and hastened to say: 'Praise be to Allah, my beloved, but what do you say? Please make me happy and warm my heart.'

'My dear mother, I now want to adapt to the remote isolation in which I live. Moreover, my work hours are very long, and the neighborhood I live in has only a few houses, with each house far from the other. Also, I cannot get married; I do not want any woman to enter my life and snatch Meriem and her memories from my heart and mind. I do not want to be distracted by another woman.'

Then the father said: 'May Allah guide you, my son. Your late wife departed to the afterlife. She is with Allah's mercy.'

'I know, Father, but I do not desire to get married. Please leave me alone.'

The mother said to him: 'Isn't your business our business, my son?'

(5)

On a cold November night, Mansour had taken over the guard duty, accompanied by two of his close friends. The three friends sat chatting and drinking tea.

Ali said: 'Do you know, my friends, that I've decided to get married?'

Saeed: 'What do you mean? But you're married and a father of four children.'

'I know. But I'm alone here in this isolated area, and I've given up on my wife coming to live with me here with the children. I've begged her repeatedly, but she strongly refuses. And honestly, I can't bear to live alone in this desolate and freezing place as you can see … I want a wife to be with me here to ease my loneliness and to take care of my needs.'

'Yes, you're right. The place is desolate and isolated here.'

'That's why my wife allowed me to marry another woman, on the condition that I never see her or meet her anywhere. She doesn't want to leave her home, her family, and her neighborhood to come here.'

'And my wife doesn't want to come here either. She says it's a scary place. I brought her here two months ago, and she said it's an isolated and scary place, and she won't be able to live here. She even asked me to quit my job and go back home. What can I do? I can't do anything.'

'How can you not do anything? Did you forget that you're a man? You should ask her permission to marry someone else, just like me. Your wife doesn't want to come here, right?'

'What? Ask Um Aboud for permission to marry someone else. I swear to Allah, if she found out that I'm considering marrying someone else, she might … You don't know her. She's the dominant force in the house.'

'Come on, man. What can she do? She might get angry for a while, but then she'll return to her normal self. Who knows, maybe she'll love you more. Listen to me and ask for her permission, or else you'll stay alone here like a bachelor.'

'Do you know what I intend to do? I'm going to get married and not tell her, and she in turn will not know or feel anything.'

'Really? Then let's look for halal girls.'

'Yes.'

'Oh, yes, I remembered … Have you heard this news? Our colleague, the warehouse supervisor Hassan, told me that a group of his friends returned from India after spending their vacations there, but the main reason for their trip to India was … do you know why?'

'Why?'

'It is said that each of them returned to marry an Indian girl, all of them beautiful and quiet, who do not speak and do not express themselves verbally because they originally do not know Arabic. They are easy to deal with, and if they want to say anything, they won't be able to, and if they say something, you won't understand them because they don't understand your language, nor do you understand theirs. Life with them will be peaceful, as they are poor girls who are satisfied with what you give them and will not increase their demands or expenses. In addition, they are skilled cooks who prepare delicious and spicy Indian food.'

'This is not news to me, I have heard it before, but now I have confirmed it with you, and I want to follow in their footsteps. What do you think? Shall we submit vacation requests for the three of us and travel to India to get married according to the way Allah and His Messenger permitted, and return with them so that we do not remain alone in this isolation on earth? But wait … are the girls Muslim or Hindu?'

'They are Muslims, my brother.'

'Praise be to Allah, then let's depend on Allah.'

They turned to Mansour, who was absent-minded, with his hands stretched out for warmth in front of the flames they lit for making tea, and asked him: 'What's wrong with you today? You haven't said a word or told us your opinion.'

He smiled lightly and said: 'You both know what I will say if I speak.'

'You don't argue now, we won't leave you. You will travel with us and get married just like us.'

'The travel plan is good. I will travel with you to see the land of India that I've heard about but never had the chance to visit even during the days of travel and maritime trade. However, the issue of marriage is not something that I want to discuss here. I beg and implore you not to bring it up in my presence. I am traveling to ease my distress, but I ask you not to discuss this matter in front of me.'

Ali felt sympathy for Mansour's state of misery and said: 'What's wrong with you, brother? Why are you harming yourself and your family in this way? This is the way of life. Life does not stop with the death of loved ones, which is the fate of all creatures. It only lasts as long as Allah wills. If the deceased knew what you were doing to yourself and your family, she would be upset. You have erased your life and stopped it. Get married, brother. Marry a good woman who will bear children for you and who will carry your name and your father's name. Have you forgotten that you are his only son who must continue his lineage? So, marry a woman who will accompany and enlighten your life. What do you say?'

Mansour felt remorse for causing his parents misery and for his circumstances, but Meriem was his first and last love. How could he let her go like this?

He bowed his head in sadness and said: 'I don't know what to say. I'm speechless.'

Saeed: 'Don't say anything, just rely on Allah.'

Mansour: 'We relied on Allah in the matter of travel, but I want you to promise me that you will never bring up the subject of my marriage again. I will never get married.'

Ali: 'It's up to your Lord to make it easy for you, brother. Just come with us.'

(6)

The three submitted their vacation request to the center for 30 days and started preparing to travel to India, specifically to the city of Hyderabad. They searched for someone to guide them on how to travel and reach their destination and found a man named Musbah Al-Muqawil (the person who receives cash commission from men to handle all their travel-related affairs, such as processing visas, bonds, travel tickets, accommodation in India, and also searches for Indian Muslim women who wish to marry Arabs to travel with them abroad and send financial aid to their poor families).

The contractor Musbah asked each of them for their passport and a sum of 200 rupees to process the visa and ticket, and his commission was 2000 rupees for each of them, in addition to travel expenses, hotel, and food. Ali borrowed a good amount of money from one of his relatives, and Saeed also borrowed money from his brothers, while Mansour did not need to borrow it because his father saved three-quarters of his monthly salary for him.

The contractor Musbah took their passports and money, and when he finished the procedures for booking travel and accommodation, he asked them to prepare and buy colorful clothes such as trousers, shirts, large bags, shoes, socks, and perfume bottles, and to leave their Arab clothing so that poor Indians would not desire them. Everyone prepared for the marriage trip except for Mansour, who did not even consider the idea of marriage. His preparation was only for the trip because travel would create an opportunity for him to relax and experience something new, and visit another land and other people.

It was the first time they had ridden the modern ship "Tara", which carried passengers to and from India. The three of them boarded with the contractor and were at the peak of happiness and the highest degree of fear and astonishment.

They arrived in the city of Bombay after a long journey that took them four days of sailing on a ship, from which they took a taxi to the train station and then boarded the train to the city of Hyderabad on a 20-hour journey. The train stopped at the city stations every two hours for 10 minutes so that the passengers could buy what they wanted from the station, such as food, drinks, newspapers, and tools. They saw the magnificent sights of the towering green mountains, waterfalls, dense forests, and wide rice fields in valleys and highlands, as well as the fruitful coconut trees that stretched over vast areas, and the many colorful Hindu temples that attracted attention. At each station, they would get off the train to see the place, the people, the different food carts, the large movie ads displayed on the roads, and the way of life in a country other than their own.

The smell and coolness of dawn and the mixed spices with the scent of the place's breath carried the scent of Indian incense, burning distant woods, and dust that had just been moistened by light rain showers. The sights and feelings were unfamiliar to them. They spent the first ten hours as spectators, enjoying the scenery, and the last ten hours sleeping in the train carriage.

'Get up … get up now … Ali, Mansour, and Saeed wake up, we have arrived.'

They got up to the sounds of train horns and whistles, and the contractor's voice, Musbah, opened the window and shouted: 'Coolie … coolie …' calling for the porter to carry their bags and luggage.

They got off the train and left the station, then boarded three horse-drawn carts (small wooden carts with a movable circular canopy that the driver pulls behind his bicycle). A cart was taken by the contractor, Musbah, with some of his luggage, the second cart that Saeed took with the rest of his luggage, and a cart that Mansour and Ali rode on. After a long arduous journey, they arrived at the hotel in which the contractor decided to stay; exhaustion and fatigue took their toll.

The luggage was moved to the next room and each one of them headed to his room to get some rest. It was past midnight and they had to get up early to start searching for a wife the next morning so that time would be used wisely.

(7)

In the morning, the three prepared to go out in their new clothes (pants, shirt, and shiny new shoes). The waiter brought them traditional Indian breakfast, which they had never tasted before yet enjoyed.

Contractor Musbah was waiting for them in the hotel lobby, and two rickshaws were waiting outside to take them to their destination. Along the way, Musbah introduced them to the city of Hyderabad, with its roads, ancient ruins, Ottoman-Turkish colonial buildings, alleys, restaurants, shops, and tombs, a mix of Ottoman and Indian cultures intertwined with each other.

Then they arrived at a street that was full of alleys. The rickshaws could not climb up the steep road, so they had to get off and walk up the hill on foot to the top, where they found a flat, wide land with cool and clean air. A residential area with houses, streets, facilities, and shops was built on that hill.

After walking for a while, they arrived at the cleanest and most elegant house compared to the other poor houses they passed on their way up the hill.

This was the house of the area's official (mayor), who took care of all the affairs of the people in this neighborhood, from resolving disputes, providing shelter for the poor, feeding the needy, repairing faults, and coordinating between the families of the girls who wished to marry Gulf or Arab men. The introduction between the Indian girl and her Gulf fiancé happened in his house, with his presence and approval. It cannot be said for certain that the mayor did not receive a material or profit percentage, but after every wedding, he visited the bride's family to receive a small share of what the girl sent from the Gulf countries.

At the entrance of the house was a large gate, surrounded by a medium-sized cement wall, corrugated and reinforced with iron rods. In the center of the house was a wide courtyard, a clean and dry space with a floor adorned with gray granite rocks in a square and flat shape with a rough texture. The doors of the rooms were open but covered with thin silk curtains.

The four entered the house's courtyard and the contractor clapped his hands twice. Then a small nine-year-old girl came out.

The contractor quickly approached and said to the mayor: 'This girl is too young to be married, and I, for my part, do not want to marry a child.'

The contractor, Musbah, smiled and replied: 'What's wrong with you? This is a child, she is the mayor's daughter, and the mayor will not marry his daughters to men from outside the country.'

Then the mayor, a round-faced man in his fifties with big eyes, a long beard from under his chin, wearing a black velvet triangular hat and tight trousers called "courtah" (a long white cotton shirt that reaches the knees), left.

The mayor asked the maid to put chairs in the courtyard for the guests, and she did so, bringing five chairs with iron frames and seats and backs made of brightly colored plastic tubes attached to the frames. She placed a small iron table in the middle of the chairs, and then the maid brought those drinks, silver cups with cold white syrup. The contractor Musbah told them that it was almond syrup, which they had never tasted before. They liked the drink, the place, and the gracious treatment. Then the mayor stood up and called one of his servants, whispered something in his ear, and the boy nodded his head in agreement and ran off immediately. Within half an hour, dozens of men entered with veiled girls. All the girls lined up while the men moved away, and a curtain in the middle of the courtyard was opened, which had been closed to separate the girls from the mayor and his guests. The mayor turned his head to the contractor Musbah as if inviting him for something. Musbah got up and took Saeed by the hand and told him to accompany him to see the girl he would choose as his wife. He complied and went with him, and they exited from the other side of the curtain where the girls were.

Saeed was startled by the sight of the lined-up girls in the courtyard and couldn't focus on any of them or choose between them, even though all the girls had lowered their heads shyly. The contractor headed towards the front row and towards the first girl who was of average beauty, slim with fair skin, and slightly prominent front teeth. She was wearing a pink Punjabi dress (a long shirt that goes down to the knee or above it with two slits on either side that go up to the waist and a head covering that covers the chest and hangs from the shoulders). She had a thick long braid that she had brought forward over her right shoulder.

The contractor Musbah said: 'Look, this is called Daulat, she is now sixteen years old, completed her education in tenth grade, and weaves clothes and cooks food.'

The contractor, Musbah, spoke to her in Urdu, pointing her toward Saeed. She approached him and lifted her eyes, allowing Saeed to see her up close. Then the contractor asked the girl to step back, and asked Saeed: 'What do you think of her? Do you like this girl or not?'

Saeed replied: 'I don't know.'

Musbah went and came back with another girl, who was tall, broad-shouldered, with long wavy black hair, a plump face, wide eyes, and rosy cheeks. She was wearing a sparkly outfit (a tight long-sleeved shirt that reached her hips, tight pants up to the knee that widened to become loose like a skirt, and a head covering that rested on her chest and shoulders).

Musbah said of her: 'This girl is called Najma, she is 17 years old, an orphan who lives with her sick grandmother. She completed the tenth grade and teaches Quran reading to children in the neighborhood to earn a living for herself and her grandmother.'

Then he asked Najma, as he did with the first girl, to step forward and lift her eyes to Saeed so he could see her well.

Najma lifted her eyes to see Saeed looking at her deeply, and she liked him as well. Musbah felt the affection between them and asked Najma to step back.

He then asked Saeed: 'Did you like this girl or do you want to see the others?'

Saeed nodded in agreement and said: 'Yes.'

'Can I congratulate you now?'

Saeed nodded in agreement and said: 'This girl is nice, and she's an orphan with no provider or support.'

'Congratulations, and may Allah bless you both.'

'We have put our trust in Allah.'

The contractor, Musbah called out to the mayor and spoke to him in Urdu, informing him that Saeed had chosen Najma to be his wife and asked the mayor to prepare the bride, as Saeed would prepare for the wedding.

Saeed returned to his chair near Mansour and Ali, and they asked him what had happened behind the curtain. He told them what had happened and they congratulated and praised him.

The contractor, Musbah, spent a long time discussing with the mayor, agreeing with him, and determining the preparations for the wedding and the matters related to obtaining Najma's identity papers so she could travel with her husband after the wedding.

When he finished his discussion with the mayor, he jumped up from his place and exclaimed: 'When is it my turn, Your Excellency the contractor?'

Musbah answered with a smile: 'Please, your turn has come, and everyone is waiting for you.'

Ali entered on the other side of the curtain where the girls were and began to examine them all.

The contractor asked him: 'Do you want me to introduce you to the girls, or do you want to choose for yourself?'

Ali replied happily: 'You don't have to worry; I'll choose for myself. Masha'Allah … Masha'Allah …'

He looked at the girls' faces several times until he said: 'Your Excellency the contractor, do you see that girl in the green shirt, the wheat-colored skin, and beautiful face, standing in the corner?'

'Yes, I know her … I'll bring her to you so you can see her up close.'

After the contractor brought her to Ali to see her up close, he returned her to the corner where she was standing, after asking her if she liked Ali.

She lowered her head shyly, and the contractor returned to Ali, saying: 'I think, Ali, that you are deeply in love with her. Every time you see her, I can tell how much you admire her. Well then, let's trust in Allah. This girl's name is Zareena. She is the daughter of the schoolteacher. She has a mother and three younger brothers. She is the eldest and has just turned fifteen. She has completed the tenth grade and is good at cooking and sewing. However, there is one condition. Anyone who wants to marry her must buy a house for her family, who live in a small room in her uncle's overcrowded house.'

Ali: 'She is very beautiful, but this house issue … what is the value of houses here?'

'Don't worry about that. Houses here are very cheap. I saw a good house at the end of this hill for 30,000 rupees, which is a small amount for you, isn't it?'

'Yes, but I don't have that amount now.'

'Don't worry, my brother. I will lend you the money, and you can pay me back whenever you can or in installments as you are able.'

'Yes, please. That's a good idea.'

'But my dear, I want you to sign a receipt that I will prepare for you, to ensure that both of us get our rights. Is that okay?'

'Yes, that's correct. Your idea is right, Mr Contractor. I have 20,000 rupees now. I will spend it on the wedding expenses and some daily living expenses until we return. I also want to buy some gifts for my family.'

'Don't worry, my dear. I agree with your plan, and I will pay for the house. You can pay me back as you wish. Trust in Allah.'

'On the blessings of Allah.'

Ali went back to his friends happily humming a tune so they congratulated him.

The contractor, Musbah, resumed his conversation with the mayor, then he congratulated everyone, and a broad smile spread across his face: 'Congratulations! Congratulations on your engagement, gentlemen. The mayor, the families of the bride and groom, and I have agreed on all the matters. Now it's your turn, Mansour.'

Mansour's heart raced as he heard the question he had always avoided, and he responded to the contractor's question with another question: 'My turn in what?'

'Don't you want to choose a bride for yourself, son?'

Mansour seemed lost with traces of anger appearing on his face: 'You know well, Mr. Contractor that I have no desire to marry.'

The contractor's smile faded gradually and his enthusiasm turned into embarrassment as he trembled and said: 'I know … but I thought maybe your thoughts had changed when you saw your friends getting married and preparing for it. Perhaps the idea appealed to you?'

Ali signaled with his eyes to the contractor and Saeed to leave him alone. Mansour became agitated, and anger rose in him. His hands began to shake, and sweat drops formed on his forehead as everyone looked at him with pity. He felt suffocated, closed his eyes, clasped his fingers, and hit his head to escape from this embarrassing situation and the painful looks. He began to recall the image of Meriem, her plea, her smile, her voice, her love, and her touch. At that moment, he felt a small, cold, soft, and delicate hand slipping between his hands. He opened his eyes and saw a familiar hand, raised his head to see the face of his beloved Meriem, with her bright and smiling face, which increased her sweetness. She leaned towards his ear, and her hair, which was playing with the breeze, moved with her.

She whispered to him: 'Do you love me this much, Mansour?'

He responded with a smile: 'Yes, my love, more than you can imagine.'

She wrapped her arms around him, covering his face with her hair. Tears gathered in his eyes, ready to fall. In her embrace, and the soft light of the sun's rays, he began to think. Had his wife been returned to him from the dead? Or was it just his imagination? He was afraid of this thought, and he held her tightly, opening his eyes to see her and make sure she was there. But the hair got into his eyes and it hurt, he groaned in pain, trying to rub his eye. The pain subsided, and he opened his eyes to find himself alone in the courtyard where he used to gather with his friends, the mayor, and the contractor Musbah. But how was this possible? Was it a dream? Or had that state of madness returned to him?

He wanted to catch up with the men who he could still hear outside the mayor's house; perhaps they hadn't noticed his absence. As he turned to leave, he saw a girl watching him from a distance, a familiar face. The girl was scared because he had caught her watching him, so she fled. He blamed himself for what he had done in that moment of absence from reality, thanking Allah that no one but him and that strange girl who seemed familiar to him was in that courtyard. He hurried towards the place where he met his friends, the contractor, and the mayor.

(8)

On the following day, Saeed brought an amount of 5,000 rupees for his fiancée Najma's dowry, and another 5,000 rupees to buy her gold and silver jewelry. He also allocated 5,000 rupees for the wedding arrangements, such as decorations, tables, food, music band, clothes, and so on.

Similarly, Ali did the same, except that he kept 5,000 rupees for emergencies. He also borrowed 30,000 rupees from the contractor, Musbah, to buy a house for his fiancé Zareena's family.

Everyone prepared for the engagement party of Saeed and Najma on Thursday evening and for Ali and Zareena's engagement party on Friday evening. On Saturday evening, a feast was held for the newlyweds (a banquet that the groom hosts in India for family and friends) to celebrate their marriage consummation in the schoolyard under the hill. The two nights of the newlyweds' engagement parties were held in the courtyard of the mayor's house.

The first night of Roses …

On the first night that was the night of Saeed and Najma, the mayor made preparations with the money given to him by the contractor Musbah from the groom, Saeed. He prepared the shadir (a carpet that covers the ground where the celebration is held) in front of his house to receive the male guests. Chairs and tables were arranged, and a small platform was set up for the groom. It was covered with red embroidered silk carpets and large embroidered red cushions. The groom sat with his companions, Ali and Mansour, on his left side, while the mayor, who acted as the bride's guardian, the Sheikh, and the contractor, Musbah, sat on Saeed's right side. The bride's relatives sat in front of Saeed. Behind the groom were red velvet embroidered curtains and some pink and red rose rings.

On the other side of the house, she put out the pots and lit the stoves to cook dinner, which were biryani rice, spicy eggplant gravy, tandoori chicken roasted red pieces, hot naan bread, and nut milk pudding.

The place for the celebration of women was the courtyard of the mayor's house, and the walls of the courtyard were covered from the inside with green cotton cover, and a platform was erected for the bride on which the silk carpet and embroidered pillows were placed. The bride wore a red embroidered wedding dress, her eyes were covered with kohl, her hair was combed into a long braid, and a rose wreath was placed around the braid.

Najma wore the golden jewelry star that Saeed brought her, with a silver anklet around her feet and silver rings on the middle toes of her feet. Around her neck, she wore a necklace of seven layered pearls, interspersed with rubies and zircon stones. She also wore a small black glass bead necklace that brides wear on their wedding night, which she would keep around her neck as long as she was married and her husband was alive. She had a thin, large golden ring on her nose, connected to a string of pearls that was fastened to her hair above her ear. Another clip, attached to her hair from the top of her head, was connected to a thick string of pearls, and at the end of it hung a dangling golden necklace studded with circular red ruby stones, with pearl beads and some small red and zircon stones on the forehead. It is said that the bride wears this pearl set on her wedding night and then gives it to another girl on her wedding night, so the girls exchange it on their wedding nights. She also had bright red dots above her eyebrows and wore sturdy glass bracelets studded with zircon and brightly colored glass. She wore ten gold rings on her fingers, four of which were among the jewelry Saeed gave her and the rest were gifts from the mayor, relatives, and friends. Najma sat with her eyes closed, her head lowered in the designated area in the middle of the courtyard on the bride's platform. She was covered with a red veil, revealing only her hands and a part of her chin. The way she sat was different, as she raised her right leg and held it against her chest, resting her chin on it, which is the traditional Muslim bride's sitting position in India on her wedding night.

The marriage official sheikh came with the mayor after delivering a sermon to the people about the marriage contract. After filling out the paperwork and getting the signature of the groom and witnesses, he went to the bride to ask her if she accepted to marry Saeed or not.

She accepted as expected, then she and her guardian (the mayor) signed the marriage contract, and the marriage was completed. The women came to her and sat beside her, congratulating her, and adorned her with garlands of roses, jasmine, and flowers around her neck and wrists, and even her head was covered with a veil of white jasmine and some red roses that dangled from the sides of her forehead.

On the other side, the groom and his companions were invited to have dinner. Saeed sat at a table covered with a large white cotton tablecloth, and in the middle of the table, a small red cloth was spread with fragrant red rose petals scattered on it. White clean dishes were distributed, and various tables with colorful and delicious smelling dishes and the rising incense were spread.

One of the bride's relatives approached Saeed and sat next to him, according to Indian customs and traditions, the bride's brother or one of her close relatives must serve the groom on the wedding night, and began to serve him food from every dish and feed him with his hands as a mother feeds her child. His friends laughed at him because they had never seen such a scene before.

After finishing their dinner, the contractor came in with garlands of roses and flowers to put around Saeed's neck, and wrists, and cover his face with a rose veil. They also dressed him in the groom's turban covered in roses and flowers. He was covered in so many garlands that he almost suffocated, but his happiness could not be described that night. He had never seen so many flowers and decorations before in his life. This night was like a fairytale for him, one that does not happen to every man in this world at that time. His bride was also special among all the girls; she was the most beautiful, and he was extremely happy with her. Then they took him to the women's celebration area where his bride was waiting for him, covered only in garlands of roses and a red veil.

The women made Saeed and his bride sit facing each other with a large circular mirror on the ground between them. They covered them both with the red veil of the bride and removed the rose veil from their faces so they could see each other's faces. When Saeed saw her reflection in the mirror, he smiled and said, 'Masha'Allah.'

And she smiled back at him. The photographer then arrived, and pictures were taken of the newlyweds with their relatives, friends, and guests.

The ceremonies ended and the wooden carriage, square in shape, open on two sides, decorated and covered with flowers, which four men carried for the bride to sit in on her way to her husband's house. The horse procession followed with garlands of flowers and shiny decorations, which would later carry the groom to his house in his bride's carriage. As the bride and groom left the mayor's house, joy turned into sadness, and everyone began to cry as they bid farewell to the bride. Even the bride herself cried heavily at leaving her family and grandmother. This was the only sad part of the happy night of the first rose night. The bride was carried by carriage to the hotel while Saeed rode behind her on horseback with music playing and drumming and dancing boys.

The second night of Roses …

On the second night of roses, Ali married Zareena in the same place with similar ceremonies and tools used for decoration, furniture, tables, and platforms for the couple. The food menu was similar except for dessert which changed to custard with dried Afghan apricots and nuts. The number of guests doubled compared to last night as Zareena's relatives and acquaintances exceeded those of Najma's family. The previous night's bride also attended wearing a pink Indian sari with her red veil from last night. All happy wedding events were repeated at Ali's wedding as well.

Mansour ended up alone both times when the groom went to his wife leaving him feeling lonely and bitter about being away from home, especially on this night when he felt truly alone. He couldn't continue through the night so he asked the contractor to arrange his return to the hotel immediately because he was exhausted.

The contractor, Musbah called for one of the boys and whispered in his ears, and then said to Mansour: 'This boy will take you down the hill and bring the carriage with him; and he will ride with you to the hotel as well.'

'Yes, thank you and what about you?'

'I will stay; I have a lot to do. Do you feel lonely now that your friends are married? You didn't listen to me when I suggested marriage to you.'

'No, it's alright, I'm used to it. I'll see you in the morning, Insha'Allah.'

'In Allah's protection.'

(9)

Mansour left the wedding place with the boy who kept talking to him, asking him and insisting on his questions. Except that Mansour did not understand anything the boy said as he spoke in his Urdu language. Mansour just smiled and nodded positively, as if he was agreeing with everything, he said … the boy pointed to his mouth and throat as if he was telling him that he feels thirsty and wishes to drink. He pointed at the store on the corner of the street, so Mansour understood that the boy wanted him to get him something to drink. Mansour nodded his head agreeing with the boy's request; the boy felt happy and held Mansour's hand to drag him to the store. Mansour bought two bottles of cold Coca-Cola to drink for himself and the boy. When they were done, they gave the bottles back and left the store. However, Mansour bumped into a girl that was about to leave the store, eggs fell out of the paper roll that she was carrying and broke. So, the girl mumbled in Urdu blaming Mansour for bumping into her, and she started crying as if she was afraid of the punishment that would befall her.

Mansour felt that the girl would fall into trouble with breaking the eggs, so he signaled to the boy to talk to her and make her stop crying. The boy did as he was told and the girl stopped crying. She spoke to the boy, complaining sadly, and Mansour understood that he should compensate her for the broken eggs. He counted the number of eggs that were broken, took out his wallet, and went to the shop owner to ask for six eggs to wrap for him. The shop owner wrapped them in the newspaper as requested, and also gave him a bottle of Coca-Cola. Mansour took the wrapped eggs and the Coca-Cola and gave them to the girl, apologizing for not noticing her when he bumped into her. The girl didn't understand what Mansour said, but her face lit up with joy when she saw the eggs, and she stopped crying. She thanked him a lot and when he handed her the bottle of Coca-Cola, she shook her head shyly, refusing to take it. Mansour offered her the bottle and urged her to take it, but she refused for the second time. The boy took the bottle from Mansour's hand and convinced the girl to drink it.

The poor girl was happy and took sips from the bottle, wiping her tears, her face blushing with shyness. The sky was dark and the stars were scattered here and there, and the lights of the shop and the simple alleyways were dim. Despite all the darkness surrounding them, Mansour continued to gaze at the girl with his bewildered eyes. Her eyes were wide and blue with thick, long lashes like those of a deer, her face was round and white like the full moon, and she had long, silky, brown, and blonde hair flowing out of her worn-out green headscarf. She had a small, smooth nose and small, plump lips. This girl's features were not just beautiful, they were beyond beautiful. Here Mansour paid attention and noticed that he was beginning to be fascinated by her, so he turned his eyes away from her and closed his eyes, suddenly Meriem appeared with her beautiful face and her image that did not leave his eyes. The feeling squeezed his heart and he was troubled, then he heard the girl's voice behind him, reaching out to him with her hand with a bottle of Coca-Cola and thanking him saying: "Shukriya" …

He turned to her to find her reaching his hand to give him the empty Coca-Cola bottle. He raised his gaze to her eyes and gasped in shock when he versioned Meriem in the girl. Mansour took the bottle from the girl as he was in shock, it felt like a dream. He closed his eyes and opened them again to see that the girl is the same and not Meriem. Nevertheless, the girl seemed familiar, as if he had known her for years. She seemed to him to be a dangerous magic, a mysterious ambiguity, a mind-numbing madness. She seemed to him very beautiful at that moment. She seemed to be related to him … A strong feeling, a pulse increasing in speed … A strange sensation …

The boy pulled the empty bottle from Mansour's hands and gave it to the shop owner. Mansour woke from his thoughts and turned to see the girl starting to disappear in the darkness of the alley. The boy kept talking to him and pointing with his hands, yet Mansour did not pay attention to the boy's signals. He just kept watching as the girl sank into the darkness of the alley, so the boy shook Mansour violently and woke him up from the daydreaming that was captivating him. He obeyed the boy who walked him down the hill and asked for a rickshaw for him. Mansour gave the boy some metal rupees and bid him farewell, and Mansour mentioned the name of the hotel to the owner of the rickshaw who gave him a ride.

As the rickshaw moved, the cold breeze surrounded him, playing with his cheeks and hair. He lowered his eyelids, and in his mind's eye, he saw the courtyard of that girl's house. Was she the same girl who had been watching him at the mayor's office that day? It was strange! Until moments ago, when he closed his eyes, he saw Meriem's face. Now it was the girl's face that appeared to him every time. He opened his eyes, trying to dismiss these new thoughts from his mind and continue to honor the memory of his deceased wife. With courage and confidence, he closed his eyes again to see the Indian girl's face once more. He was startled when he opened them again and became angry at what was happening to him.

How could a girl he didn't know to take over his thoughts?

How could he let a girl, coming from an unknown place, occupy his mind?

Perhaps she had impressed him?

Perhaps he had been occupied by her?

Is this how one becomes attached to someone after just one meeting?

Maybe it is so?

But why is he concerned with all of this?

He had pledged his life in loyalty to the memory of his departed beloved. He would remain faithful only to her and wander again wondering: 'But isn't the Indian girl a little young for me? Even so, I am handsome and in my prime youth … girls still line up in windows and on rooftops to see me …'

If he has started to be tempted by the Indian girl, what will he do with Meriem's love? Will he forget her?

Has she also been attracted to him as much as he has been attracted to her or is this just his situation?

Perhaps she is a little young but still in her prime youthfulness. She may appear poor or perhaps she is a servant in one of the houses but with her beauty … her eyes … hair … and features … she had stolen Mansour's thoughts.

(10)

Mansour entered his hotel room, and threw himself on the bed, feeling very tired and overwhelmed with thoughts. He heard a knock on the door, got up to open it, and was surprised to see someone he knew.

'Aren't you afraid? Aren't you happy to see me?'

'Yes, I'm very happy … but how did you come here?'

'You don't know what I did to be able to visit you tonight?'

'Are you here in front of me or is this a dream?'

'I am here in front of you … won't you invite me in?'

'Yes, please come in. But tell me, how did you find me, and where I was?'

She laughed slightly and said: 'Why do you care about all these details?'

'I just wonder.'

'Never mind all these details. Tell me, how are you? I see that you are better than the last time I saw you.'

'Praise be to Allah … but I still suffer from your absence.'

'I know, and I came today to comfort you.'

'Will you stay with me?'

'I can't, I have to go back to where I came from … I was suffering for your suffering.'

'Will you leave me again?'

'Yes, that's what is supposed to happen.'

Tears filled Mansour's eyes as he said: 'Don't cry my love; I don't want to see you like this. I was always the reason for your sadness.'

'Don't say that … I miss you so much, what can I do?'

'I know, I saw what happened to you after I left.'

'And yet you are leaving me again.'

'This is the reality.'

'It is not fair; don't you see that I am alone and miserable?'

'But I don't want you to stay like this.'

'What can I do?'

'You can do a lot.'

'How can I do a lot when you are not by my side?'

'Your life didn't stop because of me, my love.'

'But it did stop.'

'You stopped it, then.'

'I didn't ... I did not set for you to leave me.'

'Allah did, this is my destiny.'

'I seek forgiveness from Allah.'

'Yes, seek forgiveness from your Lord, for this is fate.'

'By the grace of Allah.'

'I will ask you a favor, Mansour. Will you do it for me?'

'Ask anything, I would give my life for you.'

'No, I shall not ask for your life ... May Allah make it long and full of joy and happiness.'

'While you are not with me?'

'Yes.'

'I don't want it ... How could I ever be happy with someone else? Have you not been certain that you are the reason for my happiness and sorrow? I don't want to spend this life alone.'

'Why?'

'I still love you, Meriem ... I live through your love.'

'I know, but I can't live with you anymore.'

'You live inside me and inside my heart, my love.'

'I know and that is a good thing, but you have ruined your life for me.'

'I can't help it ... I have lived with you since I was just a child.'

'And you are the first and last love of my life.'

'Don't leave me now, stay with me.'

'You know that it is impossible.'

'The impossible is to see you again, yet here I am looking at you, talking to you, and touching you.'

'This is temporary and for extreme need.'

'What do you need?'

'Mansour, my love, listen to me. Promise me that you will grant me my last will in life, which I was planning to do as you did before we separated.'

'Promise you what? Tell me.'

'I want you to promise me first that you will grant it to me.'

'I promise to grant you your wish.'

'You have promised me and this is your debt to pay.'

'Yes, I promised you, but what is it?'

'Get married, Mansour.'

'What? You are talking to me about marriage as well!'

'I am the one who wants you to get married and start a family the most.'

'Meriem, what are you saying?'

'I am telling you the truth; you my love are putting on me a burden that I can't carry ... I am tired of this matter.'

'What?'

'Yes, I am tired.'

'If I ever marry someone else, she will keep me occupied and I will forget about you.'

'Let it be then ... Forget about me and set me free from my sufferings.'

He choked on his breath and let out a deep sigh with hot tears, saying: 'Meriem, please don't say that.'

'Yes Mansour, I'm tired. I want you to continue your normal life like other people. Your life didn't stop with my death. You have to move forward.'

'I love you, Meriem, and I have devoted my life to you.'

'This could not be. Keep me in your memory and live your life.'

'I don't want to get married.' She held his hand firmly and said in a stern tone: 'If you want to relieve me, then get married ...'

'Marry whom?'

'That girl you were thinking of ...'

Mansour remembered the girl. His heart beat faster, the lights in his room increased, and strong rays of light shone in his eyes.

'Meriem, where are you? I can't see you ... Where are you? Meriem ... Meriem ...'

He jumped to run after her, yet he stumbled on something and fell to the ground. He opened his eyes to see himself lying between the beds.

It was a dream close to reality as if he was really living those moments. Perhaps it had actually happened, and how was that possible? Maybe ...

(11)

Mansour took a shower, got dressed and went out to the contractor's room; he knocked his door and called out to him: 'Contractor Musbah, are you here? Are you still sleeping? This is Mansour, can you hear me?'

The contractor opened the door while he was rubbing his eyes and said: 'Hello, Mansour, why are you up so early? Do you have an important matter to attend to?'

'No, never, it is just that I slept well and I could not remain in bed any longer. I felt lonely now that my friends were married.'

'Have you not become lonely now, Mansour? This is exactly what I meant when I advised you to get married. Don't you want to get married now? The opportunity is still available to you and it won't come again. We have fifteen days left before we return home. Take advantage of them and get married, my son. Then you can bring your wife back with you. If you get married during these days, we can obtain the official papers for your wife. If you delay, we won't be able to bring her with you until we obtain the papers. What do you say?'

'Do the procedures take a long time here?'

'Yes, but if you hurry up and get married, we'll take care of everything. Don't you think it's worth it? I feel that you're starting to soften, aren't you?'

Mansour remained silent, lowered his head, and pondered.

'I see that your silence means acceptance. Don't worry; I'll take care of everything. Why don't you go to the restaurant in the hotel lobby and I'll join you there? We'll have breakfast together and discuss the details.'

'Yes.'

The contractor, Musbah, entered the restaurant to find Mansour sitting in a corner near the window overlooking the Musi River, waiting for him. He ordered minced meat fried with spices, fried Indian bread (paratha) and fried black pepper beef liver, and milk tea.

Mansour was eager to discuss the marriage issue with the contractor and agree on all the details, yet the contractor spoke about all different topics except marriage. He tried to remain calm and waited for the contractor to initiate the discussion himself, but the contractor either pretended forgetfulness or indifference.

Mansour had no choice but to gather his courage and ask the contractor, Musbah: 'Weren't we talking about marriage?'

'Marriage ... whose marriage?'

Mansour's face was stained with redness, and drops of sweat glistened on his forehead. He was embarrassed by the contractor's question and decided to back out of his intention to get married. He remained silent and turned to look at the river, wondering to himself: *How could the contractor forget the topic of marriage that he just brought up? How could he forget?*

He trembled and turned to the contractor, whose loud laughter filled the place and made the restaurant patrons turn to look at him. Mansour wondered what was wrong with the contractor.

'Now do you see? I told you before; you won't be able to spend your whole life without a wife.'

'I know ... I have honestly decided to get married now. I want to have a family, a wife, and children. How long will I remain alone?'

'Good thinking, the right thing to do is to get married, my friend. Marriage is the completion of religion. But tell me, who managed to change your mind and convince you?'

Mansour closed his eyes, sighed and remembered Meriem's face in the dream and said: 'The deceased.'

'And who is the deceased? Do you mean your wife?'

'Yes.'

'May Allah have mercy on her ... but how is this possible?'

Mansour smiled and looked at the river, recalling the previous night's encounter.

The contractor surprised him when he said: 'Maybe she spoke to you in a dream. It's possible, the dead have always communicated with the living and talked to their loved ones through dreams. Or was it something else?'

'It was a dream, or at least it seemed like one.'

'Yes, it definitely was a dream. Don't worry and don't be afraid ... Did she tell you to get married?'

Mansour nodded in agreement.

'Then it's settled, my son, get married. Marriage is a blessing, believe me. Do as your friends did, and you won't regret it, trust me.'

'Yes, yes.'

'And finally, Praise be to Allah. Let's trust in Allah then. We'll go to the mayor's house to tell him that you intend to get married and choose a wife for you.'

'Yes, Insha'Allah.'

(12)

They made it to the bottom of the hill; they got off the rickshaw and walked up to the top of the hill, heading towards the mayor's house in the neighborhood. While they were walking, the contractor Musabah asked Mansour about the specifications of his life partner, and Mansour began to think about the qualities that should be present. Suddenly, they both stopped walking and talking when a girl fell in front of them. She was pushed forcefully by someone, and lay there unable to move.

The poor girl lay on the ground, trying to gather herself and get up, but unable to do so. She was crying silently, with her body trembling. A woman's strong voice appeared from behind scolding and threatening her harshly. The girl was exhausted from the beating, maybe the hard work, hunger, and poverty. Mansour and the contractor turned to see the woman standing behind them, an overweight woman with her belly hanging out of her saree, her face reddened with anger, and a long stick in her hand, ready to continue punishing and hitting the girl. The contractor tried to intervene to stop her, but she pushed him aside and charged at the girl, lifting the stick to strike her. Mansour grabbed the stick before it could hit the girl and the contractor lifted the poor girl from the ground, who was completely exhausted from the beating. Two girls from the neighborhood who had gathered to watch the commotion approached and took the girl away from the contractor Musabah's hand and lay her away.

The angry woman growled when Mansour took the stick from her hand. He turned to the girl and realized she was the same girl with the fair complexion who had occupied his thoughts the night before. It was the same eggs girl, yet her face had become pale and tired, her eyes were faded and tears had washed her cheeks. A thin stream of blood had started to flow from her small nose and cut its way down the side of her trembling lips. Despite her tears and pain, her beautiful face, blended with a reddish hue that dominated her appearance, shone like the sun with its rays, he was suddenly looking at the most beautiful girl on planet earth. Mansour watched her with a gaze of love and passion more than pity and tenderness. He watched her closely and imagined avenging her from the fat woman who couldn't possibly be her mother. He envisioned beating her with the stick he carried until she fell unconscious. He snapped out of his reverie when he noticed the contractor approaching the fat woman, trying to speak to her in Urdu as if pleading with her to intervene in their affairs. She screamed in his face, as if she were preventing him from interfering, and a woman came and pulled the poor girl to a stone chair outside her house, where she sat her down to rest. Then she brought her a glass of water to drink. Mansour took the glass of water from the woman's hand and sat next to the girl, giving her water with his hand. The poor girl was in a state of extreme exhaustion that made her tremble with fear and pain. Mansour noticed his behavior and sitting close to her, which made him feel embarrassed. He got up from his seat and returned the glass to the homeowner, who poured the remaining water into her hand and wiped the face of the poor girl with it. The other woman spoke to the fat woman in a soft, calm, and measured tone, while the fat woman opened her mouth to spew out anger and venom. After an unequal verbal battle between two women, the overweight woman withdrew from where she came, panting fire and smoke, leaving behind people huddled together whispering among themselves, while the contractor Musbah and Mansour stood facing the homeowner and the poor girl. The crowd began to disperse little by little, and amidst a great commotion, everyone went their separate ways. The homeowner took the poor girl into her house and the scene calmed down, everything returning to how it was before.

Musbah turned to Mansour and noticed tears welling up in his eyes, so he asked him: 'What's wrong? Do you want to cry?'

'Could you tell me what you understood from that overweight woman? And why was she unleashing all her anger on the poor girl?'

'The domineering woman claimed that the girl forgot the food on the stove until it burnt.'

'Is that a strong reason for the poor girl to receive such a severe punishment? She almost died, did you not notice that, O contractor?'

'Yes, I did notice, and the kind neighbor scolded the domineering woman and prevented her from depriving the poor girl of her share of rest like everyone else. The poor girl has no designated sleeping area, works tirelessly throughout the night, and extracts water from a faraway well for her mistress and her children. The poor girl only sleeps before sunrise, either on the rooftop or in the kitchen, her clothes always damp and tattered, her bed worn out and dusty. She only eats leftovers from the mistress and her children, and if there is nothing left, she spends her day hungry.'

'Do you know them, O contractor?'

'I used to know the husband of this woman who passed away two years ago. He was a good and righteous man, but his wife is wicked.'

'Yes … you are right.'

(13)

In the mayor's house, after they sat on chair in the courtyard, Mansour started by saying: 'Dear contractor, please, allow me to marry that oppressed girl.'

'But she is their maid, how could you marry her? I will search for a better wife for you.'

'First of all, she is a human being, and I don't care about her social or material status, I want her as my wife and that's all that matters.'

'I will find someone better for you, trust me. She is an ignorant servant who won't suit you, my son. You will soon see how insignificant she is.'

'Please, sir, talk to the mayor to take all necessary steps to propose to her and marry her.'

Mansour got what he wanted. The contractor talked to the mayor and told him everything that happened since they arrived at the hill. The two of them continued to speak in Urdu for a long time, and Mansour was burning with desire to know the content of their long conversation. He noticed that the contractor shook his head regretfully about something, his heart tightened, and he feared that the girl he decided to marry would not be his.

After his long patience and terrifying fear, the contractor turned to Mansour and said to him: 'Forget about this girl, Mansour.'

'What's the problem? What's wrong with the girl?'

'Her story is long, my son, and you won't like it. Let me show you other girls who are better than her, man.'

With determination and enthusiasm, Mansour said: 'Tell me her story now.'

The contractor had no choice but to give in to his request.

'Listen, Mansour, this girl's name is Niloofar, she is fourteen years old, and she is the granddaughter of the fat and unjust woman's husband. I think I told you about her husband that I used to know.'

'Yes, you told me.'

'Her mother was the eldest child of that man. She was studying in school in the tenth grade, was fifteen years old, and was a stunning girl known and described for her captivating beauty. She also had two younger brothers. On her way to and from school, she would encounter British soldiers, and she met one of them who showed interest in her. They fell in love, and they started exchanging love letters and having secret meetings. The British soldier became deeply infatuated with her and thought about escaping the military service with her to take her to his country to marry and live happily. He asked her to run away with him, because her family would not approve of their marriage since he was a foreign colonizer from a different religion. The girl agreed, and they planned to escape and get married far away from her family and the British military barracks. One day, he escaped from the military service and took her with him to a distant city, where they got married and lived together for about six to eight months. Throughout that time, he tried to find a way to escape to Britain or any other country where nobody knew them with his pregnant wife.

'However, fate had other plans, and he was arrested, tried in a military court, and sentenced to imprisonment in one of the remote military barracks in the remote colonies.

'Due to imprisonment, mistreatment, wounds, and bruises resulting from the beating he received from the soldiers when he was arrested, he contracted a lung disease which led to his death in prison before being transferred to Britain for treatment. As for his poor wife, she became lonely and sad after losing her husband, and remained alone suffering the pain of separation and pregnancy until her neighbor, an old poor woman, took care of her as much as she could until she gave birth to a baby girl. Then the poor woman became ill with postpartum fever and severe weakness, so she wrote a letter to her father explaining everything that had happened and attached her marriage contract and a paper with her father's address on it. She asked the old woman that if anything happened to her, to take the baby girl and the letter to her father's house, whose address she had written for her. She died after a bitter struggle with weakness and illness, and the old woman took the baby and came to her grandfather's house with the letter and the marriage contract. Her father wept bitterly for her and her sick mother mourned her deeply and passed away in the same month.

'When the father became responsible for two children and a baby, he had to marry a woman to take care of his children and granddaughter. However, the wife turned out to be a cruel witch who gave birth to four children and convinced him not to send Niloofar to school so that she wouldn't end up like her mother. When the man died two years ago, the two boys, Niloofar's uncles, went to live with their uncle. As for Niloofar, she was not accepted by that uncle, who considered her mother's escape and marriage to that settler a disgrace and a waste. So, the poor girl remained with her grandfather's wife to taste the bitterness of humiliation and servitude, serving her and her four children. Now that she has grown up, no one will think of marrying her because traditions here dictate that the bride's family must prepare her for marriage. In the case of pregnancy and childbirth, the bride's parents are responsible for all the expenses of the first child's birth. If the son-in-law needs financial assistance in the future, his wife's family will support him financially. Everyone here is looking for a bride from a good family. As for the Arabs, no one will accept her because she will not be nominated and they would not be fond of her clothes. Moreover, her grandfather's wife will not let her leave because she serves her and her children without compensation. Therefore, no one will pay attention to her, neither from her tribe nor from strangers. Now tell me, do you still want to marry her?'

Mansour smiled and lowered his head, letting out a sigh of victory in a fierce battle: 'I promise you, sir, that I will not return to my country without holding her hand in mine.'

Thus, with Mansour's persistence and his serious desire to marry Niloofar, the efforts of the mayor and the contractor, Musbah, succeeded in persuading the grandfather's wife, who had initially refused completely. Yet, with the charm of money, they shut her mouth and forced her to accept.

The wedding ceremony was completed quickly within just five days, and Mansour prepared all the necessary supplies for the wedding and the bride.

The third Night of Roses …

On the wedding night, Niloofar sat on the platform in the designated place for her in the mayor's house, like the previous two brides. The wall behind her was decorated with a black velvet canopy adorned with white jasmine flowers and white artificial pearl beads. Her white face shone like a moon in full brightness and completeness in a black sky full of innocent, shining stars, adding beauty to her beauty. With her Indian clothing embroidered with golden threads, she looked like a beautiful porcelain doll displayed on a shelf in a souvenir shop in India.

Mansour entered the women's wedding courtyard and saw her in all her adornment, happy on her wedding day. Her face was radiant, her eyes sparkling, her lips smiled in a way he had never seen before. He was delighted for her and himself, and congratulated himself for promising her not to shed a tear or approach any sadness. He would compensate her for all the deprivation and suffering she had endured throughout her life.

His marriage to her was not driven by infatuation with her rare and captivating beauty, the Indian and British mix, but because he had begun to aspire to her. He also wanted to save her and free her from the clutches of misery, and the most important reason of all was to fulfill the request of his deceased beloved.

Marriage proceedings were completed and the three couples went back with their wives. Contractor Musbah stayed in India for another week to tie some loose ends.

(14)

Once they made it back home, Mansour headed to his parents' house to show them his new bride and introduce her to them. He told them about her difficult conditions and the situations that led him to marry her.

His family sympathized with her when they heard her story. They rejoiced in her sweetness, beauty, and natural modesty, as well as her impeccable manners, the only flaw they found in her was her ignorance of the Arabic language. Communication and interaction with her would be difficult, as sign language occasionally made mistakes. The mother was a little upset that she couldn't pronounce the bride's name correctly.

'I don't know how to pronounce her name because it's strange and difficult. I'll call her Noura, what do you think?'

'Call her whatever you like, my mother. My wife won't object.'

Everyone agreed to call her Noura, and her name was changed from Niloofar to Noura in the Mansour family. Mansour and his bride stayed with his family for five days, during which time his mother taught the bride all the Arab domestic sciences, such as cooking, organizing, sewing, and cleaning, all the household chores that differ in detail from what she had learned in India. Mansour's mother also prepared a daily feast for the women of the family, relatives, and acquaintances during the bride and groom's stay to introduce them to the bride and to introduce her to them. Mansour's sisters each took turns preparing the bride each day over the five days, and each day the bride would adorn herself with the most beautiful local embroidered clothing, gold and silver jewelry, which they had purchased as a wedding gift for her.

During this short period, the bride learned everything her mother-in-law taught her with mastery, and learned the basics of local cooking, the names of dishes and spices, and their tools and how to pronounce and understand them since she was new to the Arabic language.

On one of the days of the feasts that her mother-in-law had prepared in her honor, some of the women were whispering and mocking the bride, and the rudest of them said aloud: 'How can a foreign woman who doesn't even understand how to read the Quran marry an Arab man and have children? In what language will she speak to her children, her native language or broken Arabic? Mansour didn't do any good when he married an Indian girl and brought her to live with us. She might be beautiful and gorgeous, yet her beauty is lacking. In addition, she is not one of us and does not come from our Arab roots. We do not lack beautiful girls here, at least they are Arab girls, with deep roots, who memorize the Quran, recite poetry, heal wounds, and soothe the soul. He will regret it later when he sees his children do not know how to interact or speak with Arabs.'

Mansour's grandmother angrily intervened: 'What nonsense is this? You are the one who does not know how to speak with Arabs. Is this what should be said? It is more appropriate for you to pray for the happiness, success, and stability of the newlyweds, instead of mocking them and spreading your poison and ill will. Look at this young and innocent girl, she can learn and become more knowledgeable than you or anyone you know. Never underestimate the weakest of Allah's creation.'

The face of that woman was colored with shame and disgust, and she began to cover up her hatred with side conversations with the others.

The days that the couple spent with the Mansour family passed by quickly. The couple bid farewell to Mansour's family and boarded the rented truck that the groom's father hired to transport them and the gifts that the bride received from her mother-in-law and sisters-in-law, including gold and silver jewelry, bed linens, pillowcases, blankets, brass and pottery dishes, pots, boxes filled with luxurious embroidered clothes, sweets, incense, dried foods, grains, and spices. Memories of welcoming and happiness accompanied them, as well as the new life skills that the bride acquired. They returned to start their new life from the starting point.

They set off at 7:00 in the morning. Niloofar learned that her life would begin as soon as she was alone with her husband in their home, and that her husband, his family, and acquaintances were her people, her original family, and that this country had become her home, not India where she was born and raised, and where she only had painful memories and people who only shared a blood relationship with her. She had to forget the sorrows and tragedies of the past and adapt to the new life.

She had to take care of her husband and work to make him happy and fulfill all his needs. She had to relieve him of the worries and sorrows of the past, which the contractor, Musbah, told her about when he visited her on the eve of her wedding in the mayor's house. She was sitting in the middle of a room full of girls who were applying henna to her hands and feet when the contractor stood with the mayor's wife, who asked the girls to leave so that the contractor could talk to her. When they left, the mayor's wife closed the door behind them and brought two low, circular chairs made of reeds cut close to Niloofar, and sat next to the contractor, who was looking at the bride with a calm smile on his face, making her feel safe and comfortable.

He asked her in Urdu: 'How are you doing, my child?'

'I am fine, Praise be to Allah.'

'I see that you have prepared yourself, and now you have prepared yourself with henna, and nothing is left except the wedding dress and decorations, isn't that right?'

The bride lowered her head in shyness.

The contractor added: 'Don't be ashamed, my daughter, for this is the way of life, and every girl in this world adorns herself to go to her husband's house when Allah wills it.'

The bride kept her head lowered, but her movement confirms the contractor's words.

He continued: 'Do you know, my child, that you are one of the luckiest girls here, because although your childhood was not happy, your youth and future with your husband and family will be bright and beautiful. Look my child, Mansour is one of the most skilled, noble, and handsome men, and he chose only you. You are really lucky because you will become his only wife in his life, unlike other girls who marry men who already have wives and children. Do you know that Mansour doesn't have a wife? He had a wife, he married his cousin because he loved her so much, and she was the love of his life as they say. Unfortunately, she became sick and was bedridden for a long time before she passed away. Fate did not allow him to have a natural married life with her nor have children with her. When she died, his mind and psyche were deeply affected by her loss, and he became ill. But thankfully, he recovered after a long treatment. So, my child, be wise and keep your words to yourself, and do not mention her with any negativity. Without her, you would not have reached where you are now. Mansour is the only son in his family, and he has no male siblings. He is the only male heir among four daughters. Therefore, preserve his dignity and reputation among his peers. Look at your gifts and your attire; no other girl among your peers has received such gifts. Know that he is generous, so keep his money safe. He is strong now and in full health, so be the renewed remedy for his vitality and youthfulness. Preserve yourself so that he will love you and not find solace elsewhere. Love him and obey him so that he will accompany you throughout your life.'

His words still reverberated in her ears, until she woke up from her daydreams to the sound of the car horn, which the driver issued to disperse the gathering of cats from one way, and she noticed that the area was dark and remote, and she turned to her husband to see him reassure her with a smile that could hardly be seen in the darkness of that pitch-black night. Then he indicated to her that they had approached the house.

(15)

As they arrived at the house, the clock struck seven for the Maghrib prayer. The journey had taken twelve hours, with stops and breaks along the way.

Mansour and his wife got out of the vehicle and he asked his wife to wait for him at the door while he turned on the lights. In moments, the darkness was replaced by electric light, and Mansour and his driver began unloading their belongings and gifts in the courtyard. Niloofar looked around and noticed that the house was in an almost uninhabited area with a large sandy courtyard containing a well and a rock basin for washing dishes and clothes. The main building sat in the middle of the courtyard, connected to the main gate by a rocky path. To the west was a small kitchen building and a closed structure.

The February sea breeze is cold, clean, and winter was still in its prime. The tranquility was comforting and she felt that this house was her new world, her eternal world. She began to plan projects in her mind to bring life to this house and her feeling of happiness drew a broad smile on her face. Mansour closed the main iron gate of the house after bidding farewell to the driver. He walked towards her, a smile still on her face, and he smiled back, influenced by it. He felt relieved by her happiness and affection.

He showed her around the main building of the interior of the house which was considered modern compared to houses of that time. It was a rectangular building with a single entrance door that closed on both sides like old houses, and a window with two wooden doors just like the entrance door. The window had iron railings and overlooked the outdoor courtyard. The entrance led to a living room with floor cushions for back support and a woolen carpet. On the right side of the living room was a door leading to the bedroom which contained a sturdy iron high bed, a window overlooking the living room covered with a linen curtain printed with large blue flowers, a wardrobe with small openings facing the bed where she hung up a mirror, as well as a circular chair and red cotton carpet covering the entire floor of the room. There was also another door leading to an alcove then to the bathroom.

The external building consisted of a kitchen with a door leading to storage room, and on one side of it there was another door leading to an alcove then to bathroom. Mansour showed her how to draw water from the well and transfer it into heating container in order for bathing or washing purposes.

She got acquainted with all the facilities of the house while she was at the height of her joy and happiness. The poor girl had never dreamed of living in a house like this, even less becoming the wife of the handsome, generous, strong young man, the owner of the house. In those moments, she forgot her unhappy past that she had lived, and she imagined that she was the princess who owned the palace, the wife of the handsome prince in the story that she been dreaming about ever since her childhood.

She awakened from her thoughts when Mansour approached her and wrapped his arms around her neck, making her look at him.

He said to her: 'Now that the house is illuminated by your presence, Niloofar, I want you to fill it with children who resemble you.'

She did not fully understand the meaning of his words, but she felt that he was expressing his happiness with her presence. She blushed and lowered her head.

The next day, Niloofar woke up early upon hearing the call to prayer for Fajr. She went to draw water from the well and led it to the corner to put it in the tank for heating water. Then she lit the fire underneath it so that Mansour could bathe.

After preparing breakfast, which she learned how to prepare from her mother-in-law, she went to wake him up gently and called him with her sweet and melodious voice using Urdu words. He woke up with a bright face and followed her as she led him by hand to the corner where she gave him a towel and waited for him in the living room during breakfast.

When he finished bathing, he came out and said to her: 'Let's pray Fajr prayer.'

She did not understand him at first but he gestured with Takbir sign so she blushed and shook her head denying that she did not know how to pray. He gestured for her to follow him so he could teach her how to perform ablution and prayer. He made ablution himself then showed her how to do it as well. Then he spread their prayer rugs side by side a little behind his own rug and gestured for her to stand straight with her right hand on top of the left on top of her stomach while repeating after him what he said during prayer. She did exactly as he did.

After finishing, joy filled Niloofar's face as she thanked him saying: 'Shukriya (thank you in Urdu).'

He sat next to her, happy and grateful to Allah for blessing him with a grace he had been depriving himself from. He pulled her wrist towards him and kissed her fingers as an expression of his great happiness with her presence.

She felt embarrassed in front of him and withdrew to the room to take out his military uniform and put it on the bed. She cleaned his shoes from the dust and shined them. She waited until he finished his meal and came to get ready for work. He put on his clothes and signaled to her that he would leave for work now and return after noon prayer. She understood that she should prepare lunch an hour before the call to prayer, when his workday ended, which may take him ten minutes during his return by bicycle from work.

She caught up with him at the main door, and before he opened it, he turned to her and kissed her forehead, saying: 'In Allah's safety.'

She repeated his sentence shyly, and he gestured for her not to open the door for anyone ever again. She understood what he meant and nodded obediently before closing the door.

He did not ride his bicycle but walked it with him until the bottom of the slope where the soil met rocks. On the way, he talked to himself, saying that this day was his first day of work since traveling to India or since getting married. He tried hard to recall memories with Meriem but Niloofar's face never left his mind. He did not love Niloofar as much as he loved Meriem, but where was Meriem now in his heart and mind?

Does love bind with living beings and forget about the dead?

But her love and memories remained with him even after marrying Niloofar. Can it be reasonable that what he expected happened: that the new wife's love would make him forget Meriem's love?

Or is it a law of life that living beings are more enduring than dead ones?

At that moment, he passed by the old woman who sat every day on the roadside selling dried fish.

He greeted her, and she returned the greeting and said: 'How are you, my son?'

'Praise be to Allah, I am fine. And how are you, Aunt?'

'Praise be to Allah, I am fine. And I Praise be to Allah very much for restoring your life and happiness. May Allah bless your wife and your marriage, my son.'

'Praise be to Allah. But how did you know about my marriage, Aunt?'

'I felt it, my son. My feelings are always true. These long years have not left their mark on my forehead in vain. Each year gives you experience, my son.'

'Masha'Allah, Allah bless you, Aunt, this is a blessing from Allah.'

'Praise be to Allah; it is indeed a blessing. And your new wife is also a blessing, so take good care of her.'

'Yes, she is a blessing. Praise be to Allah very much for providing her to me. I will see you soon, Aunt. I have to hurry to work.'

'Go with safety, but know that the living are more enduring than the dead, my son.'

He heard these words, and his features froze, and he stopped talking. He said goodbye to the old woman, got on his bike, and began to think about how the old woman could answer the questions he asked himself. Perhaps the answer came to him from heaven to reassure him that the living are indeed more enduring than the dead.

(16)

After Mansour left for work, Niloofar carried the food containers to the kitchen and placed them in the perforated food storage cabinet. She then entered the main building and emptied the contents of the boxes and bags she had brought from her mother-in-law's house, distributing all the items in their designated places. Afterwards, she went to the kitchen to prepare lunch, attempting to apply what she had learned from her aunt in preparing local cuisine. She took a handful of rice from one of the bags, cleaned and boiled it. From one of the cans, she had brought with her, she took out dried shrimp, washed it and soaked it in water to reduce its salt content. She then cleaned the house, removing dust and dirt from shelves and walls in the main building's living room, bedroom, corner (bathroom), and toilet. After that, she washed the floor of the corner and bathroom before sweeping and mopping the floors of the bedroom, living room, and inner courtyard. Later, she went outside to remove dirt from the ground before spraying water to moisten it. Finally, she returned to continue preparing food by cleaning shrimp shells and cutting onions, tomatoes, and garlic. She sautéed onions, garlic, and shrimp in oil before adding tomatoes and water to make a broth using a method, she learned from her mother-in-law …

She took out the dates from the date bundle and stacked them in a plate, covered the rice pot, and the dried shrimp broth that she had finished cooking. She tasted the broth and the taste was delicious, but she wished she had brought pepper powder or some hot pepper grains, because apparently there was no pepper in this country. In contrast to the taste of food in India, the taste was peppery, rich in spices, pepper and different tastes, and the types of green leaves that flavored the food.

Then she took the water out of the well and took it to the corner and lit a fire under it, after taking out her clothes that she had brought with her from India, the red tight cotton pants, the long shirt open on both sides, it was made of silk with prints of large red roses and a green background, and the long transparent veil that covered the chest ...

After she took a shower, she refilled the water for her husband to take a shower and wash when he came back from work.

She put on her clothes and combed her hair into two long braids. She tied each braid with a green ribbon, and lifted the ribbon to the beginning of the braid, forming a rose shape on each side of her head, just like Indian girls do. She applied kohl to her eyes to enhance their beauty and bring out the sparkle in them. She lit two pieces of charcoal that she had brought from her mother-in-law's house, along with the incense burner and incense, and filled the house with the sweet scent of incense, as she had learned from her. As the sun reached its zenith, she heard the call to prayer coming from afar. She hesitated whether to pray or wait for her husband to return and teach her how to pray. But she decided to pray in the same way he had taught her, so that she could tell him that she had prayed the midday prayer if he asked. She performed ablution in the same way she had learned, covered her hair well, and stood on the prayer rug. All of this was easy for her except for the prayer itself, as she did not remember or memorize any Quranic verses. She stood in reverence, bowed, prostrated, and said the final piece well. Even her supplication was a request to Allah to bless her and her husband and protect them from the evils of the world, and to make her a source of happiness for her husband so that he would not tire of her and leave her, as she called upon the Merciful. She also asked Allah to enable her to learn to read the Quran and perform the prayer, because her recitation in prayer consisted of only the words "In the name of Allah, the Most Merciful, the Lord of the Worlds, Allah is Great." She did not know how to read the verses, as she was illiterate and had not received any education or opportunity to learn and memorize the Holy Quran.

She put the prayer rug back in its place, she had finished all her work, so she sat waiting for her husband in the living room, leaning her back on the reclining, seeking his return. Then her eyes became heavy, she closed them, and fell asleep, dreaming that she was flying in the sky at times, crawling on the desert sands at times, walking on the surface of the sea at times, and riding the mountain at other times. She also saw that she was speaking with Mansour fluently in Arabic, praying and reading the Quran well, laughing and dancing under the rain water. In that dream, she saw all the impossibilities.

She woke up from her nap when she heard the sound of the main door opening. She ran into the room to see her face in the mirror, arranged her hair and spread it with her hand, arranged her clothes, and stood waiting for him to enter the main building through the sitting room door.

Mansour entered and smiled at her when he saw her, and she smiled back at him. She took the bags that he was carrying from his hand and he asked her to wash and clean them and put them in the kitchen in the container that preserved food. She opened the bags to see lettuce, arugula, watercress, tomatoes, onions, garlic, and the peppers she wished she had a moment ago. She was overjoyed to see the large quantities of green peppers, smiled broadly at him, and thanked him. Mansour also brought lemons and oranges, took a plate, collected some of the vegetables he brought, the orange, and asked her to wash it for him to have it for lunch. He smiled and gestured to his mouth and stomach that he was hungry. She smiled and nodded her head, asking him to wash up so she could prepare the food. She then took his work hat and keys from his hand and placed them in the closet, and helped him take off his socks and shoes. She went to prepare the food, while he went to the living room, removed his military uniform, hung it on the wall, washed, and put on his undershirt and t-shirt and lay down on the bed until she prepared his food. They had lunch together, and then he went to the bedroom to rest until it was time for Asr prayer. He and asked her to wake him up when she heard the call to prayer. She nodded her head in agreement.

She carried the lunch dishes and food, lifted what was left in the food clip, washed the dirty dishes, and wanted to start preparing dinner from now so she could finish her work quickly in the evening.

She cut onions and tomatoes, crushed garlic and pepper, kneaded the dough to later bake paratha and raised the dough …

She sat in the courtyard on the cold sand, contemplating and enjoying the warm rays of the sun. She reflected on what her situation used to be like and where she was now. She was once destitute and miserable, but now she was happy and settled as the wife of a beloved man with a high social standing and an excellent job. Her family were loving people who showed her affection and respect.

This house was her husband's or rather it was her home after having been a servant in her grandfather's house, serving his wife and children. She was grateful for those moments that brought them together and made her fortunate enough to have Mansour desire to marry her and choose her among dozens of beautiful and educated girls. This was the love of Allah for her, as He saved her from the clutches and injustice of her grandfather's wife. She was now lost in thoughts and memories.

Suddenly, she heard a knocking on the main door of the house, so she got up to open it. However, her husband's warnings not to open the door for anyone came to mind, so she hurried to wake him up from his sleep to see who was at the door. But he was tired and deep in a slumber after a hard day's work, and he had told her that he would sleep until the time for Asr prayer.

She hesitated and went back to the door, deciding to ask about the identity of the person knocking. However, she changed her mind since she would not be able to communicate in Arabic. She stood beside the door hoping to hear the person say something that she could understand. But instead of the sound of knocker, she heard the meowing of a cat from behind the door. She laughed at herself and thanked Allah that she didn't wake up her husband for a cat scratching at the door. However, it wasn't the sound of scratching, it was a strong knocking. She went to fetch water from the well for her husband to perform his ablutions and sat by his side, waiting for the call to prayer.

(17)

After two days, Mansour returned from work carrying a basket made of palm leaves filled with fresh fish that he had purchased from fishermen. Niloofar was overjoyed to see the huge number of fresh fish.

After they had lunch, Mansour went to take a nap and Niloofar began washing and preparing the fish for cutting, salting, and drying, a preservation method she had learned from her mother-in-law that allowed her to keep food for as long as possible. As she worked, she heard a knock on the main door. She remembered that she should ignore it because she shouldn't open the door. She continued working while the knocking was followed by the sound of a cat meowing again and wondered who could be knocking on the door. Was it someone strange or just a hungry cat attracted by the smell of fish? Maybe it was but who was knocking?

She decided to call out to feed the cat some leftover fish scraps since cats can jump over fences and climb walls. She held a fish tail in her hand and approached the door where she heard the cat's meowing and started calling out to her but it didn't respond. It continued meowing outside, so she heard the call to prayer for Asr and remembered her husband. She returned the fish tail to waste, washed her hands well, and began drawing water from the well for Mansour's ablution.

When Mansour returned from Asr prayer, he signaled to his wife to get ready to go out with him and asked her to bring some of the salty fish she had prepared. She was happy and went to wash up and get dressed, wearing Arab clothes and carrying the fish that she had prepared. They walked on foot in the neighborhood, and while they were walking, she looked around to get to know the place well. They found themselves on a deserted coastal area, with sandy beaches that scattered with each step, movement, or gust of wind. There were only a few similar houses scattered here and there, with no one else on the road except for them and the poor cat that began to follow them as they left the house. These scenes were the opposite of the ones she was used to seeing in her homeland, where the red sands were compact due to their fertility, with green crops and many large trees. The roads were always filled with people, but here she walked only with her husband and the poor cat. She turned to see it, what a poor hungry and sad cat he was. She wished she could feed it the salty fish she was carrying or keep it at home, take care of it, and relieve its loneliness. It was a wonderful cat, with milk-colored fur, thick hair, and a beautiful face, with a gray line surrounding its neck. It was a clean, friendly cat that seemed like it was one of them. It seemed like a house cat with good health, not like a neglected, dirty, skinny street cat.

They stopped in front of a house that was a little far from their home but in the same area. She could see the top of their house from that place.

She looked at Mansour's face in surprise, and he smiled reassuringly at her. She heard footsteps approaching and the door opening, and a man came out and greeted Mansour. She recognized the man as Saeed, Mansour's friend who married Najma and accompanied them with the rest on the trip from India to here.

Her eyes lit up and she entered with her husband, meeting her friend and embracing her. They spoke eagerly, after a period of separation finding someone with whom they could converse fluently, exchanging their thoughts and feelings. The same was for Najma, except that Najma had learned some Arabic, making it easier for her to communicate with her husband.

She rejoiced and entered inside with her husband, met her friend and hugged her, and they spoke together eagerly. Now, after a period of separation, she found someone with whom she could speak fluently, exchange conversations with, and express everything in her heart, and so did her friend. However, her friend had learned some Arabic language since she was somewhat educated, which made it easier for her to deal with her husband, Saeed, in an easier way.

As for Mansour and Saeed, they sat talking in the courtyard of the house on a carpet and some cushions, with a tray in the middle containing some dates, a tea pot, a coffee pot, cups and saucers. It was the first warm family visit for Samar, with the men in the outer courtyard and the women in the inner courtyard. After the evening prayer, the couple returned home happy, and Saeed gave them a basket full of soaked dates in delicious syrup as a gift, while Najma gave Niloofar some red pepper powder. On the way back, Niloofar was looking for that poor cat, asking Mansour to let her keep it, but she couldn't find it no matter where she looked.

At night, Niloofar woke up in the middle of the night to the sound of a cat meowing outside, but the sound was very close, as if it had entered the courtyard. She wanted to check it out and got up from bed, but Mansour's hand was around her waist, so he woke up and asked her: 'What's wrong? Where are you going?'

She signaled to him that she wanted to see the hungry cat that was meowing outside. He stopped her and asked her to go back to sleep, explaining that she shouldn't go outside at such a late hour. She felt sad for the hungry cat because she wouldn't be able to feed it.

(18)

In the early morning, after Mansour went to work, Niloofar sorted the dirty clothes next to the well, filled the bucket with water, brought soap, and sat next to the well to wash the clothes with her hands, each one separately. She heard a movement behind the main door of the house, and she remembered that it might be the hungry cat that she needed to feed. She got up and headed towards the door and made some sounds that could attract the cat, "Ps … Ps … No … No …" as she did the previous day. As soon as she stopped, the cat jumped and stood on the fence of the house. She saw it and called it, and it stood looking at her as she called it. Then it jumped towards her, approached her, wiped its body with her leg, and meowed weakly.

    She carried it and brought it inside. It started to sharpen its claws on her clothes and lick her hand. She poured some water for it and brought the pieces of fish that were left from the previous day and gave them to it.

    The cat devoured all those pieces quickly, licked every drop in the water bowl until it was finished, and then raised its head, looking at Niloofar as if thanking her gratefully for what she had given it.

    Then she prepared a place for it to rest. She brought some rocks from behind the kitchen building, some scattered woods, and an old piece of cloth that covered the small building she had built for it and made it enter its house, which she built for it. She then continued her household chores, and from time to time, she came to see what it was doing or what it wanted. When she finished her housework, she bathed, put on her beautiful clothes, and went to spend some time playing with the cat in the yard. When she felt the door opening with the key and that Mansur had come, she wanted to hide the cat from him but did not know where or how. Suddenly, the cat jumped from her hands and hid in one of the corners, as if it had heard her voice and hidden.

    Mansour noticed the small tent that Niloofar had prepared for the cat, and a small smile appeared on his face as he pointed to it, wondering who it was for.

She was flustered and didn't know how to answer, as she didn't want to lie to him, so she said it was for the cat and imitated the sound of cats. Mansour smiled and asked her about its location, and she gestured that it had been scared and had run away.

Mansour went into his room, and she hurried behind him to prepare his clothes, bathing water, and lunch. Mansour took a nap after lunch, while she went searching for the cat, but she couldn't find it anywhere. She tried calling it by making those sounds, but it didn't come.

She was saddened by its departure and guessed that maybe it was scared of Mansour, or it went for a walk and would surely return. Mansour went out in the evening to the popular coffee shop with his friend Saeed, while she stayed alone at home, as all his attempts to take her to Najma's house failed. She wanted to finish embroidering the bedspread she had started, to give it to her mother-in-law on their next visit.

She sat in the living room, turned on the radio according to Najma's instructions, who had confirmed to her that she had learned Arabic from the radio. She also said that continuing to listen to Arabic radio would increase her ability to learn and acquire the language quickly. While she was embroidering that piece of cloth, she tried to imitate and repeat every Arabic word said on the radio program that she only understood a little of. At that moment, she heard her cat's meowing and rejoiced at its return. She got up to open the door and take it out to the outdoor courtyard. As soon as she opened the door, it appeared, and she played with it before letting out a loud scream.

Mansour went with Saeed to the popular coffee shop after Asr prayer. They drank red tea, ate boiled fava beans (bagila), played dominos and cards (sheda), and sat with their friends talking about various matters.

Mansour remembered his wife and said: 'I am a bit worried about my wife, as I left her alone at home.'

'Why didn't you bring her to my wife's house? Today, Abu Sultan brought his wife to stay with us until he and his children return from Fujairah tomorrow. She seems to be in the early stages of pregnancy and won't be able to handle the burdens and hardships of travel. Umm Sultan said she will teach Najma how to knit the "tally" thread. Why didn't you bring your wife? She could have also learned and spent a lovely time with them.'

'I insisted several times, but she didn't respond. She said she would stay to finish embroidering the bedspread she will gift to my mother on our next visit to Fujairah.'

'Look, oh Mansour, the poor woman is thinking of pleasing your family and giving them gifts already. You have a great wife, my brother, a really great wife.'

'Indeed, Praise be to Allah, she is hardworking and knows how to manage the household. She takes care of all the chores and never asks for my help.'

'I ask Allah for happiness for both of you.'

'Amen, my brother, and may you have the same.'

After praying together, the evening prayer in one of the mosques near the coffee shop, they both returned to their homes.

Mansour opened the main door and entered, calling out for Niloofar, but there was no answer. He entered the main building's living room to find her sitting in a corner with a piece of cloth that she had started embroidering when he left. Now it seemed that she had finished it, and it was beautiful and magnificent embroidery, with bright and shiny colors. Mansour was delighted to see the bedspread as beautiful embroidery, and he pointed out to her that the bedspread was well-made. She nodded and smiled lightly, but her face was swollen, and the blood was evident on her forehead and cheeks.

Mansour was a little panicked when he saw her swollen face, and he put his hand on her forehead. She was indeed very hot and he felt sorry for her situation. He regretted leaving her alone as she was in good health when he left. Now, as she was sick and he was far away enjoying his time with friends, he blamed himself and reproached himself. He made a commitment to take care of her from now on and not to let her die like Meriem did, and he hugged her tightly.

(19)

The following day, Mansour got up when he heard the call to dawn prayer, the sound coming from far away from the distant Saif Mosque.

'Praise be to Allah who has given us life after death, and to Him is the resurrection. O Lord, do not deprive me of hearing your call to prayer. O Lord, make this day a day of goodness and blessings, not a day of sorrow, worry, and grief.'

After finishing his prayer, he headed to the kitchen to prepare breakfast for himself and his wife, who was sick and had been moaning in pain and shivering from the cold all night.

After breakfast, he asked her permission to go to work and apply for leave for that day and the next, to take care of her during this period of illness and weakness. At first, she didn't want him to go and leave her alone. If she wanted to stop him, what would she say to him? She couldn't even explain or clarify to him what had happened to her the previous night, not even by gesture. But she agreed, and she couldn't do anything but adapt and live the normal life she would live with her husband and wait for him to return whenever he went out.

Mansour left the main house door and closed it behind him, telling her to keep her body warm in bed and leave all the housework to him. He would bring some popular medicines from the market.

Niloofar remained in bed for a while, but she couldn't stay any longer. She got up and carried the breakfast dishes to the sink and started doing the dishes. However, her memory began to recall what had happened to her yesterday. She remembered how she was sitting embroidering a piece of cloth and listening to the radio, trying to imitate the Arabic words in an attempt to learn Arabic. She heard the sound of that cat meowing behind the door, and she jumped up to open it for him. She had missed him since he ran away from home. She opened the door, and the cat stood in front of her, begging for her attention.

Niloofar was overjoyed at the return of her cat and ran to the kitchen to prepare some leftovers from lunch, which she had saved for it. She fed the cat, which approached her and rubbed its body against her legs. Niloofar then sat on the doorstep of the main building of the house, with the cat in her hands, playing with it, petting it, and laughing with it.

Suddenly, Niloofar was startled when she saw her cat's paws and legs elongating, causing the cat to rise up and encircle her with all four limbs, preventing her from moving. Trembling, Niloofar tried to stand up to free herself from the grip of the cat, which had turned into a monster. However, it tightened its grip, and with great fear and helplessness, Niloofar let out a loud scream that shook her entire body, exhausting her completely.

Due to the intense exhaustion and fear caused by the cat's attack, Niloofar broke out in a cold sweat, with every part of her body shaking uncontrollably, including her toes. Sweat poured down her face and blinded her eyes, turning her vision into a nightmare. She tried to grab onto something or to turn around to do something, but to no avail. The cat's face was in front of hers, and its breath had turned into a hot, dragon-like exhale.

Then the cat spoke words that Niloofar couldn't understand, and this was the last thing she remembered before losing consciousness. She didn't know how much time had passed until she came back to her senses, sitting in the same place in the living room, with a fever and the embroidered bedspread in her hand. She was amazed at how she had finished the embroidery in a few hours, which usually takes ten days or more of continuous work.

It ended and she finished the last part with embroidery that was even more magnificent than before, something that she could not have done herself.

She sat in her place, amazed and not denying it, staring at the embroidered bedspread until Mansour entered and woke her up from her distraction. The situation was difficult for her, and no one could explain what had happened to her. Was it a dream?

Or was it reality?

Was it a terrifying nightmare?

Was the cat a normal animal?

Or was it under a spell?

Or was it from the jinn?

No one could exactly explain it to her.

And how could she finish embroidering the entire bedspread in the blink of an eye in just a few hours?

What was happening to her?

(20)

Her psychological questions were interrupted by the cat's voice that she heard again.

She trembled, stood rooted to the spot, and then the pot fell from her hand. She tried to stand up very quietly, run toward the main building, and did not see what was behind her; she run as fast as she could.

She was running and hearing like someone was jogging behind her, and then she fell down after the cat jumped on her shoulder to stop her. She started to weep, and then the cat uttered in a human voice something she could not understand. The cat's voice was low-pitched and quiet, as if it was trying to calm her down, until she fell silent; she kept lying down on the ground, closing her eyes, until Niloofar's arm was grabbed by a hand that made her stand up and then sit in her place. Niloofar wept again making no noise while closing her eyes, and then she felt two palms catching her cheeks. The other started talking to her in that strange language as if he wanted her to look at him; she opened her eyes very slowly and was very scared, as if her heart was going to burst due to its rapid beating.

After she opened her eyes, she was terrified of seeing him; the cat turned into a human-like creature, like a dwarf man whose skin was too white, he was fat, and had large ears and wide eyes, with a big red nose, wide mouth, and small sharpened teeth like those of fish. He looked like the clowns you see in India's seasonal festivals. He smiled at her and then said something she could not understand, which made her lose her balance, and then she started shivering. He stood in front of her, grabbed her wrists, and made her stand behind him. She managed to contain herself, stood up half conscious, not completely aware of what was happening around her. He pulled her hand slowly to make her follow him, and she did so.

He took her to the inner courtyard of the main building (the living room), let go of her hand, and started searching in the stuff. Then he brought her the embroidered tablecloth, unrolled it on the ground in front of her, and pointed out to it to make her look at it; she gazed at the tablecloth as if she was dreaming; it was like an endless nightmare; she could not do anything. He raised his hand, pointing at her, the tablecloth, and at his chest, as if he wanted to tell her that he was who embroidered the tablecloth. She trembled and fell down sitting in her place, and then burst ceaselessly into tears.

The dwarf screamed like a child, started jumping in his place and moving his hands as birds do, singing in his language as if he wanted to prevent her from crying, and reassuring her that he will not harm her, but will try to help her. He continued jumping like a clown, clapping his hands and singing, making her laugh. Her fear of him started to disappear gradually. He stopped, pulled her hand, and put her palms on his cheeks like kids do, as if he was drawing her attention and sympathy. He pulled her from her hands, made her stand, and then took her to the outside. She followed him to the kitchen, where he pointed to his mouth and belly to make her know that he was hungry. This made her sympathize with him and then she nodded in approval, let go of his hands, started frying eggs for him, took the bread out of the larder, and put it in a plate in front of him.

The dwarf sat cross-legged on the ground, and then started eating joyfully looking at her with gratitude, exchanging gazes full of sympathy and compassion. After he finished having the food she prepared for him, he ran through the outer courtyard of the house, and started singing and dancing to express to her how happy he was. She was looking at him in astonishment, but she was also happy for his happiness.

Suddenly, the dwarf ceased what he was doing and stood silent when the sound of clinking keys was heard from the front door of the house. Niloofar also noticed that sound, and was afraid that Mansour might come in and see the dwarf with her; she turned to the door and saw it being opened by Mansour whose face appeared from behind it. And when she turned again to the dwarf and found that he had climbed the top of the wall and was getting prepared to jump outside the house. She raised her hand to stop him out of fear for him, but he had already jumped off the wall. Immediately after that, Mansour entered the house, closed the door behind him, and saw her standing in the courtyard raising her hand as if she was pointing to the wall.

Mansour turned to the wall, but he found nothing, and then he turned to her, came closer and asked her: 'What are you doing here? What's wrong with the wall?'

She shook her head denying that there was anything wrong with the wall.

He placed his hand on her forehead to find that her temperature was still a little bit high; he reproached her, saying: 'Have not I told you to stay in your bed until I come back? Have I not said I will come back soon? Why have you left your bed? You are not okay, darling. I requested a leave so that I can stay here and take care of you. I also asked one of my colleagues to bring a car after Asr prayer to take you to the hospital in Dubai.'

She did not get what he said, but she felt that he is afraid for her. While he was reproaching her for leaving the bed, she was looking at the wall, and the dwarf had already left. After that, she felt very cold and her entire skinny body started to shiver. Mansour hugged her and took her to the bedroom.

She wanted to tell her husband all that had happened to her, but she realized that he will not understand her, and that even if he did, he will not believe her.

Later in the hospital, Niloofar's temperature had been too high, and after the doctor checked her, he told Mansour that she was exposed to cold air that changed her body temperature, and also told him that she should be kept warm and refrain a little bit from doing chores until she felt better. He also prescribed some medications and foods that would help her recover.

(21)

The next morning, Niloofar was awakened by the radio sound when Mansour came back from Fajr prayer. He sat in the outer courtyard of the house after putting the coffee pot on the stove, and was switching radio channels. When she went to the kitchen to prepare breakfast, he called her to sit in his place because she was not well, and said that he will prepare breakfast instead of her. He left and then came back bringing a scarf that he tied around her neck. After that, he went to the kitchen, put the tea pot on the stove, took the coffee pot off it, fried balaleet, sprayed it with water, let it absorb, and then he added some sugar to it and poured it into a glass. Then he fried eggs in a round shape, added some salt and black pepper, put the egg on the balaleet, and then poured tea into two cups and added sugar to them. In another dish, he poured some yogurt that his mother gave to him, and added some dry dates to it. He finally put all the food he prepared in a tray and took it to Niloofar. After he went in her direction, he saw her standing and looking at him; she was staggering like a drunken person, and then she fell unconscious. He put the tray on the floor, and ran to his wife; he carried her, pressed her close to him, and realized that she was still weak and faint due to fever.

But this was not the case; when he left her there and went to the kitchen to prepare food, she sat in his place and was enjoying the pleasant morning, birdsongs, and radio sound. She suddenly heard a sound of something falling into the well and splashing water. She rushed to the well to check whether a bird or mouse fell into it, and then dangled the bucket into the well hoping that she might catch what fell there. She started to move the bucket in the water for that purpose, and then she felt that the bucket has become heavier as if something got stuck in it; she pulled it immediately and it was very heavy this time. She continued pulling it with all her strength while still looking into the well, and once the bucket has been totally pulled, she saw the dwarf hanging on the rope. She let go the rope and was about to scream, but she saw the water bursting from inside the well holding the dwarf who landed next to her, embraced her with his arms, and then he jumped high in the air and they both landed on a beach. After that, he made another higher jump and landed in an empty space where there were large rocks, and then he jumped a third higher jump and landed with her on the roof of a house. After that, he made a fourth jump that was higher than the previous one and landed on a barn of sheep and camels. He finally jumped while holding her and then landed in her house courtyard, at the same place from which he took her for the first time. He let her go, and then she fell to her knees due to the horror of the situation that left her speechless while looking at the dwarf. He approached, hugged her, whispered some incomprehensible words in her ears, and then he made her stand on her feet. He ran towards the wall, climbed it, and jumped outside the house. At that moment, Mansour saw her.

Niloofar regained her consciousness while lying on the bed and Mansour was sleeping next to her. She recalled the journey that the dwarf took her on; it was a terrifying journey that made her lose her mind, although she enjoyed it. She hesitated to tell her husband about the dwarf because she did not want him to call her insane, since he will surely not believe her, and she also feared that if she tells him about the dwarf, he will separate them from each other; she did not want this to happen as the dwarf was who entertained her in her loneliness thanks to his strange way of bringing joy to her heart.

The dwarf had started to make Niloofar happy in his own way; he approached her when Mansour was not with her, as if he waited for her husband's absence to come to her, and each time he frightened her, he made up for that by making her laugh and happy, one way or another by his unusual movements that no human could do, and he also helped her in doing chores by his strange ways.

On one occasion, she and her husband were sifting sand in the outer courtyard to remove harmful stones, impurities, and dirt; they had been doing that for the whole day and even though they finished only one quarter of the sand that was in there. While they were doing that, the main house door was knocked at; it was one of Mansour's friends, and they both stood outside to talk. Niloofar was now alone sifting sand, and she remembered her friend, the dwarf, and wished that he was there at that moment to help her in that work. She thought that he might be nearby watching her, and then she looked around hoping that she might see him, but she did not. She resumed sifting the sand over and over until the sieve was taken from her hand. Her dwarf friend was the one who did that; he started sifting sand very quickly and effectively until sand dust surrounded the entire place.

Niloofar was speechless while looking at the way her dwarf friend was sifting the sand at lightning speed. When Mansour came back, he saw nothing! There was a lack of visibility so that he could not see his wife. He started calling her and sneezing due to the thick dust around him, and he was sneezing until he reached her and took her into the house.

Niloofar had worked hard last night, and then she fell into a deep sleep due to that. Thus, she could not wake up for Mansour to prepare what he needed; she even did not feel when he left the iron bed that made an annoying high sound.

She was sleeping on her back like a child at the right side of the bed, with her hair resting on the pillow and dangling to the floor; she was sleeping with the innocence of a child.

Seeing her like that melted his heart, thus he bent down to kiss her forehead, and then he left to work. That afternoon, Mansour took her on a cruise by a sailing ship and his father was waiting for them. They sailed to the middle of the sea where they stopped the ship.

Mansour stood up and started collecting the net to throw it in the sea, and then he looked at her and she was smiling. As for her father-in-law, he was sitting next to her and put a large basket to put the fish in it. He was happy for that, and this made her happy also. She turned to her husband to find that he caught a big fish that he handed to her and was delighted. She wanted to give the fish to her father-in-law, but she mistakenly dropped it in the sea.

They were all sad for what happened. Mansour cast the net again into the sea, and after waiting for some time, he managed to catch another fish that he handed to Niloofar to give to her father-in-law, but the fish was moving ceaselessly, which frightened Niloofar who dropped it to the sea for the second time. They were again sad for that. Mansour threw his net for the third time, and after some time, he caught a bigger fish this time. He put it in her lap this time so that she did not drop it again into the water, but the fish hit Niloofar by her tail and jumped into the sea for the third time; and they were all sad for what happened. After long patience, the net of Mansour became heavy, and he tried his best to pull it until he was about to fall into the sea. Niloofar wanted to get up and help him in pulling the heavy net, but she could not stand up, and her hair got stuck in something from behind; she turned to see why her father-in-law was pulling her hair, and she was terrified, to find that it was her evil grandfather's wife who was pulling her hair. This made her scream loudly, and she tried to flee, but she could not. She opened her eyes to see herself lying down on the bed, and that her hair is under the control of her friend, the dwarf, who was combing it and playing with it. She wanted to free her hair from his hands, but he grabbed it tighter than before. She surrendered to him, sat on the bed, and dangled her legs from the top of the bed while the dwarf was standing behind her, combing her hair and playing with it; she surrendered to him and suffered alone without saying a word; she considered him as a little child who wanted to spend some fun time with her, and he maybe saw her as his doll.

She would play with him and hold him, as she does with little kids; she would feed and water him, and knit nice clothes for him. He talked to her in his language, but she kept listening to him without complaining although she did not understand what he said. She did not say no to what he wanted her to do for him. If he wanted her to hold him as a kid, she did that. He made her physically and mentally exhausted, but she did not make him feel that she was tired of him. She did all what he wanted from her to keep him close to her, and he, in turn, surprised her with his terrifying journeys in the area, but those journeys made her happy; he entertained her and made her avoid feeling lonely. He would also do all the chores on her behalf very easily and quickly.

She used to feel afraid of him in the beginning, but she could not leave him now; she'd become accustomed to being with him. His presence used to be a little annoying to her, but he soon became an essential in her life; her secret friend or her comfortable invisible breathing space.

When she got a headache, or got tired from doing chores, he comforted her until she fell asleep. He showed her the care of a mother towards her kids that she had never been given in her entire life, and the care of a father toward his kids. They'd been friends for six months by now, and each of them was enjoying being close to each other. She had started to understand and pronounce some weak Arabic.

(22)

The temperature of August had become high, and so did the humidity. Niloofar woke up during the Fajr Azan and was feeling annoyed due to the extreme heat. Last night, Mansour filled the pots in the corner with water to help her in doing daily chores. She awoke him to wash himself and perform ablution before Fajr prayer, and stood next to him while he was washing to give him the towel after he finished. Suddenly, she fell unconscious into the floor, which terrified Mansour. It was actually a quite fall, only that the sound of her bones was heard when they hit the floor; he screamed: 'Niloofar, Niloofar, what's wrong darling?'

Tears soon filled Mansour's eyes, and started falling down when he remembered the illness and demise of Meriem at that moment; he was controlled by obsessions and ideas:

How can she fell ill on the same day Meriem were ill?

Can I be that ill-fated?

Is it conceivable that she is dead?

Questions from all types rushed into his mind.

He tried to touch her, but he became powerless and started to shiver from head to toe. He sat next to her and started crying like a kid; he was too weak to touch her or do anything else but looking at her and weeping.

Shortly after that, he summoned his strength and touched her, drew the curtain of her hair that totally covered her face, and noticed that sweat covered her cheeks and forehead.

He summoned his strength again, held her in his arms, and put her on the bed. He started kissing and hugging her, begging her to wake up, but all this was in vain.

To revive her, he rushed to the corner, filled his hands with water, and sprayed it on her face, and used the rest of water for wiping his face. She moaned and moved her hand.

'Darling … darling … Niloofar.'

'Hum.'

She murmured in pain, opened her eyes, and uttered some incomprehensible words that he could not understand!

'What's wrong darling? What happened to you?'

'Oh, I do not know, I lost my strength and balance …'

'How do you feel now?'

'I feel fatigued; I think I am ill.'

'No, don't say that, Allah forbid!'

'I am tired, I want to sleep.'

He was very afraid for her … and his tears started falling heavier than before.

'I feel cold. Cover me, please.'

He hugged her tightly, covered her, and let her sleep. Then he washed himself for prayer, and prayed next to her, asking Allah for her recovery soon, and that she stayed alive and lived by his side for the rest of his life.

He kept waiting until sunrise, reciting the Quran verses and invocations that he had memorized and puffing towards her. Once the sun started to send the first ray of light, he put on his clothes, covered his wife's face with abaya, carried her on the bicycle and drove her to his brother's house; Saeed.

Mansour knocked at the door of Saeed's house with all his strength. Saeed went out and was terrified; Najma was behind him with her puffy belly …

'What happened?' Saeed asked Mansour.

Mansour started weeping bitterly.

'I do not know, brother; we woke up in the morning and then she fell unconscious, powerless, and could not talk. After she regained her consciousness, she said that she feels cold. I do not want her to die! I do not want to lose her! She is who brought life back to me.'

Najma rushed to Niloofar, despite her heavy weight, to help her get off the bicycle and take her inside the house, but Niloofar was not completely conscious …

Mansour took her inside the house of Saeed, and Najma followed her. Mansour and Saeed stayed outside in the outer courtyard of the house waiting for the news.

Saeed said to Mansour: 'Do not be afraid, my brother, everything will be okay. Don't worry.'

Mansour replied: 'I noticed that she has changed and was not good lately. Now, she does not like being with others, and tries to avoid family visits. She does not like going out, and she keeps quite all the time. She also eats less and sleeps longer and deeper than before, her body has been skinny and she lost her glamour, and most of the time she does not do the chores, as she used to do before. I do not know the reason.'

Saeed replied: 'Do not say this, oh man; you have to expect everything good from Allah, do not worry. It might be because she has been in an environment that differs from the one she was born, and grew up, in. This is the first summer they spend in our country, and they have not become accustomed to the heat and humidity here yet. They must feel some difference since their country of rains and fertility is completely different from our country of high heat and humidity. Your brother's wife was also sick the last week, and I was confused since she is pregnant. So, I brought her some folk medicine based on the advice of our neighbor, Um Sultan. Look at her, she is well now. Do not worry for your wife, she will recover and be well, as she was before.'

'What if – Allah forbid – her health deteriorated? Do you know what? I will call the contractor Musbah to prepare for our travel to India to treat her there.'

'No, you will not need that, believe me.'

'Insha'Allah, I hope so from the bottom of my heart.'

Mansour turned to the other side and started weeping bitterly.

Saeed said: 'Trust in Allah, and do not do this to yourself, you have to be not that sensitive.'

At that moment, Najma went out and was smiling.

Saeed said to her: 'What's up? Tell us about Niloofar, Mansour is very afraid for her.'

'It is all good, I think that Mansour will be a father six months from now.'

Mansour rushed to Najma and asked her: 'What did you just say? Is she really pregnant, is pregnancy like this?'

'Yes, I am sure she is pregnant; she has the same symptoms that I had, which means she is pregnant. This is what Um Sultan taught me, and I can call her to come and confirm what I am saying. But, I prefer that you take her to the hospital so that she can be checked by the specialist who will open a file for her, and give her the required medication and instructions, if needed.'

'Congratulations my brother! See, she is not ill, nor does she have any health problems.'

'Praise be to Allah, and thank you my brother's wife for your efforts with us … can I see her now?'

'Yes, you can, but I think you should call a car to take her to the doctor in Dubai so that she can check her and give her the necessary medications and food that help in making her feel well.'

(23)

'Congratulations Mansour! Your wife is in her third month of pregnancy …'

'Thanks, doctor, but look how fatigued and weak she is.'

'Is it your first child?'

'Yes.'

'Okay, I hope that Allah will make it a happy ending for both of you. Me, in my turn, will prescribe some medications that help strengthen the mother and her embryo, and will also recommend some healthy food that is good for your wife in this stage, but I advise you to visit us with your wife on Sunday or Tuesday when the doctor is usually here since she is better than me when it comes to pregnancy and delivery.'

'Okay, I will bring her on the next Sunday, Insha'Allah.'

'Insha'Allah, but she should avoid doing chores that need great physical effort, but it is okay for simple chores. In this stage, she has to lie down on her back and to raise her legs so that pregnancy is sustained, even though I think that she is about to be out of danger, since she will be in her fourth month of pregnancy after a few days, as the first three months are the sensitive phase. However, and since she used to do the chores not knowing about her pregnancy, this means she is physically strong enough and that her body can maintain pregnancy together with exerting effort, but I still warn her of doing exhausting chores.'

'Now, tell me how old your wife is.'

'When we got married six months ago, she was 14 years old.'

'Yes, she is still too young for pregnancy and delivery, but do not worry; she is strong enough and will survive these phases easily. When she comes on Sunday to see doctor Sarouj, bring your and her documents so that we can register your names in the health record.'

When they arrived at home, he hugged her, kissed her between her eyes, and said to her: 'Sweetheart, you are holding my child whom my parents and I have waited for long years.'

She blushed and looked shy ...

'Hey, darling, from now until you deliver our baby, you are not allowed to do any chores; you will only prepare food; this will be your only duty from now and throughout the next six months.'

She smiled and said in her poor language: 'Who will then do the chores instead of me?'

'I will do them; every day after Asr prayer, I will do the chores until the sleeping time, and I will not go out with my friends unless you are with Najma, my parents, or with a woman we trust ... deal?'

She laughed gently and said: 'No, this is too much; your work is enough, I will work as much as I can without harming my child.'

'No, you will not do any work; I order you! I order you to have a complete rest; do you hear me!'

'Yes, I do.'

He inserted his hand in her hair to touch her scalp and started playing with her hair strands, and then he started kissing her from the eyes, to her cheeks, nose, until he reached her mouth that he kept kissing very passionately, and then his lips went down to her chin and neck. Niloofar here was aroused and felt that she was surrendering to her and her husband's desire, but she felt that she should stop that arousal that can lead to some harmful results, following the advice of her friend, Najma, who recommended her to not have intercourse with her husband in the first three or four months of pregnancy.

She interrupted the love and passion of Mansour, saying: 'I am hungry ...'

'Oh, darling! Why did not you say that when we were in Dubai?'

'I was not hungry then.'

'Oh Allah, what can I cook that fast?'

'I will prepare something to eat. You have to rest since you were with me from dawn, and you must be tired now.'

'No, no, I will bring something for us to eat. Do not worry, just lie down on the bed, and I will bring some pillows for you to raise your legs, as the doctor told us to do.'

He made her lie down, brought the pillows and put them under her legs, and then took his shoes off, and went to the kitchen.

She started thinking about her child, and how her life will be after he would come to existence. She felt that she missed her late grandmother, and thought that if her mother were alive now, she would have been happy for her pregnancy. At this moment, the room's door was being opened gently. She turned and saw that her dwarf friend was trying to open it and then his head appeared. She smiled for what she saw, and felt secure, as if he had come to tell her that he will always help her and be close to her, to make up for her grandfather's love and mother's tenderness. But the dwarf did not smile for her as he did usually. Rather, he shivered as if he was afraid of something, and then ran.

She was surprised at what he did, and then she heard his steps as if he had come back. He entered, but it was not the dwarf, but her husband Mansour, who was holding a tray on which there were two food pots. She smiled and was surprised by how he finished preparing the food that fast.

He said to her: 'It was Saeed; Najma sent you the food as she felt that you might be hungry and unable to prepare food today; she is a really good woman, and so is her husband. I was cutting bread to fry it for you when I heard that someone was knocking at the door.'

Najma had sent them Indian rice cooked with spices and ginger, in addition to chicken fried with peanut sauce, onion, and garlic.

After they finished having food, Mansour took the dishes and pots to the kitchen, and then came back to her immediately. Niloofar was very happy with the food she had until she was satisfied, and then she slept in her father's lap like a child.

(24)

In the morning, Mansour got up in a hurry, washed himself for prayer, and then he performed Fajr prayer. And then he filled the pots with water, washed the dishes, and put on his work clothes, while Niloofar was still sleeping. He kissed her between her eyes and kept gazing at her amazing beauty, innocence, and sweetness. He considered himself lucky for having her in his life.

He heard someone knocking at the door, and rushed to open it; it was Saeed and his wife, Najma, who would stay with Niloofar until Mansour came back.

'Assalamu Alaikum …'

'Wa alaykumu s-salam, thanks for being here.'

'Don't mention it, they are sisters who can help each other in such circumstances. Najma received the assistance of Um Sultan when she was in her early months of pregnancy, and now it is her turn to help her sister, Niloofar.'

'May Allah bless you.'

'Come with me, sister, to show you the room.'

He took her to the main building, and Saeed waited for her in the courtyard.

Mansour started calling Niloofar: 'Hey Niloofar, Niloofar, look who we have here.'

But Niloofar did not get up.

Najma said: 'It is okay, do not awake her, keep her sleeping, I will sleep on the floor.'

Mansour replied: 'No, please lie next to her on the bed, because you are also pregnant.'

'No, I should not do that. I will sleep on the floor, I am accustomed to that, I even sleep on the floor because I have a backache from sleeping on the bed.'

'Okay, then I will bring you a blanket and pillow.'

Mansour and Saeed went to work …

When Niloofar woke up, she found that her friend Najma was sleeping on the floor. She could not believe her eyes; was this real or fiction?

She approached, and touched her. Najma woke up, and then they talked to each other with their language: 'Have you woken up? How do you feel now?'

'I am fine, Praise be to Allah, but tell me what brought you here.'

'I asked my husband to seek the permission of your husband for allowing me to stay with you until they come back from their work, after which I will return to my house. I thought that you may need something and nobody is with you, since you are passing through a sensitive period and need care. I have also started feeling lonely and need someone to entertain me.'

'Yes, sure. I sleep deeply these days so that I do not feel who is around me while sleeping. But why have you slept on the floor and not next to me?'

'No, no, I should not do that. This is the bed of you and your husband, and no other women should sleep on it. Your husband also insisted that I sleep next to you, but I refused to do that.'

'I do not know how to thank you for the care that you are showing toward me, and you also sent us tasty food yesterday; this is great giving that I do not know to reward you for, I think that if I had a sister, she would not have been kinder than you with me.'

'No, this is my duty, we are for each other, and since we have no parents or relatives here, we have to look after each other, and I will definitely need your help when I give birth two or three months later.'

'Yes, absolutely.'

Niloofar hugged her friend Najma, and remembered her friend, the dwarf, who fled last night out of fear from her husband, Mansour. Will he come back today to visit her?

They both spent the day preparing various Indian dishes that can be preserved for a long time. They also tried to practice speaking Arabic. Every time, Niloofar tries to suppress her desire to tell Najma about her dwarf friend.

Although Niloofar was enjoying that Najma was with her, she was eagerly waiting for her departure to see and experience the tenderness and compassion of her dwarf friend after he knows that she was pregnant. She was sure that he would treat her gently and surround her with love and tenderness.

When will she experience that love and compassion? When will she see him after Najma told her that she will visit her daily when their husbands go to work? How can she meet her kind-hearted friend?

On Sunday, Mansour took Niloofar to visit doctor Sarouj in the health building. The doctor reassured them that her pregnancy had started to stabilize, and told them that Mansour would have to bring her there once a month to be checked by the doctor, and that if she felt pain or tiredness, he had to bring her immediately. The doctor also prescribed medications other than those given by the doctor she had visited first.

Two weeks had passed during which Niloofar could not see her friend, the dwarf, because when her husband went to work, Najma came to her house and stayed with her until he came back.

(25)

One morning …

'Niloofar … Niloofar … darling … come on, wake up.'

'Yes, I have woken up.'

'Hey, sweetheart, my brother Saeed is outside, he told me that Najma is having some pain and that Um Sultan will stay with her. She cannot come to you today; do you want me to take you to her?'

'No, I do not want to go anywhere, I just want to sleep.'

Niloofar was happy for that news, because she would finally have the opportunity to see her friend dwarf that she had been waiting for two weeks, as if the tenderness, compassion, and love of her husband had declined so that she waited for the love and tenderness of her friend, the dwarf.

'Okay, sleep and have rest. I will go to work and ask for a leave to come back to you as soon as possible so that you do not have to be alone. Listen, I do not want you to hold anything heavy or to do any chores until I come back.'

'No, I will not do any work that may harm me or my child, I will stay in my place until you come back.'

He kissed her between her eyes, closed the door, and went to work.

She waited … until she heard the sound of closing the main house door, after which she heard the sound of opening that door. She felt happy, raised her body, and sat in the bed, with her eyes looking directly toward the door. Her friend, the dwarf, came in and was wearing amazing colorful clothes as if it was on an Eid day. He gave her a set of nice clothes, and asked her to put them on. Then he took her to the corner and stayed in the room waiting for her. Niloofar put on the nice clothes, and then came back to the room where he was waiting for her in the corner. She stood in front of the mirror to find herself wearing a long white dress interspersed with pearls around the neck opening and hands, and her gold hair was dangling on her back with a large strand of it lying on her right side of her chest; her face has been nicer and brighter as if she was one of princesses that she used to hear their stories from her grandfather when she was a child. He approached her, pulled her from hand and walked ahead of her; she followed him and was smiling and happy. He took her from the main building to the courtyard that turned into a gorgeous and green grove, full of flowers and roses with nice and bright colors, in addition to banana, apple, mango, pear, and fig fruitful trees. Birds in that grove were uttering the best songs, and it was filled with fresh cold air. There was a swing decorated with nice flowers hanging from the apple tree. The dwarf asked her to ride that swing and enjoy her day.

She rode the swing and was grateful to her dwarf friend who showed her the happiness that she had always dreamt of experiencing. While she was on the swing, he told her to raise her head and look to the sky the color of which turned into a brilliant pink color that comforts the soul and heart. She swayed a lot until she got tired, and her friend felt that she was tired of swaying, so he stopped her and got her off the swing so that she could rest on the green ground, enjoy the perfume of roses, and sing with the birds that landed and sat around her and between her hands.

He rushed to the kitchen and brought a transparent glass plate that she had never seen like before, and then he started picking a large matured fruit from every tree in the grove. He dangled the bucket into the well that turned into a golden bucket, and then he pulled it filled with fresh pure water that was not available in any of part of that land. He washed the fruits that he picked, brought them to her, and left her while she was eating them and enjoying their sweet and mouth-watering taste. He sat next to her and was happy for seeing her happy; how delighted she is! This is what she had been waiting for ... this compassion ... this tenderness that nobody but her kind-hearted dwarf friend could offer to her. After she finished eating fruits, she turned to him to find that he had brought her a golden bucket full of pure fresh water to wash her hands with. Her eyes had been full of tears out of joy; she hugged him tightly after she washed her hands, and thanked him. The dwarf pulled her from hand with a big smile on his face and then took her to the main building of her house; she was very happy, but she was a little sad for knowing that this fun and happiness time in that grove was about to come to an end, and that her husband, Mansour, might be on his way to the house. She had never hated that her husband returned to the house like this time, but this was reality. She did what her friend, the dwarf, told her to do; he asked her to change the clothes that he brought to her and give them back to him. Niloofar came out the corner after she had changed that magical white dress and put on her old outfit, and handed it to him; she was smiling, but sadness had started to sneak into her heart.

He made her lie down on her back, caressed her face and head, and then kissed her forehead, as if he was reassuring Niloofar that he will always be close to her during her pregnancy. And then he left. No sooner had the door been closed than it was opened again; it was Mansour who had brought some food.

(26)

Niloofar pretended that she was sleeping as she wanted to keep remembering the moments she spent with her dwarf friend in the grove of the house courtyard, until she really fell asleep. When Mansour saw her, he did not want to awaken her. He changed his clothes, and headed to the kitchen to prepare food for both of them, as she must be hungry now.

He took out the lamb liver that he bought from the butcher who brought a carcass to his store to sell it to cooks and chefs. Mansour washed the liver and cut it into small cubes, added some salt and Bzar (local spices), put it in a pot on the stove, poured some oil, and kept it on fire until it was cooked thoroughly. After that, he brought down the rice that was hanged on the shelf in which he had put dates to keep it safe and away from insects, and then he added some water drops and let it be heated on charcoal. After that, he moved to the main building to awaken his wife so that she could wash her face until the food is ready.

He entered her room and walked toward the bed, and before he reached it, he felt as if warm water was under his feet. He turned on the lights to find that the floor was all red as if a bucket of blood was poured on it. He was frightened and wondered where this liquid came from.

Mansour looked at his wife and found that blood was flowing from the bed she was sleeping on. He was terrified, and when he took off the cover, he found her covered with blood, as if someone stabbed her or poured a large bucket of blood on her.

He run like crazy to seek help, and when he went out of the house, he saw a car driven by a military man who was picking up a Sheikh to Dubai. Mansour explained to him what happened to his wife, and the man expressed his willingness to render help. Mansour carried Niloofar who was like a corpse after he covered her with a sheet. He put her in the back seat of the car and sat next to her. The driver was confused and terrified while trying to reassure Mansour as much as he could. Mansour was deeply affected by what happened to his wife, and he started wondering: *I do not know what happed to her; what caused all that bleeding? Did she commit suicide by cutting her arteries? Could it be that a thief broke into the house and tried to steal something, and when she tried to prevent him, he harmed her? Could she be suffering some illness? But I was in her room before a few minutes, and everything was okay then. Oh, my Allah, why is this my destiny that when I get married to a girl, she falls ill? Am I the reason?*

He asked a lot of questions, but found no answers to any …

Niloofar seemed lifeless as a corpse, but she was breathing normally, and when they reached the hospital, Mansour carried her and took her to the doctor. The doctor asked him to stay outside, and summoned the other doctors …

One hour later, the doctor and another one went out to inform Mansour that his wife had lost her baby, because she might have eaten something that was harmful, which might have been the reason of bleeding. They also told him that she will be kept under medical supervision until she recovered completely.

He went to her room and found her sleeping peacefully, ignorant of what happened to her. He kissed her between her eyes, and thanked Allah for her safety.

Mansour left the hospital and was in a mixed psychological state, not knowing whether he should be happy for she is well, or whether he should be sad for losing his first baby. He took a car and headed to his village.

He went to his parents' house, and said: 'Assalamu Alaikum.'

'Wa alaykumu s-salam, son; in the Name of Allah, the Most Gracious, the Most Merciful! Where did all this blood on your clothes come from? Has anything bad happened to you?'

'I am fine …'

'Did you fight with anyone, or what?'

'No.'

'Then where did all this blood come from?'

'My baby has died; Niloofar lost our baby, and she bled a lot. So, I carried her with my hands to the hospital; she was like a corpse.'

His mother walked toward him and hugged him:

'I ask Allah for forgiveness, Allah forbids, do not worry my son, you are still young. Allah will send you many kids who will fill your house.'

Mansour burst into tears and so did his mother.

His father tried to calm them down: 'Praise be to Allah for everything; it is His Will and Wisdom that we cannot object to.'

'Blessed is Allah, Almighty.'

'Come on son, change your clothes and go take a shower, I will call a taxi to take us to Dubai. Me and your mother will go with you. We should not leave Niloofar alone there, since she has no one with her but Allah and us. Let's go and check on her.'

(27)

Mansour came with his parents and a brunette girl, called Sanota, who was their maid, to the hospital to check on Niloofar. It was late, and they saw her from a distance because they were not allowed to enter her room or even to be close to her. She was sleeping like a child, putting her face on her right hand, and the fingers of her left hand touching her right hand.

'You have to leave now and come back in the morning, because no visits are allowed, to maintain the rest of patients.'

'I am her mother-in-law, and like her mother, can I stay with her till the morning? We have come from a distant place.'

'No, dear, this is not allowed ... please leave now and come back tomorrow after 8 am.'

'Okay, daughter, but can you tell me how she is now?'

'She is well, do not worry, and in safe hands.'

'Insha'Allah, may Allah bless you ... come on, son, take us to your house.'

They took another car to Mansour's house.

The blood that bled from Niloofar had reached the main building, dried, and its color turned into black brown. Mansour was deeply sad for seeing the remains of his child who had never been born ...

Mansour's father said: 'There is no might or power except by Allah. Hey, Sanota, please go with your madam and clean the house. Me and Mansour will sit on the sand until you finish.'

Mansour's mother and the maid started cleaning the dry bloodstains that were on the floor.

The maid took the bed sheets and the mattress and put them next to the well, filled a large pot with water, poured boiled water and salt on them, and left them until they were soaked so that they become clean.

After they had dinner prepared by Mansour's mother, Sanota spread the mattress in the inner courtyard, and they all went to bed.

In the morning, Mansour and his parents went to the hospital in Dubai to visit Niloofar, and Sanota stayed in Mansour's house to do the chores and prepare food for them.

When they entered from the door of the long room where nurses gather, they noticed that doctor Sarouj was standing there. When she saw them, she raised her head and looked at them. Niloofar turned and saw her husband and his parents, and then she got up and ran as fast as she could to her husband, threw herself in his arms, and started weeping bitterly for her lost baby.

'My child has died … died!'

Mansour hugged her tightly and tried to not cry, but he failed. Mansour's parents tried to calm them down, together with the doctor and nurses who rushed to take Niloofar back to her bed since her health condition had not been stable yet.

That was a really touching moment, and Niloofar was deeply affected; she wept, screamed, and whined a lot, and then she was given a calming injection that helped her fall asleep.

The doctor said: 'Praise be to Allah that you are here to check on her condition by yourself; this is how most of the women who lose their babies feel. I am very sorry that you lost your baby, hoping that Allah will make up for this loss, Insha'Allah.'

'But how did this happen, doctor? Have not you told us that her pregnancy has become safe? So, how did my child die?'

'The embryo did not die without a reason. It seems that she ate something or took medication by mistake, which led to the death of the embryo.'

'How did that happen?'

'Allah only knows. She says that she had no food but that she ate with you, isn't this right?'

'Yes, that's right.'

'Never mind, now you have to take care of her in this period. As you know, she is too weak and has lost a lot of blood. If her condition has become stable by tomorrow, you can take her home.'

Mansour and his parents left the hospital and came back home.

Mansour's father said: 'How about that we keep Niloofar in our house for some time? And I will personally take care of her until she recovers.'

(28)

Niloofar had moved unwillingly to live at her parents-in-law's house.

And even though she didn't want to be away from her dwarf caring friend nor her loving husband, it wasn't up to her to decide; she had no choice but to comply with her husband and his parents' request.

During the time she spent with them, she was successfully recovered, her cheeks and lips restored the lovely pink color again, and she got even prettier.

Moreover, she learned all about local food recipes, absorbed the Arabian lifestyle, and reached an advanced level in Arabic speaking skills. She was also able to memorize some short Surahs from Quran by the help of her mother-in-law, learned well how to pray, and became more and more attached to her husband's family. As for Mansour, he was constantly visiting them to check on her.

Days continued to pass calmly yet a bit heavy on Niloofar's heart as she was missing her dwarf friend, and it was also the same for Mansour who had to endure the difficulty of travelling over and over to his wife and family.

One day, Mansour decided that the next time, he will take his wife back home. His parents didn't mind it, and his wife was over the moon who was desperately waiting for that day to come to get back her home and her caring friend.

A week before Mansour came, Niloofar went out with her sister-in-law to feed the goat at the farm, and all of a sudden she felt nauseous and fatigued. That's how Mansour's sister found out about Niloofar's pregnancy; by noticing her pregnancy symptoms.

That was her second pregnancy, which became even more special as it came like a gift to make it up for the loss of the first one.

It came along with an exceptional joy from her side as well as her husband's family's side after the heart break she went through by losing her baby who she was blessed with. Everyone was thrilled by this pregnancy news, especially Mansour who felt like Allah had made it up for him with that baby.

Mansour's mother had sent Sanota, the nan, with them to take care of Niloofar and their needs generally. Niloofar was a bit upset at the beginning about Sanota accompanying them as she won't be able to meet her dwarf friend easily while having Sanota around. However, she realized how exhausting the chores were besides the fact that she needed to fully rest especially at this stage, maintain this pregnancy and keep it safe.

The three of them made it home on Friday evening, and Niloofar was finally in her home that she hadn't seen for over two months. She kept looking around in the place, seeing herself in every corner in it with her friend. Lots of memories she had made with her dwarf friend that she didn't know yet whether she could meet or not.

She walked to her room, recalling what her mother in low had enjoined them with before leaving the house: 'Noura, my dear, now you're about to get in the car for a very long time that it will take you almost the whole day to make it home. That's indeed a long travelling time for a woman who has just became pregnant. Once you make it home, I want you to lie down, keep your legs up to rest your back and hold the fetus in place. Lie down and keep your legs up using this pillow. Don't try to hold or move it yourself as it is very heavy, Sanota will hold it for you and get it to the room. I also enjoin you, my daughter, to forget all about the chores as Sanota will take care of everything. So, all what you need to do is keeping yourself and your baby safe.'

Indeed, Niloofar did follow all her mother in low instructions; she walked to the room, lay down with her legs up using that pillow which Sanota put under. She felt exhausted owing to the long trip, and let herself to go asleep while hearing sounds of the doors being locked by Mansour who was making sure that they were well locked before heading to sleep.

She also heard him telling Sanota: 'From now on, you will be sleeping here (the inner yard – living room).'

'Noted, Uncle.'

Niloofar suddenly woke up in the middle of the night to the sound of the cat mewing over and over as if it was calling her. She then realized it was her dwarf friend that was deeply missing her for being away all that time, and it was same for her. However, she couldn't answer the cat's call and go out to meet it in the outer yard as Mansour was keeping her in his arm as a way of keeping her safe, along with Sanota who was sleeping outside the room as if she was her bodyguard. Even if she could slip out of Mansour's arms, she won't be able to sneak out of bed without avoiding the metal bad squeaking.

So, she closed her eyes and tried to fall asleep again while feeling her heart break over her dwarf friend that always tried to make her happy.

In the morning, Mansour kissed her lips and forehead, then went out to work after getting a shower and praying Fajr prayer. She got up upon the sound of locking the main door, and immediately jumped out of bed to make sure that he left, but she got spooked standing by her room door as she heard a loud snoring sound coming from Sanota. She then felt relieved by the snoring sound knowing that it will help her to be aware whenever Sanota wakes up as the sound will start to fade. When that happens, she will just go back to bed or go to the kitchen pretending that she's cooking some food. Eventually, she sneaked out to the outer yard while continuing to hear the snoring sound.

Finally, she felt the freedom, excitement, and thrill she has been waiting for over two months. With the sunlight slowly getting to every spot on the ground, she lay down on the sand waiting for her dwarf friend that hasn't showed up yet.

She kept on waiting till the snoring sound of Sanota faded away, hence she ran out to the kitchen to pretend that she's cooking food. Within few moments, Sanota came, opened the main door and went looking for her mam till she stepped into the kitchen.

'Aunt, what are you doing here?'

'Nothing, I was just frying some eggs cause I'm hungry.'

'Why didn't you wake me up?'

'No, I didn't want to interrupt your sleep. I preferred that you wake up at your own comfort.'

'No, Aunt, please don't say this. I'm here to take care of your needs, and the last thing I want is you or what's in your womb getting hurt.'

'Don't worry, we won't get hurt, Insha'Allah.'

'Set aside, Aunt, and let me finish this. Go back to your bed please.'

'Okay, I will, thank you.'

(29)

Ten days had passed, through which the dwarf friend kept showing up as a cat at night, mewing for her to meet outside while, on the other hand, she pointlessly waited for him in the morning. That hard-headed friend seemed to be playing mind tricks on her challenging her hopeless case, and waiting for her to figure out a way to meet together at night. She had to find a way to do so without causing a noise that could raise doubts.

She thought she could use her back as an excuse, and argue that the bed was causing her a back pain, therefore she'd prefer to sleep on the ground. This way, Mansour will let her sleep on the ground thus avoiding the metal bed squeaking. She will also use the room temperature as an excuse for leaving the door open, thus leaving Mansour alone on the bed with Sanota's snoring sound nearby him.

She carried out her plan; everyone slept but her who kept waiting for her friend mewing to go and meet outside. She waited for too long that even the cat mewing time passed. She kept waiting, but then she decided to get out of the room hoping she could hear the mewing as maybe it wasn't clear because of Sanota's snoring sound.

She stood up calmly, looked back at Mansour who was totally asleep, then she got out of the room after putting the pillows in her place and covering them to make it seem like she was sleeping. As for Sanota, she was asleep with her mouth open and unaware of anything that was happening.

She headed to the main door of the inner building, but she couldn't hear the mewing. She, however, did hear a sound of something moving. So, she tried to listen carefully, and all of a sudden, there were light knocks on the door. That made her freak out, but she knew it was her friend. She looked back to make sure it was still quiet, then opened the door quietly, got out and closed it. She sneaked to half of the yard looking in the dark, but she didn't find him. She had a feeling that something was getting close to her, thus waited till it got closer. She looked at him right after he grabbed her wrist, to find that his face was covered with tears. Hence, she bent down and gave him a hug, he jumped right at her so violently that she almost screamed. Rather, she just closed her eyes with no resistance.

Couple of seconds later, both of them went down to wide green lowland that was full of flowers and fruit trees. It also had a running river falling down from a waterfall at the mountaintop, white rabbits playing over the place, colorful ducks swimming with their offspring in a little swamp, beautiful golden frogs jumping along with amazing shiny group and some big friendly deer.

Her dwarf friend walked towards her, holding her hand with a grumpy face. When she looked at him, she kissed his cheeks, gave him a hug, smiled at him and went to run happily in the green area ahead of her while he was running, jumping and singing happily because of her happiness.

She ran after the rabbits, grabbed a frog and kissed it, held the baby duck and touched her cheeks with its feathers and hugged the deer gently.

She was so overwhelmed with joy that she didn't – at that moment – care about Mansour or Sanota feeling that she was missing. She was distracted, and kept playing with her friend and the lovely animals in that fantasy place. When she felt exhausted after too much running and playing, she lay down under a huge pomegranate tree with her friend next to her.

Deep inside, she wished she could taste that tree fruits. Suddenly, he jumped high to the top of the tree, and got her some red, yellow and green pomegranate fruit. That made her delighted and she started to peel the fruits and eat what's inside till she was full. One by one, it was getting sweeter.

The dwarf stood up, held her and jumped high, while she was feeling fearless with absolute tranquility. Within seconds, she was in her house's outer yard. He left her happy as she indeed was.

She hugged him whispering in Urdu: 'Don't ever get mad at me again please, I couldn't meet you only because I'm not staying alone at home anymore as you know. Just be sure that you're always missed as you're my one and only safe home in this life.'

He nodded his head as if he was telling her that he knows and he's no longer mad at her.

She whispered again: 'Do you know I'm expecting a baby? This is, indeed, my second time being pregnant as I lost the first baby the same day we met for the last time.'

He sadly nodded his head as if he was consoling her. He then gave her a hug and ran away.

She freaked out thinking that Mansour was on his way to them, therefore, she got up and somehow jogged till the main building. There, she heard the sound of the bed squeaking and Sanota's snoring thus thought to herself like: maybe he was just rolling from side to side on bed. She quietly got into the building, locked the door behind, walked and stood next to Sanota's head who was peacefully asleep. She smiled at her and remembered when she used to work as a nanny for her grandfather's wife, even though Sanota's state was much better than hers back then.

She felt fatigued and dizzy, and was afraid to pass out. So, she leaned against the wall, swinging till she made it to bed and fell asleep.

Mansour woke up to the sound of Sanota screaming …

He ran towards her to find that she's sitting close to a pool of blood with a terrified look on her face …

'Oh gosh, what's that? Where all this blood coming from!'

'I don't have a clue, uncle. I just woke up heading to the bathroom, and was shocked to see this scene.'

Mansour ran towards his wife whose body color turned to blue and who was in the middle of another pool of blood connected to the first one with blood spots.

Niloofar was admitted to the treatment room in the healthcare facility, while Mansour was still under the effect of what happened to his wife.

He ran towards Saeed who brought them to the healthcare facility as he had already started to drive his work car.

'Don't you worry brother; hopefully it will be fine, Insha'Allah.'

'I just don't know; why does my wife keep suffering from this bleeding every time she gets pregnant? I truly hope she didn't lose the baby this time too. She's taking the medication exactly as the doctor prescribed; moreover, she neither works at home nor makes any effort, so how is this happening?'

'Don't you worry brother, maybe she didn't lose him? Let's wait till the doctor shows up.'

'I hope she didn't. She's young, could that be the reason? But the doctors have assured me that she has a strong body, and can withstand the exhausting nature of pregnancy and giving birth to the baby.'

After minutes, Dr Sarouj got out and found that Mansour and Saeed are standing by some corner, thus, she headed towards them.

'I don't know where to start. How can I explain this to you? Look, all I can say is that she has miscarried her second pregnancy this time, just like the first one – after eating a poisoned nutrient. The toxins level in her blood and stomach was high enough to kill her, but it only terminated the fetus life. After all, Niloofar's medical situation is critical because we need to quickly carry out a blood transfusion in order to be able to replace the poisoned blood as fast as possible.'

'What! How did that happen?'

'I think you are the one who should answer this, right?'

'Yes, but we were asleep. When did she eat the poisoned food? I must have eaten it with her because the last thing that went down her stomach was last night dinner which everyone ate and no one got hurt from. She even said that she has back pain and a sense of high body temperature before going to bed.'

'I don't know, but all the lab tests and examinations prove what I'm saying … and in such case, we usually leave the whole thing to the authorities to get involved and resolve such mysteries. However, we won't do this, rather, we will let you figure out the whole thing on your own.'

Saeed interrupted the conversation saying: 'Oh no, not a crime, please, things can't be this messed up doctor!'

'Mansour, I didn't accuse anyone of anything. Maybe she is just a bit sad or depressed.'

Saeed asked: 'Sorry doctor, I didn't get what you mean by that?'

Mansour answered: 'The doctor means that she, Niloofar, may have wanted to get rid of her life or the baby's life. Oh gosh, I'm about to lose my mind! How is this happening?'

He then got out straight to the street as he couldn't keep it together and couldn't help crying.

Saeed went after him saying: 'Oh, my brother, remember Allah, that's Allah's will and there's nothing in our hands to do other than praising Allah.'

'Amen … the doctor says that she ate poisoned food.'

'I don't think so, trust me, it's just Allah's will.'

'I really hope so.'

(30)

A week later, Niloofar had successfully completed the treatment …

On their way home, there were sad vibes filling up the air and the silence wasn't interrupted by anything except by the car engine noise through the road.

Niloofar was the one to end this silence saying: 'Saeed, my brother, can I go and visit Najma now? I really want to see her and the baby, Butai. I truly miss her.'

'Oh, yeah … yes, but …'

'No, brother. You shouldn't be visiting her now, at least not now …'

'Why not? I'm fine now.'

'No, you're still fatigued and it's all over you face. I wouldn't prefer that Saeed's wife sees you this way. Get better first. You got me?'

'Yeah, I got you …'

'Hold on, Mansour, don't say this. My sister-in-law, look, I promise when you get better, I'll bring her and the baby to you myself.'

'Okay, hopefully, Insha'Allah.'

She got back into the sad silent mood, and thought to herself that he doesn't want her to meet his wife and baby as – by losing her baby twice – she might be sort of a bad luck for them; Najma and her baby.

Of course, she didn't miscarry on purpose; it was just her destiny and what was meant for her. If her first pregnancy had been maintained, she would have been in her seventh month now, counting down days left till the time of delivery.

With these thoughts, she felt down and her eyes were full of tears that started to fall down, but she tried to stare at the horizons to hopefully get her tears back in their place again.

After that, days went heavy on her heart and everyone who was around. She didn't get out of the room unless it was urgent, and even her dwarf friend was whining with her as he was visiting her in the room while Mansour was out and Sanota was busy with the chores.

He just kept an eye on her, or sat next to her, patted her shoulder and passed his hands through her hair to give her the feeling that he was here supporting her. As for her, she lost that passion towards life and whatever it came with, and – during some wild awful moments – she even planned to end her life. Moreover, Mansour had begun to become emotionally cold as he suspected that she was doing the miscarriage on purpose.

One day, she woke up to the sound of the house's main door closing, while Mansour was leaving to pray the afternoon prayer.

She felt really pissed off and severely depressed, and Sanota was taking her nap in the inner yard. So, she got up, walked to the outer yard till she reached the well, and stood there staring at its water, darkness and depth. She thought to herself that if she deliberately fell down into it, no one would feel a thing, and she would stay there till her body floats on the surface of the water. She stood over two rocks till the top of the well became at the level of her lower abdomen, meaning that she could easily throw herself down.

She held onto the two sides of the well edges, slowly bending and leaning forward the well wall from inside while being afraid of the well's darkness and depth till the point where the rocks she was leaning towards started to shake owing to her body weight.

She started to let gravity take control, but her grandfather's face came across her imagination and it looked sad and afraid. That's why she felt afraid of death all of a sudden. She then started to hardly get back to the right standing position, and she even was afraid that she can't trust these shaky rocks that started to wear out leaving this mud weld.

She was so in awe of the whole scene that she fell on the ground trying to recap the moment in her head.

Why did she ever take that step?

Why was she about to end her life?

Why didn't her life and life itself matter that much?

She was brought back to reality by Sanota's voice that was running towards her asking: 'Aunt, what's wrong? What are you feeling?'

She desperately tried to hide what she was going through and what she was about to do: 'Nothing, I'm all good, just trying to enjoy the fresh air.'

'It's cold here, Aunt. It's almost winter time. Come on, go back inside so you won't get sick.'

'I know it is, but I loved it.'

'Do you want me to get you something?'

'No, no, just sit down and chat with me a bit, tell me something.'

Sanota became happy and laughed.

'What would I say?'

'Whatever you have on mind.'

'There's nothing I can think of.'

Then they both heard knocking sound on the main door.

'Aunt, someone is at the door.'

'Yes, go and find out whom, but ask the person who she or he is and don't open the door.'

'Noted.'

Then she ran towards the door.

'Who is this?'

'This is … This is Musbah, the contractor … Is Mansour here dear?'

'No, sir, Uncle Mansour went out for the afternoon prayer, and he will get back soon.'

'Well, I'll wait for him.'

'Okay, but excuse me, sir, I can't open the door for you till Uncle Mansour gets back home.'

'Never mind dear, I got you. Don't worry I'll wait for him here.'

Niloofar immediately ran towards the door when she knew it was Mosbih, the contractor.

She talked with him behind the door in Urdu: 'Hello, sir, how are you doing? I'm Niloofar.'

'I'm fine, dear, what about you? I came here to see you and I also have some news.'

'Really! You came to see me?'

'Yes, and I'm waiting for your husband … Oh, here he is, I can see him, he is coming …'

Moments pass slowly while she is waiting to hear Mansour's voice. She ran towards her room, put on the long head scarf and quickly got back to where she was standing.

Within minutes, she was able to hear Mansour greeting the contractor: 'Oh, Musbah, the contractor … how are you?'

'I'm fine, son, what about you?'

'I'm all good, thanks to Allah. It has been a while since we met, sir.'

'Right, it is because I spend six months in town while the other six months in India, trying to earn a living you know.'

'Yes I do, may Allah bless your provision.'

'Come on, get inside.'

Mansour then opened the main door, and let the contractor in.

(31)

In the inner yard, Sanota had already set on the dining table; she put on the tablecloth (circular food rug, made of palm fronds , and on top of it, she placed a plate of dates, Buckthorn fruits, tea and coffeepot, some cups and small tea glass cups.

'Sir contractor, Allah bless you. Come on, come closer to the table.'

'Allah bless you too. I'm close enough, don't worry. I came here today to talk with Niloofar, could you please call her to come over and sit with us? The whole thing is about her.'

'Yes, sure. Niloofar, come here and sit next to me. The contractor wants to talk to you.'

Niloofar was standing by the wall behind the door, and upon hearing him calling her name, she got out and sat next to him.

'First of all, I want to point out that I have noticed Niloofar being able to speak Arabic, therefore, let's us speak in Arabic.'

'That's right.'

'May Allah bless you dear … how is your marriage life? Are you happy with your husband?'

'I'm all good, and more than happy to have my husband, but the thing is; I miscarried twice, and I feel that Mansour is slightly mad at me thinking that I miscarried deliberately.'

'Mansour, is she serious! Oh, my Lord, there is no capability nor is there any power except with Allah!'

'Yes, he believes I did that.'

Mansour said with a slightly angry tone of voice: 'Niloofar, shut up! You shouldn't be talking about this stuff.'

She was scared as she wasn't used to this tone of voice from him.

'Son, leave her alone. I'm just like her father, so say whatever is on your mind, dear. I care about listening to what cheers you up as well as what puts you down, and don't ever worry; I can keep a secret.'

Mansour bowed his head when he saw her tears going down her cheeks …

'Don't you cry, dear, just have trust in Allah, your husband, and me.'

'I didn't do it on purpose, I just did not, rather I wish to have a baby to enjoy his company and help me to strengthen my bond with this life in which I was deprived from a lot of things.'

Her words touched Mansour's heart, and made him think that he might have been unfair to her because of his suspicions and concerns.

So, he said: 'But the doctor is saying that you did eat toxic substances that are harmful to pregnancy.'

'No, no, she didn't, she didn't deliberately cause harm to herself neither her fetus.'

'You should ask me in this matter, I know better. Some women's bodies that aren't capable of handling pregnancy try to get it rid of it as soon as possible, and only after being pregnant for one or two times, the body will start to get used to it and maintain the fetus till the time of delivery. Don't get mad at her son, you're the only one she has in this life, aside from Allah.'

'Amen, Allah is me suffice. And, Insha'Allah, I'll be the perfect husband.'

'Praises be to Allah, as you see, dear, your husband truly loves you, and he is just a bit worried about you that's all. Now it's all good, right?'

'Yes, all good.'

'Now, look, I came here today to deliver a letter that was handed to me by the sheriff to give it to you. He says that it is a letter that your late grandfather handed to him to keep safe and away from his unfair wife, and hand it to you when you're old enough to properly realize things. The sheriff forgot about the letter thing back in the wedding days, but he remembered it now.'

'What is this letter about, sir?'

'It's a very old letter, as old as your age. Your late mother wrote it for you while being severely ill in her last days. Through it, she wanted to write some bequests and other things she wanted you to be aware of.'

'My mother?'

'Yes, your mother …'

'She wrote to talk to me personally?'

'Yes, she did.'

She was overwhelmed with joy and almost fell in Mansour arms to hug him, who also felt the same.

Finally, the time has come for her to get close to her mother's entity. She had always thought that she will never know a thing about her parents especially her mother, the one who she grew up hearing offensive words about as a quote unquote, vilifying mother. Whoever she was, the fact was that she's her mother and that was all that mattered.

Mansour and the contractor kept talking while she was lost in thinking about the faded blue color of the envelope and the daydreams she had that now became more colorful and brighter.

What possibly could have been written by her mother for her?

The love she had for her, what could it possibly look like?

What were the feelings she went through when writing this letter?

Dozens of questions all over her head, and she kept trying to come up with answers herself while feeling so proud and good about her situation.

Time passed while she was yet lost in her fantasy, till Mansour and the other guy got up and were on their way out.

Mansour woke her up from her deepest thoughts and called her saying: 'What's up with you woman! Why aren't you answering the contractor?'

'Oh, I didn't hear a word he said.'

'Leave her alone, son, she's overwhelmed with a joy Allah only knows how it feels. I need to go now; I don't want to stay here in the area when it's dark as I know that I won't find someone to give me a ride. I place you in Allah's trust and wish you farewell.'

'If you'd prefer; I can drive you to Saeed's home. He has a car and can give you a ride to Dubai or the main road.'

'No, no, don't worry about it, I'm in a hurry and I need to go right away to not to be late. Praise be to Allah that I handed in the trust, everything else can be taken care of.'

'Seriously; why don't you change that old house and build a new one in Dubai? Sheikh Rashid – May Allah bless his life – is currently giving away houses to citizens. Go and capture that opportunity now!'

'If I stayed in Dubai, I would be really far away from my job.'

'Go buy a car then, so you can go there and get back.'

'I do really want to, but a car would cost a fortune, and I won't be able to save enough money for it in two or even three years.'

'You will, and Allah will help you. It would be the same for you as it as for your peers.'

'Yes indeed, or I may even be given a car from work just like Saeed.'

Their conversation was interrupted by Niloofar who said: 'I'm lost for words, thank you from the bottom of my heart, may Allah keep you safe. You went through a lot to find me and hand in my mother's letter. May Allah please and bless you.'

'Thankful for your words, my dear. Take care of yourself, your home and your husband. May Allah make it up to you in the best way possible.'

'Amen.'

(32)

After the contractor went out, Niloofar sat on her bed, started to joyfully kiss and smell the letter while trying try to carefully and slowly open the envelope. She brought out, from the envelope, an old picture of her parents from it; her mother was beautiful, had wide eyes and some of her features. As for her dad, he was a tall handsome British man with a delicate moustache, long tiny nose, blond hair and blue eyes just like hers. It's a perfect picture that seemed to be taken the moment they got married.

On the back of the picture, there were some words that she wouldn't be able to read at this time. She also brought out three papers with different sizes; two were large and one was tiny. All three papers were full of words and numbers, therefore she felt furious regarding her lack of knowledge, and put the blame on her unfair grandmother for not letting her be educated like the rest of people.

She carried the envelope and ran out of the room, but then found Mansour getting back from outside and locking the big door …

'Tell me, can you read this letter?'

Mansour took it and gave it a try.

'It is written in Urdu, the letters look Arabic, but the handwriting is different, and reading in Urdu is truly difficult for who doesn't have a clue about the language.'

With sorrow and hopeless look in her eyes, she asked: 'Would the contractor be able to read it?'

'He may do, indeed, I'm certain that he can.'

Immediately, she opened the main door and ran out with Mansour right after her. Both were running and calling out loud the contractor's name who had already got on the tiny van with the loud engine that drove him away with enough speed to set him away from who's trying to run after the van. He was gone and couldn't hear their voices neither their calls.

The two of them got back disappointed as she wouldn't have a chance to know what's written in that letter, her only legacy in this life.

'Why don't we take it to Najma? She is Indian and will be able to read the letter for you …'

'Did you forget what Saeed told you the other day? He made me feel that they are scared of me and think that I might be sort of bad luck for his daughter and wife.'

'Yes true, we also don't want to annoy him as he seems scared already. Let's just leave him alone.'

'Who can help me now? I always wished I could go to the school that I wasn't allowed to attend; I would have been able to read and write thus understanding what did my mother wrote for me in her last days.'

'Do you wish to learn how to read and write?'

'Yes, I do.'

'I will look for who is capable of teaching women at their home.'

'But till that time comes, I would be dead out of yearning waiting to read this precious letter.'

'Hopefully, you won't, Insha'Allah, and tomorrow I will start looking for someone to read this letter. Don't worry.'

He grabbed her wrist, took her to the room, and locked the door behind.

Days after that, Mansour came in the house while Niloofar was sitting in the inner yard sewing clothes with the manual sewing machine that her sister-in-law gave to her to spend some time on.

'Salaam alaikum "Peace be upon you".'

'Peace be upon you too, Uncle, would you like me to serve lunch for you now?'

'And what have you cooked for us today?'

'Today I cooked Harissa "a popular street food" with the meat that our neighbors send us in the morning.'

'Masha'Allah, have they sent us meat?'

'Yes, they have.'

'May Allah bless their days with joy. Where is Niloofar?'

'She's inside, sewing clothes.'

'Okay, get the food ready, please, I'm starving.'

'On my way to do so, Uncle …'

He went inside to his wife with a joyful face saying: 'I have some glad tidings for you!'

'Oh, tell me, please?'

'First, tell me, where the letter is?'

'I'm keeping it in the closet.'

'Well, get ready to have guests over in the afternoon.'

'Who are these guests?'

'My friend, Ali, do you remember him?'

'Yes, I do, how can I ever forget him and his beautiful wife, Zareena.'

'Well, couple of days ago, I talked to him and he said that his wife was sick. Today he came to tell me that he will come over with his wife to read the letter.'

She picked up all pieces of cloth, lift up the sewing machine and put it in the room. She then started to joyfully clean up the place that she didn't even have lunch.

(33)

The smell of incense was all over the room when Mansour came back from the afternoon prayer at the mosque. In the inner yard, the tablecloth was set on and on top of it there were the dates, Harissa, Khabees sweet, teapot, coffee, cups and glasses as if it was Eid …

Niloofar put on a red polka dot embroidered Kandora with thin longitudinal blue threads (Emirati Jalabiya embroidered with silver threads over the chest and hands), a black head scarf embroidered with plastic shiny stars, and a golden pair of earrings in addition to the Meria (the long golden necklace which is a chain of gold granules that ends up in a flat semicircle studded with colorful shiny stones and butterfly shaped gold plates).

She dressed up with all what she was gifted from her mother-in-law's house, and painted her blue eyes with Kohl as if she was a bride waiting for her morning guests to come and greet her on her wedding night. She was full of joy, and if Ali and his wife hadn't made it today, she would have died out of sorrow.

The couple sat for a while in the inner yard waiting for the guests, till they suddenly heard sounds of knocking on the main door. Sanota ran out as she was also on tenterhooks, waiting for the glad tidings.

Mansour went out to welcome the guests, and right behind him, there was Niloofar who truly was on tenterhooks!

The men sit in the inner yard, while Niloofar went with Zareena to the bedroom.

'Oh, Niloofar, you look beautiful, like really gorgeous.'

'You too, Zareena. You were blessed with the loveliest facial features as well as traits.'

'I came to know that you miscarried twice.'

'Yes, true.'

'That's destiny, we can't do something about it. As for me, I have no clue why didn't I yet have a chance to get pregnant. My first wedding anniversary is soon and I'm still not pregnant.'

'Don't worry dear, we are satisfied with whatever Allah has destined for us.'

'Amen, Allah is sufficient.'

At that time, Mansour knocked the door saying: 'Niloofar, bring the letter and come outside.'

'Okay …'

Niloofar brought out the envelope and went out together with Zareena to sit beside their husbands while Sanota was standing by the door.

Zareena has opened the envelope and brought out the picture and the three papers …

'I'll be translating what I read into Arabic so that everyone can follow with me and understand what I'm saying. Niloofar, look here; this is a picture of to your parents, isn't it?'

'Indeed, it is. Would you please what was written on the back?'

'Your mother wrote that this picture was taken right after they signed their marriage contract in the first of August, year 1948, meaning that it was 15 years ago.'

'Well, what about what's in this paper?'

'This one? Oh, let me see. This is a marriage contract registration paper between your mother Habib El-nessa Nazia and Gerald Gabriel Moore. As I said, it was issued on the first of August, year 1948. From your father side, the first witness was Jack Birman Bishop, and the second was Simon William Black while form your mother side, the first witness was Coldip Brim Sing and the second was Santosh Narian Divam and name of the judge was …'

'There's no need for all these details, just read out this paper for me, please.'

'This is a letter that was hand written to you by your mother. Oh, what a beautiful handwriting she had! Listen … "Niloofar, my beautiful daughter, I hope my letter finds you well, safe and happy. I also hope that you turned 15 so you can properly understand all what I'm about to tell you. First, I want you to know that I named you this name that I truly admire which means the gorgeous girl, and that was after I saw your entrancing beauty and the eyes you inherited from your father. The name fit you perfectly, may Allah keep you safe from all the earthly evils."

'I'm writing this letter while watching you peacefully asleep, knowing that you won't know about it till fifteen years from this moment.

My story began with seeing your father for the first time as I was on my way home with my classmates, while he was standing with his mates at the street corner drinking tea. Our eyes met and I instantly felt a unique affection between our hearts and knew that he is the one for me.

'After that, we kept exchanging glances and the eye contact continued for days. A step forward, he started throwing some papers in my way as he wrote in those papers, in a poetic way, about the love he had for me, and that I was the one he has been waiting for his entire life. At that time, I was so into him with all my emotions, and so I was responsive, gave him the green light, and lived our love story that literally changed my whole life. It was the once in a life time story that would be of interest to all lovers someday or would simply fade way and get forgotten the same way as some major events in life.

'My classmates were always warning me and saying that my relationship with Gerald will tragically end up causing a huge mess. However, I never would have cared about them or what they were saying simply because I never would have let go of the love of someone who gave up his entire world just to build a world full of joy for me.

'The relationship was then taken to the next level; from letters to secret dates, and these dates solidified our love bond and pushed us into thinking how can we strengthen this relationship and make it last forever.

'On a rainy day, and under a big Ficus tree, Gerald asked me to marry him. I was thrilled by his proposal and felt out of this world as I realized his true intentions regarding this relationship. However, I couldn't see how would my family ever allow this marriage and bless it. Gerald was a Christian, and he was also British which makes him, from my family's perspective, a brutal cunning settler, one that we cannot possibly trust let alone make a family member!

'I opened up to him and shared my concerns and worries as my family will not only turn his proposal down and reject it, but will also have a set of retaliatory responses. First things first, they will be forcing me to leave school then compel me to get married to another man as soon as possible. As for Gerald, they may kill him and get rid of his body or hurt him somehow. Back then, I couldn't compete against any concerns, I could only hope the best for our love which has grown till the point we cannot hide it anymore.

'Gerald showed me his escape plan as we didn't have a choice other than saving this love and getting away with it. We just couldn't take it anymore, couldn't handle that distance with our love and yearning kept getting bigger and bigger day by day.

We did really plan to escape for the sake of saving our love.

'I started to be gentle and treat my parents and siblings nicely, showing them love that will remind them of me when I'm no longer here. My heart was aching and getting broken day after day for having to say goodbye to them, however, the love I had for Gerald surpassed my grief, the sense of belonging and love I had for my family.

'One day, Gerald told me that he was fully prepared to escape the following morning. So, when my family to bed, I packed my all clothes and necessities into a bedspread as if it was a suitcase, and throw it out of the house between the wild trees.'

(34)

'In the morning, and while I was getting ready and on my way to get to school, I put on clothes under the uniform. I hugged and kissed my mom goodbye then went out with a heavy heart for leaving my dearest people behind. I carried my suitcase and walked through thick trees under the hill till I reached the main street intersection where the bus stops – heading to other India states – are located. There, I took off my school uniform and threw it away with the school bag. Gerald showed up in civilian clothes while also holding his suitcase. We took the bus heading to the city of Mysore, and then it took us 24 hours to get there. By that time, I was certain that my family knew about my escape as they noticed that I was late in school, didn't get back home on time and my closet was empty.

'They went out looking for me, asking my classmates and perhaps one of my mates told them about my relationship with Gerald. I couldn't imagine how furious they were back then.

'Upon reaching Mysore, me and Gerald took a rickshaw to an office that handled civilian marriage procedures. There, at the office, we weren't asked to provide any identity documents as they had a purely business policy, and their aim was to get the marriage procedures done without any contradiction whether the religion or the nationality of the couple matched or not. Moreover, they eased the obstacles and provided witnesses when needed. Gerald had already enquired all about this information beforehand, before we started our journey from our city, Hyderabad. There were also two of his friends waiting to assure us all our things were running smoothly. After the marriage contact was completed, we took the picture you're seeing, and his friends went back to Hyderabad before anyone got suspicious. From Mysore, we took a train to Pompeii so we could travel by sea to Britain, Gerald's homeland.

'From Pompeii, Gerald started to send telegraphic messages to his close family and relatives saying that he was heading back to them with his Indian bride, and that he will be working on issuing fake documents for both of us so we can be able to travel. The responses to his letters were denouncing me as a person, the marriage, and the fact that he ran away from the military service this way like a coward.

'Days after days passed after these attempts.

For me, I lived the best days of my life in only seven months with him. We lived in a room behind a Hindu temple of Krishna in a small village in mountain Kandla away from the public eyes.

'They were indeed beautiful days that not everyone is blessed with from God.

O my daughter, I was truly lucky to love and marry Gerald, he is indeed an angel on this earth.

'I became pregnant with you after a month of marriage, and circumstances were really harsh in the beginning. Gerald started to run out of money owing to costs of travel, food, housing and telegraphic messages.

'Austerity was worse day after day, and we even began to eat half a handful of rice per day. Gerald went to work in the agriculture field in one of the rice farms to provide us the daily sustenance and enough money to buy tickets to travel to Britain by sea whenever the fake documents expire.

'As the days went by, Gerald's family began to search with us for safe ways that would enable them to get us to Britain. Rather, they were eager to meet us, especially after they learned the news of my pregnancy and that I was expecting to have my child in the next three months. Their support for us increased, and the love they showed us was a strong motive to move forward with what we aspire to.

'The letters continued between Gerald and his family, and I used to memorize all those letters because they carried a lot of love and sublime meanings, and I imagined the environment from which Gerald came for his permanent description of it, a large house built of red bricks, with long windows, surrounded by a low iron wall, and behind the wall rose trees were planted. The white gardenia, which is the opposite of all the gardenia trees in the world, displays its flowers in all seasons of the year, even in the winter, and from the gate to the main entrance is a large patio whose floor is paved with sandy-colored granite stones, while the door is a wooden door made of oak wood and has a percussion hammer in the shape of big dragon head, how I wish the three of us, you and me and your father Gerald, lived in that house …

'And good tidings began to follow us, as after Gerald's family accepted our marriage and blessed it, Gerald was finally able to obtain the fake papers, and he was also able to pay for the tickets to travel by sea to Britain, and he planned to go out the next morning to Pompeii to buy them, and that night he showed me the most wonderful night, and it was a long beautiful night of love that I will never forget as long as I live.

'In the expected morning, the sun rose, but it was the sun of parting. He left my arms to go to Pompeii to buy tickets, and there he was arrested by the British forces who were looking for him for escaping from service, and all that was because of me, because he loved me …

Fears of his arrest always bothered and disturbed him, as he told me a few days before: 'If I go out and don't come back to you, know that I have been arrested, and to be sure, ask one of my friends, but you don't care, just try to communicate with my family in Britain and leave the rest to them. They are the ones who will free me from prison and return to you and our son.'

'On that day, when all the hours of the day passed and Gerald no longer came, I realized that he had been arrested, and I would not find a way to ask about him or investigate his news, nor did I have the money to send telegrams to his relatives in Britain or even to his friends.

'So, my feet brought me to that temple, the temple of Lord Krishna, in which religious ceremonies and banquets are constantly held, and contrary to my religion, I entered this temple and sat down on the stairs, so that I might see a coin falling here or there or an extra morsel from someone. I was sitting around the passers-by, then suddenly they started to give me coins thinking that I'm a beggar, and I did not care at that time what others thought of me except that I could save an amount with which I could save myself and my husband from the predicament in which we were put, then I was given a plate of food as if they knew my condition, and I ate what I could eat and kept the rest, and I took my money and went back to my room.

'I repeated what I did for days and days until I managed to send two telegrams to your father's family in Britain and to his friends in the city of Hyderabad. I received a response from his friends that he had already been arrested by the British forces and would be brought to a military trial in one of the military barracks in one of the remote colonies, and then he would be imprisoned as a punishment for the crime he had committed as soon as possible.

'I spent two months in this state going back and forth to that temple until I almost worshiped like the rest of the Hindus, and no one helped me or healed my wounds, and I was counting the days until my husband would return. When do we leave this country? When will we hold you in our arms, the two of us? When will his family come and save us? When and when?

'Then, I received a telegram saying that Gerald had died in prison, affected by his pain from pneumonia, which he had suffered due to inflammation of the wounds and bruises he suffered as a result of his resistance to the soldiers on the day of his arrest, and that telegram was the one who sentenced me to death because I realized that my life had ended with the end of Gerald's life. There were days left until my due date, but I had given up and no longer cared about me or you, so I stayed in my room and no longer felt hungry, thirsty, or anything, just deep sadness, and heavy silence.

'After two days or more, one of them knocked on the room door terribly and started shouting at the top of his voice. She told me that the gang of mountain thieves had robbed the rice stores in this village and were burning everything in front of them: 'Bring what you can carry, let's go to another area, there is no safety here.'

'I got scared, I don't know why and what, but I got some marriage papers and the picture you see and Gerald's shirt that he wore the last time he was here, and I left everything else behind, and I don't know why?'

(35)

'We moved to another dreary place in a cold flat land by a riverbed in sticky, damp huts, and I lived with the good, kind, tender lady who cared about me, fed me, and blessed me till the day you were born, and then I was overtaken by a puerperal fever that could not be controlled or relieved in this place and had no cure, I resisted a lot, and I wished at that time to recover my health in order to breastfeed you, in order to take care of you, in order to raise you like other mothers, but it seems that my time is about to end, so I wrote you this letter so that you do not hate me, my love, the most beautiful child on earth, please forgive me that I am not with you right now. But it is beyond my ability and energy. I will go to my husband and the love of my life, but you will remain without parents, except that Allah has compensated you so far. Do not worry my little rose. I hope that my parents and brothers have raised you well and have been kind to you, and have given you all the love that you deserve until that prince who kidnaps you on the wings of happiness comes to you. I hope that you have completed your school education and enrolled in university studies. I hope that you will be among the outstanding students and that you'll be in one of the best medical universities in Britain. This was the dream of your father and me to make our children go to study medicine, but unfortunately, we did not give birth to anyone but you, so be my love, a successful doctor, and make our dreams come true.

'Look, my daughter, I have enclosed for you that little piece of paper that your father had written down for me in his own handwriting, and below it was his signature. When you grow up and travel to Britain to get to know your family, just show them this paper and the picture and they will definitely recognize you …

'I love you so much, may Allah protect you, my love, and inshallah, we will meet in heaven.'

Everyone turned to Niloofar, whose face had become red, and her eyes were almost dripping with tears. Poor Sanota cried at hearing this sad letter, and she approached Niloofar and hugged her, and the two burst into bitter tears.

Mansour later turned in the bed to see Niloofar sleeping on her stomach with her face towards the wall …

'What's wrong with you, dear? Are you still crying?'

'No, No … I'm not crying … I'm just thinking.'

'What're you thinking about?'

'I think of the suffering of my poor parents, how they died far from each other, my father did not even see my face, and all the suffering that I had lived in my grandfather's home because of his evil wife was nothing compared to their suffering. Was their destiny like this?'

Tears ran from her eyes and fell fast and heavy on the bed.

'Don't cry, dear. May Allah rest them in peace.'

'May Allah rest them in peace.'

He held her in his arms and brought her to his chest.

'You know I was thinking about how to fulfill your parents' dream of making you a doctor.'

'Are you serious?'

'Sure.'

'So, what can we do to achieve this dream, since I am illiterate and ignorant and do not know the difference between a number and a letter?'

'I've had an idea … What do you think when I return from work tomorrow that we go to the health building and ask about how to make you a doctor, what I mean by entering the school and university that would make you a doctor …'

'What a wonderful idea! I'm ready to be a doctor!'

'Yes, you're going to be.'

'You know, I want to visit my family in Britain as my mother told me.'

He looked into her eyes.

'I was also thinking about the same thing. I want to take you to get to know your family in Britain. You're the daughter of their son. They should see you and get to know you.'

'How can I do it?'

'I'll see what I can do, I can ask some British soldiers, maybe they will help us in this matter.'

'You're very kind and caring.'

'You're amazing and pure.'

She smiled shyly and rested her head on his chest and fell asleep.

There were three Arab nurses sitting in the reception of the health building when Mansour talked to them: 'Hello!'

'Hello!'

'Could I meet the healthcare professional here?'

'Who is the patient, you or your wife?'

'Neither of us. I just would like to ask the doctor some general questions, if possible. Could he help us?'

'What is the matter?'

'It is about my wife.'

'You can ask us. If we know the answer, we'll tell you about it.'

'Alright! My wife is from India, she is 15 years old, she is not educated at all, we want her to become a doctor, what are the steps followed to become a doctor like the doctors here?'

The nurse laughed and winked at her colleague …

'I don't know the answer to this question. My colleague will answer.'

'My opinion is that she should do nothing better than start learning … First, she has to speak Arabic, and then she has to study medicine for seven years. I think she will grow old before she joins the school of medicine, and if you want, ask this colleague of mine.'

She laughed sarcastically and pointed to the third nurse, who expressed her displeasure with the previous two nurses.

The couple felt that they had made a mistake, and really regretted when they took this step, as this will always be the reaction of people. Mansour whispered to his wife in her ear, and they took a step back, and the third nurse called them and took them to the resting place …

'I heard what happened in the reception area, and I apologize for my female colleagues' attitude. We should alleviate people's suffering rather than exacerbate it, and comfort here does not mean only physical pain reduction, but everything related to humanity … It is admirable, sir, that you instill ambition in your wife, who is not originally Arab, and raise her to be an educated and accomplished woman, and the profession of medicine is a decent and honorable one.

'By curing people's sicknesses and alleviating their suffering, one rises to the highest levels of humanity and purity, and be certain that I am here after your husband, my sister, and one of the supporters of this idea. I'm not sure how to advise you because women's education in this country is still in its infancy. I want you to go and ask the directors of the Al-Khansaa School in Deira and the Khawla Bint Al-Azwar School, so that perhaps you will find the solution in your enrollment in primary education with children … and after you finish your school education in tenth or eleventh grade, look for the best medical universities in Egypt, India, or Sudan. Do not be concerned; our hearts are with you; just work hard and endure, and Allah does not waste a seeker's work.'

They smiled at each other, and the couple now had a great and bright hope. They called the nurse and thanked her for her kind and reassuring words, and on the way out, they heard the nurse scolding the two previous nurses: 'It was not appropriate for two nurses like you to say what you said or act like ignorant people. You really looked like idiots. We should not ridicule or destroy people's dreams. You will see how great that girl will be, I saw that in the sparkle of her eyes.'

(36)

Days passed, and Mansour accompanied his wife to the principals of Dubai's two sole girls' schools, hoping to involve his wife with the pupils of the first grade, which had more than ninety-nine students in each class. According to the two principals, all of the female students were too young to be in the same class as a married girl.

Then he searched for private tutors for her, and he found nothing but volunteers, and the volunteer would not serve the goal of teaching her and making her a doctor.

They searched for long days, until they despaired of this subject in principle, and began to discuss the issue of traveling to Britain to visit her relatives, and this research journey was longer and more difficult than the first, so they had to go through several experiences and ask many people and start corresponding with Niloofar's family in Britain. They also had to search for people with knowledge of Britain or even groups of English residents in the region, and they rented a good house in the old neighborhood of Dubai, where they had to live in Dubai because of the proximity of all facilities to them. Mansour also got a work car to make it easier for him to travel the long distances he used to commute daily.

Niloofar became pregnant for the third time at the time, and everyone was concerned about how to keep the pregnancy going. Mansour's route was diverted from his main purpose during his search for educational possibilities and a trip to Britain by looking for a middleman who might connect them to Niloofar's relatives in Britain. This coincided with his meeting three British partners of a citizen trader named Saif Al-Sunaidi at an Al-Shindagha firm for the trade of canned products imported from overseas, so he shared his work with him and became involved with the company he joined.

Their income increased, but so did the distances between Niloofar and her husband, and she no longer met her dwarf friend, did not leave the house, and returned to the same loneliness, impatiently waiting for the time when she gave birth to her child to begin the journey of searching for a school to learn and get to know her family again. Mansour's interests changed.

One night, Mansour started his conversation with her, saying: 'How are you, honey?'

'I'm good.'

'How is our son?'

'He is okay as well.'

'What's wrong with you? Why are your responses dry like this? Do you complain about something?'

'No, I am only fed up with loneliness.'

'Do you feel lonely while I'm with you?'

'You're only with me now, then we go to sleep, and wake up in the morning to find myself lonely again. You go to work before sunset, and after that, you go to the firm. I only see you at midnight before sleeping or during sleeping.'

'Oh my God! It seems you're upset.'

'No … Not at all, I'm happy with my loneliness.'

'My love, do not be upset, please. What I am doing is to provide you and the child with a happy life and all means of comfort.'

'I didn't object to anything, I just want you near me for at least an hour a day, I want to talk to you.'

'I'm all yours, honey; don't worry, I'm not leaving, and whenever you need me, just send Sanota to call me at the corner of the street that overlooks the firm, and I'll come to you right away … I have some extremely wonderful news for you, Niloofar.'

'What is it?'

'Saeed told me that Najma is going to prepare a feast for the circumcision of her child tomorrow, and she has invited all the women in the neighborhood, and you are the first to have a special invitation, as Saeed told me.'

'Really! I missed her so much, and I thought she had forgotten me or didn't want to see me anymore.'

'No, my love, whoever sees this pretty face must always want to see it …'

She smiled shyly and said: 'I'll go to the feast, and we should give the child a gift, shouldn't we?'

'Sure, but what kind of gift should we buy for them?'

'I don't know. What is the tradition here? We're in India, and on occasions like this, we give the baby some silver or gold jewelry, as well as new clothes for the kid and his parents, and we bring rose wreaths to put around the baby's neck and his parents' necks, as well as a box of sweets.'

'No, we don't do that here. We just give them money, or if you like, we can buy a goat and a sheep for them. What do you think? I can go to the sheep market on my way … or we can give them money, I will give you a hundred rupees to give to the child, okay?'

'I think it's a good idea. I'll go get ready, and I'll inform Sanota from now. When you go out to work in the morning, take me and Sanota to our old house, to take a break and then get ready for the feast. Sanota can also clean the house that hasn't been cleaned for weeks, and when it's time for lunch we'll go. She and I will walk to Najma's house, and then we will return to our house. When you finish your work, you will come and take us back here with you … What do you think?'

'You command, and I obey, Ma'am.'

(37)

Mansour took them the next day to their old house and went to work. Niloofar and Sanota entered the house, and Sanota started cleaning the main building of the house from the inside so that her mistress could enter and rest in it until the time for the feast. Niloofar, on the other hand, proceeded to one of the house's outer courtyard corners to await the arrival of her dwarf friend, whom she was delighted to meet. Then the friend arrived. He was missing her and began hugging her so tightly that he's nearly suffocating her, kissing her so warmly that his saliva wet her face, and as soon as he stopped, she laughed at him.

'How long will you remain a child like this, when will you grow up?'

He referred to her as tall, implying that he is a huge guy, not a child.

'No, you are still a small child and I feel like your mother, and you know, my child, I have good news for you.'

He sat in front of her waiting to hear her news with a wide smile.

'You know? I'm pregnant. This is the third time, and every time I lose the baby, except that this time the doctor assured me that she injected me with an injection imported from Iran to stabilize this pregnancy and I will not lose it, Insha'Allah.'

His smile shrank little by little and seemed to have felt a little jealous of the next child, but he tried to force himself to smile and pretend in front of her to be happy.

He lay in front of her on his stomach and asked her to sit on his back.

At first, she refused and even laughed at this idea, but with his insistence she acquiesced to him and mounted his back, and he flew with her like a bird, she rose slowly to see the courtyard of her house getting smaller, then her house getting smaller, and here was Sanota carrying water from the well to the main building … how small she looked! The neighborhood had become smaller and the coastal area was getting smaller and smaller, and from that height the main street was visible. Here was her husband's workstation, as small as a matchbox.

The whole area was too small in her eyes, and the air above was so beautiful. He took everything flying in it with his cool breeze. She saw that this trip had brought happiness and comfort to her depressed heart, and she felt its lightness, as if from smoke that had become lighter than a feather. She became free from all restrictions, even from the body, her spirit free and unfettered, no one could catch her, no one could catch up with her. She was now transparent and inaudible, wondering to herself how many people have happened to them like what happened to me?

How many people could reach what I have reached?

How many people dream of what I got?

I'm really lucky!

And so, she remained up there, flying and flying, until the dwarf began to descend little by little, pulling her from her daydream into reality. Things grew bigger in her eyes, and the air breezes got hotter little by little, and as for her, the feeling of melancholy returned to her, increasing little by little.

'Why don't you take me home now? I want to go back now … take me back from where you brought me …'

When she reached the roof of the house, she heard Sanota crying out to her: 'Aunt Noura, Aunt Noura, where are you?'

She ran to the main door, opened it and ran out, looking for her outside the house …

Then the dwarf lowered her into the courtyard in the corner behind the wall.

'It was a wonderful and beautiful journey. I don't know how I can thank you.'

She hugged him tightly and kissed his cheek while she was about to stand up. He grabbed her by the wrist and gave her three large oranges. She was very happy when she saw their sizes and bright red-yellow colors.

'Is this all mine?'

He moved his head affirmatively.

She thanked him very much, and she heard the sound of the door closing, and he climbed the wall of the house and jumped outside, hid the oranges, tied them at the end of her belt, and put them behind her back.

'Aunt Noura, where have you been?'

'I'm here, Sanota.'

'Here where I do not see you?'

'I'm here in the corner behind the well.'

She came in panting after her run.

'I searched for you a lot, my Aunt, and I came here too, but I did not find you, where were you? I got scared.'

'I'm here, dear.'

'And how so? I don't know, maybe I didn't see you.'

'Never mind, tell me, what do you want from me now?'

'Nothing, I just came to tell you that I've heated water for you in the corner so you can take a shower and get some rest before we go to the feast.'

'Oh yeah, I feel the need to take a shower right now.'

She hid the oranges in her handbag and took a shower.

After the afternoon prayer, Niloofar returned home with his daughter, and Mansour was sitting in the living room waiting for her.

So, she initiated him by saying: 'Here we go, did you eat the lunch I sent you with Sanota?'

'Yes, it was delicious.'

'Najma asked me to send you food with Sanota, you must be hungry.'

'Well done! Now let's go to Dubai, I have a lot of work to do and you should get some rest.'

'Okay, let's go.'

They entered their house in Dubai at the sound of the Maghrib call to prayer.

Mansour said: 'I'll change my clothes, then I'll pray and go to work as my colleagues are waiting for me. Take a rest, honey, and I'll be back to you once I finish my work. Do you know what is going to happen tomorrow?'

'What?'

'Tonight, I will receive my profits from trading for the previous period, and tomorrow I will take you to the gold market to buy you some gold jewelry. What do you think?'

'Really? I'm very happy. You're very kind and generous to me.'

'You deserve all the best. We have been married for a year, right?'

'Yes, our anniversary was two months ago.'

'Yes, right. I love you so much.'

'I love you way more.'

He kissed her forehead and left the home.

(38)

She took the oranges out of her bag and climbed onto the roof of the house and sat down on a wooden chair looking at the clear sky, enjoying the coolness of the damp March, and remembering that beautiful journey above the clouds, how she wished her dwarf friend could come to this place. If he could repeat this trip and the other two trips, her life would be complete and she would not lack anything other than knowledge and acquaintance with her relatives in Britain.

She peeled the orange and ate its slices, while she was enjoying and savoring the taste.

Then Sanota went up to her and said: 'What do you do here alone, Aunt?'

'Nothing, I'm just enjoying the fresh air.'

'What do you eat, Aunt?'

'I'm eating the oranges that I got from the feast "luncheon".'

'I haven't seen any oranges there, maybe they didn't give them to all the people. Also, the oranges are strange in shape and their size is much larger than the sizes I used to see.'

'Maybe, do you want to eat some?'

'Yes, if you don't mind.'

'No, I don't mind. I have three slices left, eat them, please, I'm full.'

'Really? Thank you so much, Aunt.'

She put the orange slices in her mouth and chewed it a little, and her facial expression changed as if she disapproved of the taste.

Then, she spit a lot, and screamed: 'Aunt, what is this orange? It is like a poison! It's rotten, how did you eat it? Plus, it smells like mold? Why did you take it? Where did you get these oranges?'

'What do you say so? How? It is delicious. This orange is very sweet and fragrant, this is a fresh fruit.'

'No Aunt, you are wrong, throw it away, it is a bad orange, very bad, I smell the rotten smell even from the peels, I will go down to wash my mouth from this bad taste because I am starting to feel nauseous.'

She was astonished by Sanota's words, and how she could say this when she still feels the sweetness of the orange in her mouth.

Is it possible that the orange that I ate is rotten?

Could she have eaten something before she ate that orange to feel so uncomfortable?

Could she be the deceived one?

But from whom?

Could it be her dwarf friend?

Every time she became pregnant, he brought her on one of his unusual trips, and on every trip, he gave her something strange in shape and taste, and every time, after eating the fruits, she slept and woke up, and her pregnancy had miscarried.

When she told him she was pregnant, his facial expressions altered and he did not display excitement at the news.

Could he be the one harming her baby?

Could he be jealous that she will have a baby that will keep her busy?

Her heart began to beat rapidly due to the severity of her fears of her thoughts. With heavy steps, she walked to the stairs and descended the stairs with caution, but the blood had come before her.

In the health building, which had been renamed into a clinic, Dr Sarouj and the doctor in charge were trying to find out the reasons for Niloofar's third miscarriage. They were waiting for Niloofar to end her severe breakdown with pain and bitter crying over the loss of her children, whom she had unintentionally killed.

Niloofar did not know what to say, she preferred silence and decided she would put an end to her pain and sorrows.

She decided she would never meet this monster again, and if he tried to make her happy, he very likely killed her children and ruined her and her family's happiness.

She returned home in great grief. Her grief over her miscarriage was not as great the previous two times as she was this time. She finally discovered the secret of her abortion. She was the one who contributed to this crime, how foolish she was!

How reckless she was?

How did she get so carried away with her feelings so naively?

She will wait until she got pregnant, and this time she will not see his face, not during her pregnancy or even after, she will never see him again.

Ten days after her miscarriage, she opened her eyes to see Mansour wearing his military uniform and getting ready to go to work.

'Mansour …'

'Yes, dear.'

'I'd like to go to the clinic with Sanota.'

'Why? How do you feel?'

'No, I'm okay. I'd like to visit the doctor to talk with her a little bit.'

'What topic do you want to talk to her about?'

'I don't think you care about it.'

'What is it about?'

'I want to find a way to enable me to travel to meet my relatives in Britain.'

'Are we back to this again? I told you I'm looking for a way to do that.'

'Give it a try and see what you can do! But know that you have asked for permission to go out to the clinic only, and then you have to return home immediately.'

'Yes, sure.'

'You know that I love you so much, right?'

'Yes, I love you too. You're my everything in this life.'

'See you in the evening, darling.'

'Sure.'

(39)

Mansour went out to work after he kissed her on her cheeks, so she got out of bed, washed and put on her clothes, then took the letter and the papers attached to it and put them in her handbag.

Sanota had made hard-boiled eggs for her, tortillas (local bread kneaded with water and spread a thin layer on a frying pan to cook without oil to become a light crispy wafer), a cup of red tea, and some dates.

She ate her breakfast and Sanota was waiting for her to go out together to the clinic. They walked in the long alleys on their way to the clinic, and she saw the shapes and faces of people and recalled her childhood days as she walked in the alleys of her country crowded with people, so she began to talk to herself:

'Here too, the alleys are crowded with people, men here more than women, women here are few wearing black abayas, women carrying food, women sitting on the floor selling food, women cleaning their homes, women screaming at their children, women walking with their children, girls running, little girls playing, life is warm here, but are the hearts of all women stable and happy? Are the women here satisfied with what Allah has decreed for them? Or rebel against reality? I did not know a woman who rebelled yet, other than my mother, may Allah have mercy on her, is the girl who caught up with her love and lost everything, except that she got the love she wished for, the love that resulted in a girl who does not know what days are in store for her. Could my parents now know my news from that world of theirs?

Could they be praying for me like other parents?

Can I meet them someday, even if it was in dreams?

I imagined their appearance a lot, but I did not imagine their appearance as in the picture, my mother is beautiful and my father is very handsome.'

Niloofar and Sanota stood at the reception of the clinic, waiting for Dr Sarouj to come.

After a long wait, the doctor called them to her office: 'I'm sorry, I'm late, I had a lot of reviewers today, and I'm done now until it's critical.'

'Don't worry, Doctor.'

'Tell me, can I get you something, tea or water?'

'No, thanks, we had breakfast before we came here.'

'Well, tell me how are you today? How do you feel now? Did the bleeding stop? Do you suffer from pain or something?'

'I am fine. The bleeding has decreased a lot, and I feel that I am regaining my strength little by little.'

'So, why are you visiting me today?'

'I've come to you with something else and I don't know anyone else who can help me with that.'

'What is it, dear ... tell me, please.'

'I heard you on that day speaking with the other doctor in fluent English, I need you to listen to my story.'

Then, Niloofar told her the whole story, as well as the story of her mother, and showed her the letter, picture, and the other papers.

'I need your help, doctor, to write a letter to my relatives in Britain in the English language to send it to this address. I also need you to write my mother's letter in English so that I can attach it to the other letter.'

'Sure, I'd love to help you. I will write them this evening after I finish my work. Could you please visit me tomorrow to give you the letter and the English translation of your mother's letter, and I'll read them to you.'

Niloofar replied happily: 'Sure, doctor ... take your time. We will be back tomorrow. I don't know how to thank you; I will never forget this favor as long as I'm alive.'

'Don't worry, this is the least I can do for a very humane cause like this, but what I want you to focus on now is your health first and then your education, so strive to fulfill your parents' wish to become a doctor like me, right?'

'Sure, sure ... I wish I could make this dream come true.'

Niloofar and Sanota went out, and they were at the height of happiness, due to the glimmer of hope that the doctor showed to Niloofar.

'How perfect is the medical profession in which one is stripped of all grudges and selfishness and devotes themselves to serving humanity!'

'I'm very happy because you're happy, Aunt.'

'You're a good girl, Sanota ... I pray to Allah to make you happy as you make me happy and help me.'

In the evening, Mansour came home late, and she said to him: 'I'm very happy today.'

'I hope your happiness is eternal.'

'Thank you! What's wrong with you? Why are you looking sad?'

' I am sad because my partner, trader Saif Al-Sunaidi, is very ill, and he has not visited the trading firm for more than a week.'

'What is his disease?'

'I do not know, but he suffers from chest sensitivity since childhood, and his chest sometimes becomes aggravated by the change of weather conditions, except that this time he fell ill a lot, and I do not know when he will recover until the burden is lightened on my shoulders, and the three English partners want to sell their partnership to us to return to their country.'

'Never mind, he'll be okay, don't be worried, my love.'

'I'm very tired, I need to sleep.'

'Do you need me to bring you something to eat?'

'No, no, I'm not hungry ... I just want to fall asleep.'

'Okay, my love. Sleep and don't be worried. Allah will handle all the difficulties.'

(40)

The next morning, Niloofar tried to wake Mansour up:

'Mansour, my love … won't you wake up now? Won't you go to your work, the sun has risen and you're still sleeping.'

'No, I will not go to work today. I have applied for three days' leave and I will be traveling with my partner Saif and some friends today to a new Canadian hospital in Al Ain which is said to be good. He might find his cure there.'

'How are you going to travel and leave me here alone?'

'You're not alone, Allah is with you, Sanota is also with you. Don't worry; I'll travel for only three days.'

'I'm not worried, but you've not told me before about this trip.'

'I'm telling you right now.'

'Now? Before you travel?'

'Don't fight with me please, I didn't tell you about it because we planned to travel yesterday.'

'How did they plan it yesterday when you asked for leave on Thursday morning?'

'I mean, we talked about it yesterday morning, and yesterday I went to work and asked for permission to take a three day leave, and when it was approved, I went back to my friends to tell them that I was ready to travel, and we rented a car to take us to Al Ain this morning.'

'Who are your friends who will accompany you?'

'You don't know them.'

She felt very distressed, Mansour did not have to plan such big things before consulting her or even telling her, just as he had never spoken to her in this way before, and she got out of bed when she felt that she wanted to cry, and she chose to cry in complete secrecy, she resorted to the bathroom and unleashed her tears whose flow was stopped only with difficulty. Then she washed and lit fires under the pots of water for Mansour, and went out to see him trying to prepare his luggage for travel.

'Do you need me to help you?'

'Yes, dear. I want you to put me some clean kandoras, I think three will suffice, undershirts, and if you have a small towel too, I don't want to carry too many things.'

'Sure.'

Mansour entered to take a shower, and she began to put in the bag what he asked for, and as soon as she finished, Mansour came out of the corner and hugged her tightly from behind.

'Excuse me, my darling; I'm lost in thought and don't know what to say. Do you realize that if something awful happened to my partner, I would lose everything? Don't be sad, please, you're my everything.'

Tears gathered in her eyes again, but she did not want him to see her tears before he left, and she did her little trick to hold her tears in her eyeballs.

'Don't worry, I'm not mad at you, I'm just going to miss you so much.'

'I will also miss you very much, you know if we had children you would have been busy with them and ignore me, but Allah is wise. I love you so much, and I adore you. You're the most beautiful woman on Earth.'

'I want to ask your permission to go see Dr Sarouj again today, and I may visit her again while you're not here, and I also want to search for a school that will accept me.'

Then she fell silent, and he remained silent too, turning his face to the other side. He thought and answered her with a smile.

'Go wherever you like, I trust you, but I don't want you to be out after midday, and you must take Sanota with you wherever you go. I forgot to tell you that I will leave the boy called Moftah, who works in the firm, at your disposal so that you don't need anything. You will find him sitting outside the home at all hours of the day; feed him when you eat and don't worry about him; he is a dependable and helpful boy. If you want to buy something, simply ask Moftah and he'll deliver it to you, and I'll leave you some money.'

She smiled and cheered up …

'I promise you.'

'Promise me that you'll take care of yourself.'

'I promise you; you also promise me that you'll take good care of yourself. Promise me that you'll keep me in your eyes and your heart.'

He smiled and hugged her.

'I promise you that I will not see, hear, or love a woman other than you.'

He kissed her on the lips, the taste of which lingered in her mouth all that day, to remind her of his promise.

(41)

After Mansour left, and when the sun was about to set in the middle of the sky, they went out to the clinic with Moftah behind them. As soon as they entered the clinic gate, Dr Sarouj looked at them with her cheerful face.

'I was waiting for you, dear.'

'I deliberately delayed a little so that you could finish checking your patients.'

'Yes, I've just finished. You're smart, dear.'

She took her by the arm and led her to her office while looking at the face of that good nurse.

Niloofar sat across from the doctor, and she read to her the content of the letter in Urdu so that she could understand it, and she had explained in it everything that she had heard from her. She also translated the mother's letter into English, and wrote on the envelope the intended address.

'Look, my dear, I have put the stamp. I myself will make sure to send it with the clinic mail, to make sure that it arrives.'

'Thank you so much. It means the world to me.'

'You have to reward me.'

'How, doctor? I will do every effort to do anything for you.'

'I want you to get out of here, go to the house of Sheikh Saeed bin Hamdan, and ask to see Dr Mohammed Ayoub, who is an Indian military doctor, and after you see him, give him this paper, and tell him that you know me well and he will do something good for you.'

'Why should I go to him, Dr? I'm feeling good.'

'I know … go to him and you will know how to reward me.'

'Should I go now?'

'Yes, now.'

'Okay, should I visit you after I go to him?'

'Yes, I'll be waiting for you tomorrow at the same time.'

She went out of the clinic, and asked Moftah: 'Do you know where Sheikh Saeed Bin Hamdan lives? I want to visit him right now.'

'Yes, Aunt, it is near here, in the vicinity, follow me, please.'

She was following him, noticing Sanota's unaccustomed silence and Moftah's stealthy looks, and she felt that some feelings had stirred between them.

They arrived at the house, which consisted of two floors, the ground floor was crowded with people and the patients. The second floor made sounds as if they were classrooms in a school.

Moftah asked one of those present about Dr Mohammed Ayoub, so he guided him and took Niloofar to him. At that time, the doctor was in his hands, a man had handed him his head to drop some drops in his eyes from a small bottle in his hand, and as soon as he finished, he asked the patient not to rub his eyes or wash them until the next day and come back him to check his eyes.

Then, he looked at Moftah and asked: 'Hello … What are you complaining about, son?'

'I'm not complaining about anything, but my aunt here wants to talk to you.'

'My daughter, how can I help you?'

So, she spoke to him in Urdu: 'Are you Dr Mohammed Ayoub?'

He answered in the same language: 'Oh, do you speak Urdu, how did you learn it?'

'I am originally Indian and married to an Arab.'

'Do you believe that I thought you were an Englishwoman who wore Arab clothes?'

'My father is English, and my mother is Indian, but I was born and raised in India.'

'Let me guess … your accent is Hyderabadi, you're from Hyderabad?'

'Yes, sir, that is true.'

'It's nice to meet you!'

'Yes.'

'Well, tell me, what brings you here?'

'Dr Sarouj sent me from the clinic and asked me to give you this piece of paper.'

'Let me see.'

He read the paper and looked at it, thinking for a while.

'Dr Sarouj asks me in this letter to enroll you in our education classes, and that you have never attended schools, and you never learned to read or write.'

She felt very happy, and her eyes widened …

'Really? this is what she wanted from me, what a considerate person she is … Yes, sir, what Dr Sarouj mentioned is correct, as I had never attended schools before, not even Quran classes, except that my mother-in-law helped me to memorize some Quran.'

'Did you memorize it by heart?'

'Yes.'

'Great! Do you know how to pray?'

'Yes, my husband taught me how to pray, but I don't know whether I pray properly or not.'

'I am really proud of you, my daughter. You have the desire and the will to learn, and this is an excellent thing. I want you to come here every day to enroll in education classes, but I want to ask you why you did not try the government schools for girls. There are two new schools that teach girls, and they also follow the internationally recognized system. It is a two-semester system throughout the year, which we do not follow yet in our school.'

'I tried to enroll, but they didn't accept me because of my age, and because I'm a married woman.'

'Okay, never mind. Come here every day at 2 pm to attend the classes.'

'I can't leave home after midday, my husband told me not to go out after midday.'

'Oh … so, what is the solution?'

She started to feel sad …

'I don't know.'

He thought for a while …

'Look, my daughter, I will allocate a special class for you, first, you have to learn the Arabic language, and I will make my wife, the one who teaches you Arabic, the Quran, and prayer for the first three months, then you take an exam and if you pass it, she will teach you the Urdu language for another three months, and it will not be difficult for you. If you learn Arabic, and you take an exam after that, so that you can join the first classes of the English language, which my daughter Perween will teach you for a period of three months, and this will require you to attend constantly and focus to move to the major classes, which I will teach you, as you will learn the sciences of mathematics as well as other sciences in English, and in those classes you take exams continuously until you finish the course, and that will take you three years or more, and if you pass with good marks, I will write a letter to a college in India for you to join to learn primary academic sciences, and then you can choose which university to learn medicine is your dream, right?'

'It was my parents' dream, may Allah have mercy on them both, before it was mine.'

'Is it your dream now and your goal?'

'Yes it is.'

'So go and achieve it, for life is upon you, and knowledge is indispensable and indispensable.'

'Insha'Allah, but what about the attendance and departure times?'

'Oh yes, that's right. I want you to be here every day in the first year at exactly 7 am until 1 pm, and then, Insha'Allah, I will convince your husband myself to let you join the evening classes with the rest of the students.'

'When is 7 o'clock, how long is it after Fajr prayer?'

'Don't you know the time and how to read the clock?'

'I don't know the time here, and I can't find any clocks anywhere. In India, I only saw a clock in the mayor's house, but I didn't know how to read the time.'

'Okay, wait for me for a moment.'

He left the room and came back after a while with a small clock hanging on a chain.

'Look, my daughter, when the small hand is pointing to this number (and he pointed to the 7), and the big hand is pointing to this number (and he pointed to the 12), that means it's exactly 7 o'clock. You should be in your seat in the classroom at that time. Calculate how much time it takes you to wake up in the morning and travel from your home to here. And now that you're leaving, count how many numbers you've passed with the big hand. That's how much time it will take you to get here. Do you understand what I'm saying?'

'Yes, I understand, sir.'

'Please don't call me sir. Teacher will do, or Dr Ayoub, as you prefer.'

'Okay, Teacher.'

'I'll see you here tomorrow at exactly 7 am, or a little before, to introduce you to my wife.'

'Insha'Allah.'

'Allah bless you, my daughter. Niloofar is your name, isn't it?'

'Yes, Teacher.'

'It's a beautiful name that suits your beauty and intelligence.'

'Thank you, Teacher.'

(42)

She left the teacher's place while following the rays of hope for the future, which shone brighter with every step She took. Sanota and Moftah followed them in the paths of love, which began to take shape.

When they reached home, she addressed Moftah: 'Moftah, wait; don't go. We will prepare lunch in a few minutes.'

'I am not hungry, Aunt, but I will sit here outside until evening. Maybe you will need something.'

'You must have lunch here, and I will send you a chair to sit on.'

'Yes, ma'am. Thank you very much. Don't worry; I'm here whenever you need me.'

'I don't think I'll need anything today, but I want to tell you that I have to leave before twenty minutes to seven in the morning to get to school.'

'I'll wait for you here after the dawn prayer, but I want to tell you, Aunt, that you will need a notebook and a pen for school.'

'Yes, please. Can you provide them for me?'

'Of course, I'll bring you the notebook and pen from the institution.'

'And how much do you need from me?'

'No, Aunt, I don't need anything. There are plenty of notebooks and pens at the institution, and it won't hurt to take one for you.'

'Okay, that's a good idea. May Allah bless you, Moftah. You are so helpful.'

The next day, she woke up to the sound of the dawn prayer, washed, and made supplication to Allah Almighty to aid her, and headed out to fulfill her parents' dream of education. Then she found that Sanota had prepared breakfast.

'How did you sleep, Sanota?'

'I slept well, Aunt.'

'I doubt that.'

'Why do you doubt it?'

'I feel that you didn't sleep well. Maybe there was a beautiful thought on your mind.'

Sanota blushed and ran to the kitchen …

'Why did you run away? Eat your breakfast quickly, but before that, take the food out to Moftah, the poor man, he might be hungry now.'

She looked at the clock, it was showing quarter past six, so she had her breakfast, put on her cloak, and went out of the house to see Moftah standing and waiting for her.

Sanota ran to him shyly to take the tray of food from his hands.

'How are you, Moftah?'

'I'm fine, my dear aunt.'

'Did you sleep well last night?'

He smiled and understood her meaning, nodding his head.

She turned to Sanota, who had shifted her face to the other side, trying to hide her smile.

'Okay, let's go then.'

At school, she met the teacher and his wife Nasreen, their four daughters, the eldest being Bureen, followed by Jubin, Tahseen, and Farheen, and their three sons, Mustafa, Mohsin, and Mushtaq, all of them were students. Their ages ranged from five to seventeen years old.

She entered a small room with a blackboard hanging on the wall, and she was the only student with Farheen, the teacher's five-year-old daughter.

She began her first lessons in Arabic letters and simple words, learning quickly due to her eagerness to learn and her intelligence as a helpful factor. On the first day, she returned to Dr Sarouj after one o'clock to tell her what had happened, and the other was pleased with the good news.

Mansour returned after three days to find her waiting for him.

'My love, how are you?'

'I'm fine, I missed you so much.'

She ran to him and threw herself into his arms.

'I missed you more, tell me how did you spend your days?'

She hurried to her bag, took out a paper and a pen, and wrote the word "I love you" on it and gave it to him.

He was happy when he saw what she wrote.

'My love, Masha'Allah, you learned how to read and write in three days.'

'I didn't learn them well, but I'm learning.'

'And how did you do that, tell me?'

She told him everything she did, showed him her notebook and what she wrote, and the teacher's notes. She also told him about the doctor's subject and the letter she sent to Britain.

He embraced her tightly and kissed her:

'In just three days, you did everything that I couldn't do for months. You are truly a great woman, and I am lucky to have a beautiful and intelligent woman like you.'

'And I am fortunate to be the wife of a loving and loyal man like you. Tell me, how was your trip? And how is your friend doing now?'

'What can I say? The trip was tiring, and my friend's health improved a little while we were there, but it worsened on the way back. In fact, the doctors asked him to stay longer for treatment, but he refused and came back.'

'I feel for him because staying in the hospital is difficult. I've experienced it three times. What will you do now?'

'We'll wait a few days, and if his health doesn't improve, we'll take him back to the hospital and keep him there even if he refuses.'

'Yes, but what about me?'

'What about you? You handled your affairs like a brave woman in just three days, and you'll handle them again in the future. Insha'Allah, nothing will harm you.'

'I know, but I need you.'

'I'm with you, my love. My heart and soul are with you. Don't worry and never doubts about it.'

(43)

The days passed by quickly and happily as Niloofar successfully completed her first education and excelled in it. In the first three months, she learned how to read and write in Arabic, as well as how to recite and memorize many Suras from the Quran. She also learned and mastered the important principles of the Islamic religion, including prayer. Additionally, Allah had blessed her with a fourth pregnancy, and this time she did not worry much about maintaining it, as she believed that Allah would keep it for her. She did not want to be swayed by her emotions or secret disputes and leave that creature to exploit her kindness and affection for him.

During that time, Mansour's frequent trips to Al Ain to treat the merchant Saif Al-Sunaidi, and to Fujairah to visit his father who had been suffering from a stomach illness that made him lose his appetite and constant depression, continued. He refused to go to the hospital to receive treatment and was in a constant state of weakness.

As for Niloofar, despite her preoccupation with her pregnancy and education, she was aware of what was going on between Sanota and Moftah. She sensed the atmosphere between them, and the days proved her feelings, despite Moftah's silence and Sanota's shyness. She turned to Mansour to intervene and bring them together in holy matrimony. Mansour did not neglect her request and began to mediate between his father, who owned Sanota as a slave, and Saif Al-Sunaidi, who owned Moftah after obtaining the consent of the lovers. The wedding night was beautiful in the narrow courtyard of Mansour's house, attended by some neighbors and relatives of Moftah and his friends. Mansour had allocated the store that was built with the corner and the bathroom to be the newlyweds' house and built a wall to separate their house from his.

And the atmosphere was filled with the joy of the newlyweds and the joy of Niloofar's success in excelling in the second stage of education where she learned the Urdu alphabet and simple words. This was the sweetest educational period as she would quickly return home after school and try to spell out her mother's letters.

She had three months left to give birth to her child whom she had waited for nearly two years and more than three times.

In the third stage of education, which was the first stage of learning English for another three months, things became a bit difficult for her as the delivery date approached, little by little. Due to her ignorance of it and not practicing it in her daily life, but she quickly adopted it and adapted to it. Afterwards, she took the exams that Dr Mohammad Ayoub had rescheduled so that she could pass them before the delivery date. This was so that the school could grant him a four-month leave to travel with his family to India to wed his eldest daughter Ruwain. As for Niloofar, she rested and waited for the delivery date.

One night, she woke up in a panic to find herself in her old house in the coastal area, with Mansour sleeping beside her. She was surprised, how did this happen?

When did we come here?

And how did this happen without me feeling it or even remembering it?

I was sleeping in my house in Dubai, not here. What's happening? She heard groans coming from outside, and she was afraid, thinking that it might Sanota, could something have happened to her during especially that she is at her early pregnancy? Could that creature have harmed her?

But how was this possible?

She rushed out into the outdoor courtyard to see the sun's rays shining brightly and strangely, as if it were a hundred suns and not just one. She couldn't look at it because her eyes were blinded by the intense light. She tried to find the source of the sound but couldn't until her eyes adjusted to the bright rays, and she eventually found someone lying on the ground moaning.

When she approached, the creature grabbed the bottom of her dress and said: 'Don't touch me. Don't come near me or I'll kill you, do you understand? Please don't go.'

'What? You're speaking our language now?'

'Let go of me, let me go. If you harm my child, I will kill you, I swear to God, I will kill you.'

'You won't have to kill me because I'm dying now.'

'Then die, I'll be very happy after you killed my three children.'

'I'm very sorry for the harm I've caused you and your children, but I was crazy in love with you. I wanted you to be my mother alone.'

'You wanted me as a mother for yourself? Are you insane?'

'I was really crazy … I longed for a mother's affection and love, and I didn't find it in anyone but you.'

'Do you know that I hate you? I don't want to see your ugly face.'

'Please forgive me and don't say you hate me; I don't want to leave this world with you hating me.'

'Die … die and take my hatred with you until Judgment Day.'

'Please forgive me … I'm dying … I won't cause any harm to you or your family from now on, please forgive me. I'll leave you with my most precious possession to compensate you for all the pain, and just as I killed the dearest person to you, I'll save the dearest person to you.'

She managed to free her dress from his grip and ran to her room, crying and screaming, and closed the door behind her, still hearing his screams growing louder until they almost deafened her, so she kept screaming and screaming until Mansour woke up.

'Niloofar, Niloofar … wake up, my love, what's wrong? Are you feeling pain? Is it time for delivery? You're trembling.'

She opened her eyes to see Mansour's face.

'What? Was I dreaming or what?'

'I thought you were in pain from labor.'

She placed her hand on her swollen belly, making sure her pregnancy was fine.

'No, I'm fine, Praise be to Allah. It was just a terrible nightmare.'

'May Allah make it a good one.'

'Insha'Allah.'

'Come, sleep in my arms.'

She rested her head on her husband's chest, feeling as if that nightmare had been real, and that creature had indeed been calling her.

(44)

In the morning, before Mansour left for work, he asked her to check on her.

'Niloofar, my dear Niloofar.'

'Yes?'

'How are you feeling now?'

'I'm fine, thanks to Allah.'

'Do you feel any pain or any symptoms of childbirth?'

'No, I don't feel anything.'

'Praise be to Allah. Do you know, I was thinking of telling you to go to the old house so that you could gather all our remaining belongings there because I will be handing over the keys to the center, and we won't need it anymore.'

She screamed emotionally: 'No, I will not go to the old house as long as I live!'

'In the name of Allah, what's wrong?'

'Nothing, but I don't want to go there ever.'

'Okay, okay, calm down, if you don't want to go, I will go alone and gather the belongings and I will keep Sanota and Moftah with you, you may need it, don't worry.'

'Don't go alone, please.'

'Why?'

'Just promise me that you won't go alone.'

'What's wrong, Niloofar? Did you see anything in the house or something?'

'No, I didn't see anything, just promise me that you won't go there alone.'

'Okay, I promise I will take Saeed with me to gather the belongings. Does that make you feel better?'

'Yes.'

'See you in the evening.'

After two days and after having breakfast, Sanota asked her: 'Have you finished your breakfast, Aunt?'

'Yes, Sanota, I have finished. Praise be to Allah.'

'Aunt, I'm feeling a little unwell. May I please take a nap and then get up to prepare lunch?'

'What's wrong, my dear?'

'I'm feeling nauseous and weak.'

'Yes, my dear, these are pregnancy symptoms. Go and rest, I will prepare the food today, don't worry.'

'No, Aunt, I will prepare the food. I just want to lie down for a bit.'

'No, my dear, listen to me and obey me. You rest, and I will prepare the food. I want to work because the doctor said it would facilitate the delivery.'

(45)

She was energized and went into the kitchen to see that her husband had brought a large, fresh tuna fish and that Sanota had soaked and boiled the rice. She cleaned the fish, gutted it, and washed it thoroughly.

Then she chopped the garlic, onion, and coriander into small pieces, separated half of the onion from the rest, mixed the vegetables with salt and spices, stuffed the fish with the mixture, and sewed it back together. She salted the fish well on the outside, put it in a large pan, covered it tightly, and placed the pan on the stove. She placed hot coals on top of the pan's lid so that the fish would cook evenly and not need to be flipped to ensure it was cooked through.

She heated water in a large pot, salted it, added the soaked rice, fried the remaining half of the onion in oil, and added turmeric powder. She removed it from the heat and, as soon as the rice was cooked, drained it and spread the onions with turmeric powder on the bottom of the pot. She returned the rice to the pot and left it on the heat, placing a thick iron divider underneath the pot to prevent direct exposure to the heat and prevent the onions and rice from burning.

She added more wood to the fire and increased the embers on top of the fish pan's lid.

She remembered the items Mansour had brought from the old house and went to empty them.

As she was emptying her pockets, she found a red cloth bundle among her clothes that she had not seen before. When she opened the cloth, she pulled out a shiny, unpolished circular stone larger than her fist. She was afraid when she saw it. Could it be?

Could this be the compensation that the midget had told her about in her dream?

Could this stone be a precious gem?

How could she be sure and whom should she ask?

She was afraid and imagined how she would tell Mansour if what she suspected was true.

How could she get rid of it or make use of it?

She walked to her room searching for a place to hide the stone, until she found a hollow in the closet covered with an iron panel fixed with screws. She tried to remove one end of the iron panel from the nail but couldn't. She brought a long iron clamp from the kitchen and removed the iron panel from the bottom of the closet until the nail came out. She pulled the iron panel out of that corner and inserted her hand to see that the hollow was large. She wrapped the stone in the red cloth and put it in the hollow, then reinstalled the nail to secure the panel and put the clothes back on it.

She sat on her bed wondering if the dwarf had really died. And if that had happened, what could she do now? He gave her this stone that she did not yet know how it could be useful.

She lay down on the bed and got lost in thought until she fell asleep. After a while, she woke up in a panic when she remembered the food she had left on the stove, and ran to the kitchen to see Sanota sitting by the fire.

'What's wrong, Aunt? Why did you run?'

'Did the food I prepared burn?'

'No, not at all. I've been here for a long time. I removed the rice from the heat after it evaporated, and now I'm waiting for the fish to cook.'

'Praise be to Allah it didn't burn. This is our lunch and dinner for today. You didn't tell me how you are feeling now?'

'I'm fine now, Praise be to Allah.'

'Praise be to Allah … ah … ah …'

'What's wrong with you, Aunt? How do you feel?'

'I feel like something is about to explode in my stomach.'

'What? Is it time for delivery?'

'I don't know, but I feel like I'm going to lose my balance.'

'Aunt, come with me to the yard, lean on me, I want you to sit down so you don't fall.'

'Sanota, help me, water is coming out of me, I think the time for delivery has come.'

'What do I do, tell me?'

'I want to go to the clinic; I want to see Dr. Sarouj.'

'How can I take you there? Can you walk?'

'No, I can't. The pains are increasing, Sanota. Go and call a driver to bring me a car to take me to the clinic.'

'Okay, okay, Aunt.'

Sanota ran outside to the corner of the street to call a driver from the commercial building, but she returned before reaching there because she saw Mansour's car coming towards the house, so she ran towards him.

'Uncle Mansour … Uncle Mansour …'

'What's wrong, Sanota? Why are you running?'

'Aunt Noura is in labor, Uncle …'

'What's wrong with her, tell me?'

'I think she's giving birth!'

Mansour ran to her and carried her while she was moaning in pain. Sanota held her with her cloak after placing a sheet between her legs. At the clinic, Mansour, Sanota, and Moftah waited outside the delivery room, Mansour was anxious waiting for the good news of his wife and child, and poor Sanota had washed her cheeks with tears. As for Moftah, he kept saying, "'May Allah help you.'"

(46)

After an hour had passed, Dr. Sarouj emerged from the room with a beaming face and spoke in broken Arabic to Mansour: 'Congratulations, Mansour! May Allah compensate you for your patience and long suffering. Your wife has given birth to a healthy baby boy, Masha'Allah, like a full moon!'

Mansour felt a difficulty in breathing and a tickling pain in his stomach due to the magnitude of his joy, but he was worried about Niloofar.

'How is my wife, Doctor?'

'Praise be to Allah, your wife is fine, but she's a bit weak. Take care of her so she can recover her strength.'

'Yes, Insha'Allah. Can I see them now?'

'Of course, please come in.'

'You go first, Uncle, and check on her. My son and I will come in shortly.'

Mansour entered the room to find Niloofar lying on her back with her eyes closed and her hair falling on the pillow. Some strands of hair were wet, and her face had turned pale and tired.

'Niloofar, my love.'

'Yes.'

He showered warm kisses all over her face.

'Praise be to Allah for your safety. How do you feel now?'

'I'm fine, but I feel tired.'

'You'll recover soon, Insha'Allah.'

'Insha'Allah.'

'And where is my little son?'

'He's here. Come over to this side and see him.'

Mansour carefully held the baby in his arms.

'Little Mohammed, I have waited for you for years. Praise be to Allah.'

'Praise be to Allah. He's so beautiful. He inherited your beauty, my darling, but his eyes look like mine.'

'Aunt Noura, Uncle Mansour …' shouted Sanota from outside.

'Oh, I forgot about them. Come in, Sanota. Come in, Moftah.'

'Praise be to Allah for your safety, Aunt.'

She bent down and kissed her head, saying: 'Masha'Allah tabarak Allah. Can I hold him, Uncle?'

'Sure, but be careful, he still little.'

'May Allah make him the joy of your life.'

'Thank you, Moftah. Now it's your turn to wait for the crown prince.'

'Yes, Uncle. Allah is generous. Did you give the baby's call to prayer?'

'No, not yet.'

'Then give him the call to prayer, Uncle.'

'I was waiting for them to leave the hospital so I could take them to my father to do the call to prayer himself.'

'There's no harm. You can give him the call to prayer now, and then the older uncle can give him call to prayer too.'

'Okay.'

On the third day after giving birth, Niloofar and her baby left the hospital and headed to the Mansour family's home in Fujairah, where they would spend the forty-day postpartum period at Mansour's mother's house upon her request, so that she could take care of Niloofar and the baby. Mansour visited them once a week because of his busy work and trade and Sanota stayed with her husband Moftah at home to take care of Mansour's affairs and food.

(47)

The family and acquaintances of Mansour celebrated the birth of his child by holding feasts, sacrificing animals for his health and Aqiqah (a Muslim tradition of sacrificing an animal on the occasion of a child's birth), and giving him many gifts. Mansour's weak father was the happiest of them all, as he had been eagerly awaiting the birth of his first grandchild, who was named after him. He would not sleep without holding the child in his arms, and would lift his hands in gratitude to Allah whenever someone entered the room, feeling that the child was the remedy that brought back his joy and love for life.

However, his health deteriorated over the following days, and before the forty days had passed, Mansour's father passed away, leaving behind the small grandchild he had become attached to in his final days.

Two weeks after his father's death, Mansour returned to Dubai with his wife, child, and mother, who had no one else after her husband's passing. Her four daughters were settled at their homes.

They all moved back into the Dubai house, which was starting to feel cramped, so Mansour decided to buy a piece of land to build a big house for himself and his family, as he had become their sole provider. After his father's inheritance was divided according to Islamic law, Mansour received a share of six hundred thousand rupees.

As he began to execute his plan of buying the land and starting to build, Dr Sarouj urgently summoned Niloofar and one of the workers to her clinic.

Before leaving for the construction site in the afternoon, Mansour gave Niloofar permission to go and visit the doctor who had urgently summoned her without telling him the reason. She carried her child and walked with Sanota who was in her fifth month of pregnancy to the clinic.

Niloofar, the child, and Sanota were waiting in the reception area when one of the nurses entered to inform Doctor Sarouj of their arrival.

It was only a matter of moments before the doctor came out to them, almost running, and screamed in Urdu: 'Niloofar, please come with me!'

The three followed Doctor Sarouj, who led them to her room and closed the door behind them.

She gestured for them to sit down and said: 'I want to tell you something very important, but first, tell me … is everything okay? Are you having any problems with breastfeeding or experiencing any uterine pain?'

'Thankfully, everything is fine.'

'And what about the baby? Is he sleeping well now? Does he feel any abdominal pain?'

'Praise be to Allah, he's latching well, and his health is good, but he sleeps during the day and doesn't sleep at night. He stays awake and plays or cries for breastfeeding.'

'That's normal for newborns. Did you have him circumcised yet or not?'

'Yes, when my son completed his seventh day, he was circumcised, and a man who works in a barbershop in my husband's country performed the circumcision. He's the one who circumcises babies there, and the wound appears to have healed.'

'Let me see … You shouldn't have done the circumcision outside the clinic, but it seems the procedure was done correctly, and the wound has healed completely. Praise be to Allah.'

'Praise be to Allah that my mother-in-law is with us at home, and she guides me on how to raise and care for the child. I'm not afraid with her around, Praise be to Allah … Now tell me, Doctor, what's the reason for calling me today?'

'Listen, Niloofar, God has answered your prayers. After almost a year of sending your letters to your relatives in Britain, they have responded now.'

'What? Really? And what do they say?'

'They want to see you and get to know you!'

'And I want to do that too. How can I do that?'

'Excuse me … I opened it to read its contents … I am very happy with it …'

'It is alright, you have done the right thing, read the letter to me, please.'

'This letter is from your uncle, Mr Connor Gabriel Moore, the elder brother of your father, Gerald Gabriel Moore, and he says in the letter:

"Dear Niloofar ...

I hope this letter finds you well. First, I would like to thank you for reaching out to us. I and your grandmother, Mrs Betty Gabriel Moore, the widow of Mr Cedric Gabriel Moore (your grandfather), who passed away four months ago, shortly after your letter arrived. If your letter had arrived a little earlier, it would have made him very happy, and he would have done anything to meet you. I want you to know that we had traveled to India in the same year that we learned that our younger brother had married and was expecting a child. We made every effort to search for you and your mother, who had become a widow of our younger brother. We went to the area where they both lived, but all the houses had turned to ashes because the area had been burned down, and all the residents had migrated. We learned from some people there that your mother had migrated with those who had left. We searched for your mother and the newborn for months, and we even published your parents' picture and story in all the Indian newspapers, but we did not get any responses. We even hired some detectives to search for you both throughout India, but all our efforts failed.

And now, after sixteen years, God has honored us by informing us of your news through the letter you sent.

My mother, Mrs Betty Gabriel Moore, is in poor health, and since she learned about you, she has been eagerly wanting to see you and get to know you as soon as possible. Therefore, I would like to inform you that I will travel to India next month, as it is easier to reach than the country where you live. I want to meet you at the Taj Mahal Hotel in Mumbai, and I will wait for you there for the next six months, as my response to your letter may be delayed.

I also expect you to come with your husband, Mr Mansour, and I will take care of all the travel arrangements and expenses for our trip back to our home country, the United Kingdom, where we will meet your mother, your grandmother.

Note: We received your letter dated April 12, 1963, six months later, specifically on October 10 of the same year. It seems that your mail service is very slow.

Best regards to you and to my son-in-law, Mr Mansour.
Yours sincerely and lovingly always,
Your uncle, Connor Gabriel Moore.
Date: October 20, 1963."

(48)

Niloofar's joy knew no bounds, as she had achieved her goal.

'Isn't it wonderful news, my dear?'

'It's more than wonderful, Doctor. My words fail me, I can't thank you enough.'

'Don't thank me now. I want you to hurry and tell your husband to make the necessary arrangements for your trip to Bombay, as your uncle may have already traveled there or be on his way, since Connor Moore's letter is dated a month and a half ago. Hurry, my dear.'

'Okay, thank you very much.'

Niloofar hugged the doctor and hurried back home. At home, she told her mother-in-law everything that had happened to her.

'Praise be to Allah you found your family. I hope Mansour agrees to your trip.'

'Insha'Allah.'

'I want you to convert them to Islam when you see them, and tell them that it is their salvation from the fires of hell.'

Niloofar wanted to laugh, but she held back to avoid embarrassing her mother-in-law, who was unaware of the world outside her country.

'I'll tell them, Insha'Allah. Don't worry, Mother.'

'Yes, may Allah bless you. Give me the baby and go take some rest.'

'Okay, if you need anything, just call me. I feel a bit weak.'

'Okay, don't worry.'

Niloofar went to her room to pack her clothes for the trip, but she was afraid that Mansour would refuse her request or not allow her to travel alone due to his many obligations. She sat and waited for him to come.

After the evening prayer, Mansour returned home. Nilofer ran to him to see her mother-in-law, who was telling him about the situation.

'Travel to them and make them convert to Islam, they are unbelievers and living in a land of disbelief.'

'Okay, Mother, excuse me, I want to rest for a while.'

'Don't you want to eat something?'

'I'm not hungry.'

He kissed her, kissed the child and entered his room, Niloofar followed him. She lifted the headscarf and untied the buttons of his kandura.

'How are you, my dear husband? You seem bothered by something.'

'Not at all.'

'Don't hide anything from me. If you tell me, I can understand what you're saying.'

'There's nothing. I felt uneasy because I was busy with building the house. On top of that, one of the English partners sold his partnership in our establishment to us, and the other two are on their way to do the same.'

'And what's the problem here, my dear?'

'The problem is that this way, the company loses a partner, and the other two partners are on their way to dissolve the partnership. The merchant Saif Al-Sunaidi is in poor health, and the management in this case is solely up to me. With my work conditions, I feel a great burden on my shoulders.'

'I think you can handle things well, as you always have. You're capable of these tasks, you're intelligent and wise, aren't you?'

He smiled and embraced her.

'Yes, you're right, my dear. But sometimes a person feels great psychological pressure.'

'True, but Allah is always with us.'

'And yes, Allah is great.'

'Tell me, don't you want another child?'

'Yes.'

'When? If not now?'

'Give me some time. Our child is still very young.'

'Okay, tell me then about the news that my mother told me.'

'Yes, listen.'

And she told him about the contents of the letter and the offer she received from her uncle during his trip to India and then to Britain.

He was silent for a moment …

'I think it's a good idea. I was already thinking of traveling to India for trading purposes, and since we have received an invitation to go to the UK, this is an opportunity that doesn't come often.'

'Really? Are you sure?'

'Yes, we'll leave Mohammad with my mother and the two of us will travel.'

'No, that's not possible, the child is still a baby.'

'Don't worry, we can find a nursemaid for him for a fee.'

'No, I can't leave my son, and besides, they will be happy to see him.'

'As you wish, but taking him with us will be a burden on you.'

'Don't worry, I will take care of my child.'

'Tomorrow, I will look for someone who can provide us with tickets to travel by boat to Dorka or Tara, to Mumbai, and when the departure date is set, I will apply for leave from work, and so on.'

'My love, I don't know how to thank you?'

'Don't thank me, just love me.'

'I don't just love you, I adore you!'

(49)

Mansour obtained travel tickets for himself, his wife, and child on the Tara steamship to Bombay, then returned home early and met his mother.

'Peace be upon you.'

'And peace be upon you, my son. Are you okay? Why did you come back early from work today?'

'I went to work and applied for a leave request for forty-five days, returned the car to them, and then went to book travel tickets to Bombay.'

'Masha'Allah, Noura told me that you will travel.'

'Yes, we will travel as you know. Do you want to come with us?'

'No, my son. I'm afraid of traveling. I have never traveled except for Hajj, and I'm still in the waiting period, and I'm not allowed to go out or see anyone, not even Moftah can enter here.'

'You're right, I forgot.'

'Your father used to travel to Bombay a lot in his youth for diving trips, may Allah have mercy on him. I miss him so much.'

'May Allah have mercy on him. I'm not happy to leave you during this period, but it's urgent.'

'It's okay, my son. I'm fine. I'll stay here with Sanota because she's pregnant as you know and may need me.'

'May Allah bless you, Mom, and prolong your life for us.'

'And yours too, my son. Tell me when is the travel date?'

'We will travel the day after tomorrow, Insha'Allah, early in the morning.'

'By the grace of Allah. Do you need money?'

'No, Mom. Praise be to Allah; we have been blessed by Allah from his widest gates.'

'May Allah increase it with surplus of his gifts and generosity.'

'Amen.'

'Why don't you take Noura to the market to buy her some beautiful clothes and gold jewelry, because she will meet her family for the first time, and we don't want them to say that she lacks anything.'

'Insha'Allah, I'll tell her to get ready to go to the market after Asr prayer.'

'Uncle Mansour, Uncle Mansour, are you inside?'

'Yes, Moftah, I am coming to you. Wait for me. Excuse me, Mom, I will go out to see what Moftah wants.'

'Yes, Moftah. Tell me, what's wrong?'

'Uncle Saif is waiting for you at the company.'

'Masha'Allah, he came to the company after all this time. Well, I am going with you to see him now.'

'Let's go.'

When they arrived at the commercial company, Mansour greeted Saif: 'Salaam Alaikum.'

'Wa Alaikum Salaam.'

'Masha'Allah, you are here today. How are you feeling now, Abu Khaled?'

'Thanks to Allah for everything.'

'You have lightened up the company with your presence.'

'The company is lightened with your presence.

'Thank you.'

'How is the Crown Prince?'

'He is fine. I thought of bringing him to you so you can see him, but he is sleeping now.'

'Insha'Allah, I will see him. May Allah bless you with him.'

'Since you are here, I want you to take a look at the accounting books and examine the profits yourself.'

'I have reviewed the books, and it seems that you have done a great job. I am not worried about the company when you are there. As soon as the two English partners sell to us, we will have more freedom with our money and business. I wanted to ask you about something else.'

'I am at your service.'

'Thank you, but tell me where is your car?'

'I returned it to the center, as you know it's a work car.'

'Why did you return it?'

'Oh, I forgot to tell you, I was planning to visit you at home this evening to tell you, do you remember the issue with my wife's relatives in Britain?'

'Yes.'

'We received a letter from them inviting us to visit her sick grandmother in the United Kingdom, and we will travel the day after tomorrow, Insha'Allah, to Mumbai and from there we will travel to Britain.'

'So, you are planning to travel?'

'Yes.'

'I wanted to go with you tomorrow morning to the court to grant my wife's sister, Umm Khaled, a power of attorney to manage my shares in case of my illness or disability.'

'May Allah heal you and grant you a long life.'

'Thank you, but ages are in the hands of Allah, and we praise Him in all circumstances.'

'Praise be to Allah, I have no objection, I will come to you tomorrow morning, Insha'Allah.'

'Insha'Allah.'

'I excuse myself now, I have a lot of work to do before traveling.'

'Yes, rely on Allah, but I want you to take the keys to my Land Rover that I haven't used for almost a year, my health doesn't allow me to drive it.'

'No, that's not possible, you will recover soon and drive it yourself.'

'Who knows? May Allah provide what is best, but for now take it and use it for your needs.'

'I don't know how to thank you, but I will take good care of it for you.'

'Go now to complete your work, and I will return home to rest, I will see you tomorrow morning at the court, Insha'Allah.'

'Insha'Allah.'

(50)

Mansour took the merchant Saif Al-Sunaidi's car, which had been parked for over a year in the closed garage of the institution, and brought it back home.

Upon his arrival, his wife asked him: 'Where were you? I was breastfeeding the baby in the room when I heard your voice, and when I went out, I didn't find you.'

'I was talking to my mother until Saif Al-Sunaidi summoned me to the institution.'

'Why did he summon you?'

'For a matter related to trade. You don't have to worry about these things.'

She realized that she had crossed the line and shouldn't have asked that question, so she remained silent.

'I want you to get ready after the afternoon prayer so we can go out to the market together.'

She wanted to ask him why the market, but she settled for saying: 'Okay.'

He approached her with a gentle smile and said: 'I want to buy you some gold jewelry as I promised you before, and I also want to buy you some beautiful clothes for travel so that you don't lack anything in front of your peers.'

She smiled shyly and said: 'I don't want you to buy clothes for me from here. I will buy them from India, where the fabrics are beautiful and the colors are vibrant.'

'As you wish, we will only buy the gold jewelry for you.'

Following her choices, he bought her six gold bracelets to wear on her right hand, all of the same shape with small perforated patterns, and a sturdy bracelet with tapered plates and some colored stones to wear on her left hand. He also bought her a long necklace with a large tulip flower pendant, two rings, one with a medium-sized pearl in the middle and the other with a medium-sized square-shaped ruby in the middle, and two dangling earrings.

Niloofar was very happy with the jewelry that Mansour bought for her as a gift for the first time, as he had never bought her gold jewelry before. She had received some jewelry from her husband's family on their first visit.

Mansour's mother was also happy to see her, saying: 'Let me see what your husband bought for you.'

'Here you go.'

'Masha'Allah … Masha'Allah … These items are very beautiful, they will add to your sweetness, O dear mother of Mohammed. Their weight is good, not light, may Allah bless you, my daughter.'

'May Allah bless you too, Mother.'

'Wait, I'll be back to you immediately.'

She entered the small room Mansour had built for her in the courtyard, and came out after a while carrying a red cotton cloth bundle in her hand.

'Take this, my dear.'

Niloofar opened the bundle to reveal two hair clips made of gold studded with small diamonds, and small gold beads.

'Let me put them on for you.'

Niloofar turned her back to her mother-in-law for her to fasten the clips in her hair after she had untied her braid.

'Your golden shiny hair is beautiful, I won't say that the clips have added to its beauty, but your hair has increased the shine and beauty of the clips. My hair was beautiful one day when the late fastened them in my hair and gave them to me when Mansour was born. May Allah have mercy on him, my dear.'

Tears filled Niloofar's eyes, and she turned to see her mother-in-law's cheeks wet with tears, so she hugged her and kissed her forehead and hand.

'May Allah prolong your life, my dear mother.'

'And your life too, my dear. First, listen to me. I want you to wear these jewels when you get to your relatives' house, and don't wear them when traveling, because I know there are many thieves who don't hesitate to kill a woman or harm her to steal her jewelry. Please be careful.'

'Insha'Allah, I will, O my dear mother.'

'May Allah bless you. And where is Mansour? He hasn't come in yet …'

'He said he would go to see the house construction and recommend the contractor to authorize Moftah for the building matter.'

'And what does Moftah know about such matters?'

'Mansour will tell him all the details, and where is Sanota? I haven't seen her since I came back.'

'Sanota, my daughter, feels nauseous all the time. She is weak.'

'Poor thing … I don't know how we can help her?'

'Allah will take care of her, don't worry about her. She is a strong and active girl, but pregnancy exhausts even the strongest women. This is the first period that will pass, and you will see how she will run around the house.'

'Insha'Allah, Mom.'

And the child cried …

'Excuse me, Mother, I will enter the nursery, the baby is hungry, and I haven't breastfed him for more than three hours, and he has wet his clothes …'

'Why don't you breastfeed him here, why do you keep running inside every time you breastfeed him?'

She blushed and reddened her cheeks …

'Well, if you're shy, go and breastfeed him … and bring me the radio, I want to listen to the radio.'

(51)

The next morning, her husband rushed her, saying: 'Niloofar, please come out, I need to take a shower. I'll be late for my appointment.'

'I am getting dressed now, and I'll get out immediately.'

After a while.

'I've heated the water for you. Come in and take a shower.'

'When will you leave for your errands, and when will you come back home?'

'I'll leave after you do and come back quickly.'

'Alright, take care of yourself.'

'Insha'Allah.'

Mansour went to take a shower, and she picked up the sleeping baby and took him to her mother-in-law, who was reading the Quran. She put the baby next to her, kissed her head, and went to the kitchen. Sanota had just finished preparing breakfast.

'How are you today, Sanota?'

'I'm fine, Aunt. I just finished preparing the food. Should I set the table now?'

'Yes, prepare it, because your uncle Mansour will eat his food and go out straight, and tell Moftah to eat his food quickly and prepare to go out with him.'

'Alright, but dry your hair so you don't catch a cold.'

'Yes, thank you. You get ready as well. We're going to the clinic together. I want to say goodbye to the doctor because I'm leaving tomorrow morning. I'm also going to the school to leave a letter for Dr Mohammed Ayoub because the new school year will begin next month, and I don't know if I'll be able to come back before then or not.'

'Understood, Aunt.'

She left with Sanota after breastfeeding the baby and leaving him with her mother-in-law.

At the clinic: 'Peace be upon you, may I see Dr Sarouj, please?'

'Yes, but she is in the delivery room now.'

'I will come back later after finishing some work.'

'Do you want me to tell her that you came to see her?'

'Yes, please. Tell her that I came to bid her farewell as I will be traveling tomorrow morning to Bombay and then to Britain.'

'Okay, I will let her know.'

They then went to the school to deliver the letter that she wrote to Dr Mohammad Ayoub, asking for permission for her expected absence next month due to her sudden travel circumstances.

Before the call to prayer for Dhuhr, they had already returned home.

'Your mother has arrived. Take him, my daughter, and breastfeed him. He doesn't want to eat the food you prepared for him.'

'What food is that, Mother?'

'Rice with tomatoes and ghee.'

'Isn't he too young to eat such food?'

'No, my daughter, he has completed his third month and needs food to supplement his mother's milk.'

'But the doctor told me to feed him mashed food without fat after he completes his fourth month.'

'Don't worry about what the doctors say. Their advice never ends. I fed Mansour and his siblings at this age, and they were never harmed. Their health was good, Praise be to Allah.'

She smiled when she sensed her mother-in-law's annoyance.

'Insha'Allah, I will feed him. Please don't be angry, Mother, you are my source of goodness and blessings.'

'Take him and breastfeed him now. What is this bag you have in your hand?'

'It's the gift that Dr Sarouj gave me, some clothes for the baby, and a set of clothes for me.'

'Let me see.'

As soon as she saw the clothes, she said: 'The baby clothes are beautiful, but why is this dress so short, and why are the pants so tight?'

'It's the Indian outfit (Punjabi), and the pants are tight because it's worn that way.'

'Is this dress covering?'

'Yes, because the shirt reaches above the knee.'

'But it's a little tight.'

'Yes, I agree with you, I will not wear it if you do not want.'

'No, wear it if is worn like that, but not here, of course. Wear it in your country and with your relatives.'

'Alright Mother, I beg your permission, I will go in to breastfeed the baby.'

She kissed her on the head and entered her room.

(52)

Mansour went to the court with Moftah and met the merchant Saif and his wife Umm Khaled, as well as the English partners there, and they signed the contracts that granted Saif's wife the management of the establishment in case her husband was absent.

After they finished, Saif took Mansour to one of the corners and took out a paper from his robe pocket.

'Take this, Mansour, as a gift for the crown prince.'

'I don't need these formalities, my brother.'

'This is my duty.'

'And what is this paper?'

'See for yourself.'

After reading it, Mansour said: 'My God, Abu Khaled, why did you burden yourself with this? I don't need a car now. When did you register the car in my name?'

'Today before you arrived.'

'You shouldn't have done this.'

'You are my brother and dearest to me, and I haven't driven the car for a year due to my health conditions. Also, I couldn't find a better gift than this for the child's father who stood by me in times of hardship.'

'Don't say that. We are brothers.'

'May Allah bless you, your child, and the car.'

'Thank you. I don't know how I can repay your favors.'

'Just take care of my children if anything happens to me.'

'Allah forbid. May Allah bless you with a long life, good health, and well-being. You will take care of your children until they grow up and see your grandchildren and great-grandchildren.'

'Insha'Allah.'

And he thanked him a lot and said goodbye to him.

In the car, Moftah said: 'Congratulations on the car, my uncle.'

'Thank you. And how did you know about this? The man was whispering to me.'

'I knew his intention beforehand. He wanted to register the car in your name for a while, and when I saw him take out the paper from his pocket, I knew it.'

'You're so smart, Moftah.'

'I would impress you, my uncle.'

'May Allah bless you.'

'I noticed something strange today.'

'And what is that thing?'

'Today, for the first time, I saw my Aunt, Umm Khaled, the merchant Saif Al-Sunaidi's wife.'

'How did you not see her before when you were owned by Saif the merchant?'

'That's true, but I'm just a servant in the company and I never entered his house or saw any of his family, they are all from Qatar, he came alone from Qatar to start his life here.'

'Yes, I heard about this.'

'Did you not notice that Umm Khaled is a young woman compared to her husband?'

'No, I did not pay attention to her.'

'Yes, she is young, tall, and beautiful. I saw her when she lifted the cover from her face when she was signing the papers, and she was stealing glances at you.'

'What?'

'Yes, that's what she was doing.'

'I don't know, and I don't care because my wife is one of the most beautiful women in the world, and we have no right to talk about other people's wives or look at any female. Do you understand?'

'Yes, Uncle, I apologize.'

'Let's go to the construction site, then to the bank to convert our rubies to Indian rupees, then we'll go back home to pack our bags.'

'Let's depend on Allah. Do you want me to drive for you, Uncle?'

'No, no need, I want to drive myself.'

(53)

After the Fajr prayer the next day, Mansour returned from the mosque and Niloofar had just finished bathing.

He asked her: 'Did you take a shower?'

'Yes.'

'Where is the baby?'

'I bathed him, breastfed him, and took him to Mother's room so I can take a bath and get ready.

'Then pray and get ready to say goodbye to everyone and we'll go to the port.'

He went to his mother's room, she had finished praying and the little one was sleeping next to her.

'How are you, Mom?'

'I'm fine, my dear. I'll miss you all.'

'We'll miss you more. Please take care of yourself. I've instructed my sisters to take turns in coming with their children to stay with you for a week until we return safely, Insha'Allah.'

'Insha'Allah.'

'Please take care of yourself and your family.'

'I will, don't worry.'

'Don't leave before you have breakfast. I've prepared porridge, yeast bread, and milk tea for you.'

'Did you prepare it for us?'

'Yes, and I also packed some long-lasting foods for you in the luggage so you can eat them on the boat.'

'When did you do all this?'

'Before the Fajr call to prayer, I didn't sleep all night.'

'You didn't sleep just to prepare food for us? My dear, my beloved mother.'

'Yes, my son, you are my most precious child, just as I would have done the same if one of your sisters were in your situation.'

'May Allah make you a crown on our heads in this life and the Hereafter.'

'May Allah be pleased with you, my son.'

'And may Allah be pleased with you, my dearest mother. My sister Amina and her children will come to stay with you for a week.'

'May Allah bless her. But I will miss my little child the closest to my heart, don't forget to feed him well and massage his head with oil and keep him warm.'

'Yes, Mother, I will listen and obey.'

'Where is Noura? She is getting ready to leave now.'

'Okay, you stay with your child, I will go and see if Sanota has woken up from her sleep or not.'

They all had breakfast together, and then Moftah took the suitcase to the car, and then the crying began … the mother was crying, Niloofar was crying, and Sanota was crying more than anyone. Mansour's heart was torn apart by the separation and his mother's crying, he hugged her tightly and kissed her cheeks, head, eyes, and hands.

After the prayers for a safe and blessed return of the three, the mother entered and her tears had soaked the neckline of her dress, and Sanota closed the door while sobbing.

The car, driven by Moftah this time, moved, while Mansour was sitting next to him and Niloofar was in the back with her child, praying to Allah to protect her mother-in-law from all harm.

(54)

The port was filled with English, Indian, and even Arab travelers. They boarded the ship after bidding farewell to Moftah. They entered their cramped cabins where they stayed for four days, only leaving to eat, and did not mix with the people who welcomed them to speak and get closer to them until they reached the port of Bombay.

They arrived in Bombay on Monday, March 30, 1964. Niloofar and her child stood at customs while Mansour went with one of the customs officials to clear their personal belongings. Beggars gathered around Niloofar, who stood bewildered and afraid of their number, thanking Allah that she wasn't wearing any jewelry.

She glimpsed a man among the beggars who resembled her friend, as if he were him, and he stared at her with piercing eyes, causing her to tremble. She scanned the area, searching for her husband among the many travelers, but she couldn't find him. She wanted to walk and change her location, but she couldn't due to the large number of beggars around her. She anxiously 175ashed the midget approaching her. She started pushing the beggars to get out of this circle, but she couldn't because there were so many of them. Her child began to cry hysterically, and she didn't know what to do or how to escape as the midget approached her more and more. She was afraid for her child and hugged him tightly, almost suffocating him, and began to scream when the midget approached her and reached out to touch her. Suddenly, Mansour appeared in front of her.

'What's wrong, Niloofar? Why are you screaming? Why are you so afraid? They're just beggars, they won't harm you. Give me the child and come with me to leave this port.'

She turned to see that the midget had disappeared and was no longer there. He was one of her greatest fears that accompanied her wherever she went, while the customs official forcefully removed the beggars from them.

And then he returned to Mansour to receive his payment and said in Hindi: 'Please don't wear Arab clothes during your stay in Bombay to avoid bothering beggars and the danger of thieves.'

'Alright, thank you.'

And he gave him his tip.

'Thank you very much, sir. This is very generous. Please come with me. I'll take you outside to the taxi so that beggars won't bother you again.'

He walked with him, and in front of them was the porter pushing their luggage cart outside, and taxis were lined up waiting for passengers.

'Where are you going?'

'We're going to the Taj Mahal Hotel.'

And he ordered the owner of the first taxi parked in the queue: 'I want you to take them to the Taj Mahal Hotel, but be careful and don't take them through the narrow shortcuts. Do you hear me?'

'Yes, sir. I understand.'

They got into the taxi after the porter placed their bags in the trunk of the car, and the child was crying loudly …

'What's wrong with the child, Niloofar?'

'I don't know … he seems upset, maybe afraid?'

'Breastfeed him to quiet him down.'

'I can't do that now.'

'Why not?'

'Because we're in the car, and it will attract attention.'

'Don't worry, cover yourself well and breastfeed him.'

'I don't want to breastfeed him in front of people.'

'The baby will die from crying.'

'Don't say that, please.'

'Then breastfeed him, and I'm with you, don't be afraid. No one will look at you, and if anyone looks at you, I'll gouge out their eyes. Please breastfeed him.'

And she breastfed him after covering herself and the child with the cloak, which was like a tent.

After a long distance, they arrived at the hotel and the child had fallen asleep. Mansour paid the taxi driver, and the luggage was carried to the hotel lobby.

'I want to book a room, wait here.'

'No, I'm coming with you.'

'Sitting here is better for you.'

'No, I want to go with you, and I also want to ask about my uncle.'

'Okay, let's go.'

Mansour took the room key after filling out the guest registration form and depositing their passports with the receptionist.

In Urdu, Niloofar asked the receptionist: 'Excuse me, I want to inquire about one of your guests.'

'Yes, madam. Please give me his name.'

'Mr Connor Gabriel Moore.'

'Let me see … Yes, Mr Moore, the Englishman, is staying in room 450 on the fourth floor, but he is not here now.'

'Where is he?'

'He went on a business trip to Goa and will return after two days.'

'Oh, and are you certain that he will return?'

'Yes, I'm sure, as some of his belongings are still here. He has been staying with us for four months and said that his stay at the hotel may continue for another two months. Do you want me to leave a message for him?'

'No, thank you. I will wait for him for another two days.'

They headed to the elevator, but the receptionist called out to them: 'Excuse me, sir and madam, please …'

They turned back to him.

'Mr Moore left a letter for a girl named Niloofar. He said she is his niece and is waiting for him. I noticed in your passport that your name is Niloofar, as he said.'

'Yes, I am his niece, Niloofar.'

'Yes, madam. It is for you. Please give me a minute to get it for you.'

He gave her the letter and they thanked him before going to their room with the hotel staff.

(55)

In the room, Mansour said: 'I really like this city, but it's very crowded with cars, buses, and people.'

'Yes, it is.'

'That's right, unlike your city of Hyderabad, it's a historical city, and there are few people, carriages, and cars. It's a peaceful city.'

Niloofar began to stare at the envelope.

'I want to read my uncle's letter.'

'Try to read it. You have learned English, haven't you?'

'Yes, I have learned words, letters, and simple conversation, but my uncle's handwriting is similar to Dr Sarouj's, and the letters are intertwined with each other a lot.'

'Try, my dear, but not now. Look at this beautiful room. Put the baby on the bed and come to me.'

She woke up in the afternoon of that day to the sound of the baby announcing his hunger by crying, and she began to breastfeed him while thinking about what her uncle wrote in the letter. She wouldn't be able to read it completely as his writing was small and stuck together. She thought about solving the letters and rewriting them on another sheet of paper so that she could read them.

After she finished feeding the baby and changing his wet clothes, and he began to laugh, play and make baby noises, she executed her plan and untangled the intertwined letters into words that she could read. And her uncle had written in it …

"Dear Niloofar,

I hope this letter finds you in good health. I have been waiting for you in this country and in this hotel for four months now, but you have not yet arrived. I do not blame you, my dear, as it may be that the mail has been delayed in reaching you, as usual. I am fine, and my mother, Mrs Betty Gabriel Moore, is eagerly looking forward to seeing you and your husband. She has also expressed her desire to travel to Bombay to wait for you with me here, but I did not agree because she is unwell and will not be able to bear the rigors of travel and change of climate.

I hope you will come soon, or else I will do my best to travel to the country where you live and search for you myself. I am traveling for a week today to the city of Goa because two years ago I bought a small building and turned it into an inn, renting rooms to tourists there. The trip will not take more than a week. I hope to find you waiting for me at the hotel upon my return.

Note: If you arrive before my return, please go and see the city of Bombay. I assure you that you will enjoy the atmosphere.

Your loving uncle, Connor Gabriel Moore.

Date: March 2."

She was very happy and almost jumped for joy.

'Mansour, please get up.'

'I'm tired, my dear, let me sleep a little.'

'You've been sleeping for more than five hours. Get up, I'm hungry.'

'What do you want to eat?'

'I think I'll have Indian food that I haven't had in a long time.'

'Okay. Have you taken a shower?'

'No, I'll go now. The bathroom here is great, clean, cool, and the water comes directly from two taps, one hot and the other cold. We won't need to heat it up like the hotel we stayed in Hyderabad when we got married. Remember?'

'Yes, I remember. Our new house in Dubai will be like that, Insha'Allah.'

'Really?'

'Yes.'

'Lucky me.'

'Praise be to Allah.'

'Take care of the baby until I finish showering and come back.'

'Okay, come on, my son.'

'Don't fall asleep and let him roll off the bed.'

'Don't worry, I won't sleep.'

When she came out of the bathroom, Mansour was asleep, and the baby was playing on his stomach.

(56)

After Mansour finished showering and went out, she had put on the Indian clothes that Dr Sarouj had gifted her.

'You look wonderful, my dear.'

'Your eyes are wonderful.'

'You won't wear the abaya, will you?'

'Yes, I don't want to encounter beggars again.'

'That's true, but you should carry a large scarf to cover yourself when you breastfeed the baby.'

'Yes, that's true. Look, I got you this brown shirt and navy-blue pants.'

'Good, thank you.'

'Hurry up, I'm hungry.'

'Insha'Allah.'

'And you promised to buy me Indian clothes, do you remember?'

'Yes, my lady, I haven't forgotten about it.'

They left the hotel to find the nearest restaurant and came across a Madrasi restaurant (Madrasi city in the state of Tamil Nadu in southern India) where they had vegetarian Indian meals.

When they finished, Mansour asked her: 'Do you want to walk or take a taxi?'

'I really want to walk, but the baby is heavy and my hands hurt.'

'Then we'll take a taxi to the nearest women's market.'

The driver took them to Behindi Bazaar (the famous women's market in Mumbai) where the storefronts displayed women's clothing with bright colors, beautiful patterns, and bright lights that quickly attracted women.

'Look at how beautiful the clothes are, Mansour.'

'Choose whatever clothes you want, my dear.'

'How many sets can I buy?'

'I don't know, it depends on the prices here, but I can suggest that you choose ten sets, that should be enough. And don't choose the sari because you won't wear it, it's not modest clothing and it's not appropriate for Muslim women to wear.'

'I won't wear the sari because I hate it. Can I buy shoes?'

'Yes, why not? Let me choose two pairs of shoes and a woman's bag for you.'

'I am so happy; I don't know how to thank you.'

'You already thanked me earlier today, but you can thank me again when we return to the hotel.'

She didn't comment on what he said and handed the child over to him. While she searched through the clothes, Mansour found one of his colleagues, who had also brought his Indian wife to shop here and started chatting with him.

When she finished selecting what she wanted from clothes, shoes, a bag, some cosmetics, and colorful glass bracelets, she returned to her husband for him to pay. They returned to the hotel after finishing their shopping.

Mansour asked her: 'Are you hungry?'

'A little, and you?'

'I'm starving. Do you know if they serve food in the rooms?'

'I'm sure they do. This is a five-star hotel, as stated on the hotel's sign.'

'Then let me go down to reception to order food.'

'No need to go. We can just press this bell, and the worker will come to us.'

After Mansour pressed the call bell, the worker came shortly and took their dinner order. He also gave them an advertisement sheet and left.

Mansour closed the door and said: 'Look, Niloo, the worker gave me this paper, and it seems to be a movie advertisement with posters and other things.'

'Let me see … Oh, how wonderful! The hotel is offering us a list of the movies that will be shown this week so we can choose which one we want to watch. We can also buy tickets from the hotel here.'

'Do you want to watch the movies?'

'Very much, when I was young, my late grandfather used to take me and my cousins to the cinema to watch beautiful movies.'

'Then we are going to the cinema, what movie did you choose?'

'Let me see … hmmm, we will watch this movie that looks wonderful, "Oh, Khon Tayh" (who is that woman?) which stars my favorite actress named Sadna.'

'When can we go?'

'I have set options for the show times: the first show is at 10:00 am, then 1:00 pm, and then 4:00 pm, every three hours. What do you think of going after we have lunch, at 4:00 pm?'

'Good, let me inform him when he returns with the food.'

When the worker returned with the food, Mansour informed him about the movie and its timing, and the man nodded in agreement and left.

The two of them sat down to eat.

'This chicken is delicious, why don't you cook for us like this?'

'The spices here are different for each dish, so the taste changes in each dish. Take me to the market to buy a large quantity of ready-made spices so I can prepare a variety of delicious dishes.'

'Oh, I got an idea. Why don't I buy quantities for the food establishment? These spices are in demand in our country, both Arabs and English love them.'

'True, and I will also buy from your establishment.'

'Yes, we will ask about the spice market tomorrow morning. It seems like a profitable deal.'

'My love, I know that I have burdened you with many requests, but I hope you accept my last request.'

'Please, my dear, tell me your request.'

'I really want you to take a picture of us, like the picture of my father. What do you think of us going after the cinema to take a picture of the three of us?'

'That's a great idea. We haven't taken a picture together except on our wedding day.'

'True, and I also want to wear the jewelry you gave me.'

'Why not … Carry it with you in your bag, and wear it in the photo studio, or I carry it in my bag that I put in my coat pocket so that it won't be stolen from you, as women are stolen easily.'

'Good.'

(57)

Mansour woke up to find the child next to him, and turned to see his wife standing by the window, watching the street and passersby.

'Niloo … how long have you been awake?'

'For a while now, and I didn't want to wake you.'

'What time is it?'

'It's nine in the morning.'

'Alright, I'll go down to greet them. I want to ask about the spice market.'

'Do you want me to come with you? Will you be able to explain it?'

'I'm not sure. You go ahead and get ready, we'll go out together, have breakfast downstairs, and then ask about the spice market.'

'Don't forget that we have to be back before four o'clock to watch the movie.'

'Oh, right. Then let's postpone the market until tomorrow, have breakfast here, and lunch, and then go to the cinema. I'll call the worker.'

They had breakfast and went back to sleep until lunchtime. After lunch, they got ready to go to the cinema. In the hotel lobby, the receptionist addressed them.

'Excuse me, sir …'

'Come, let's see what the receptionist wants.'

'Good evening, sir.'

'Good evening.'

'Are you going to the cinema now?'

'Yes.'

'But it's 2 pm, and the movie you've chosen starts exactly at 4 pm.'

'Yes, we thought we might not find the cinema easily.'

'It's close to here, just two buildings away from the hotel. Do you have the tickets that the hotel worker brought for you last night?'

'Yes, I have them.'

'Would you like to spend some time in the hotel's backyard until 3 pm, then I will personally send the worker with you to guide you to the cinema.'

'Yes, why not.'

'Please, sir, you will enjoy an hour of your time in the backyard as there is a small festival for tourists going on, so go and have a look, please.'

'Come on, Niloofar, let's see what's there.'

The yard was filled with colors, popular Indian songs, and small moving doll theaters. Some women were doing henna tattoos on the hands of foreign women, while others were gathering around women reading palms. A man was singing and playing music on a wooden box, and some were tattooing names on their hands.

The two sat on a bench watching everything happening in the square, and even the child was enjoying the atmosphere.

A man approached them carrying a cage containing a green parrot.

'Hello sir, hello madam, would you like me to read your fortune?'

'Yes, that would be lovely. I'd like that.'

'Are you crazy, Niloofar? This is not allowed, it's forbidden.'

'I won't believe what he says; I just want to see what he will say. Please.'

'As you wish, it's not my concern. You will bear the sin.'

'Okay, could you read my fortune, my brother?'

'Please, madam, choose nine cards as you wish. Come on, bird, come out of your cage and read the beautiful lady's fortune.'

The bird flew out and picked the first card, which had a drawing of a man holding a sword on it.

'Your husband loves you very much, but other women have their eyes on him. Keep him close to you so that he doesn't go to another woman's nest.'

'In the name of Allah, what is this man saying?'

Mansour laughed and said: 'I didn't say it, the card did. You don't know your husband's value. I'm handsome and women have been attracted to me since I was a little boy.'

The bird then picked the second card.

'Your destiny, Madam, is made of gold. Everything you experience in life would be doubled; happiness and sadness, wealth and poverty, education and ignorance, and both lowly and high status in her life.'

'Maybe what he says is true, let's see.'

The bird then picked the third card.

'A little genie had become attached to you, my lady; he loved you like a son loves his mother. The genie had not allowed you to have children so that she would not be distracted from him, but he had died of grief at your separation and had left you a gift.'

Niloofar became frightened and her face changed.

'What are these witchcrafts? Could what he said be true? Do you want to hear more?'

'No, no, that's enough. Let's leave.'

'Let's go.'

Mansour agreed and gave the fortune-teller his share of the money before they left the hotel lobby.

(58)

They arrived at the cinema at 3:30.

'Here is the cinema, sir. No need to stand in line, you have movie tickets. Please proceed inside directly, and you will find a cafeteria selling snacks and drinks.'

'Thank you very much. Here you go.'

'Thank you, sir. See you at the hotel, have a good time.'

'How much did you tip him?'

'Three Indian rupees.'

'Okay, let's go in.'

'Did you know this is the first time I've ever been to the cinema?'

'Yes, you told me. As for me, I used to go with my late grandfather a lot in my childhood. Watching movies in the cinema was great. The people in the movie seemed huge and larger-than-life.'

'Let's see.'

'I want popcorn and a Maaza juice.'

'Me too. Wait here, I'll go get them for you.'

'No, you stay here and hold the baby. My hands hurt, and I'll go. Give me the money, please, and hold the baby a little.'

The movie lasted for two hours and forty-five minutes, including a ten-minute break. During the break, Mansour went to get his wife some French fries and another Maaza bottle, while she took the opportunity to breastfeed the baby so he wouldn't wake up and cry during the movie.

When the movie ended and they left the theater: 'Wait, I'll call for a taxi.'

'Why?'

'Did you forget that we were going to take the picture you requested?'

'No, I didn't forget, but I'm tired after watching the scary movie. Also, the baby has dirtied my clothes with his vomit. Let's go back today, and tomorrow, Insha'Allah, we'll go to the photographer first, then the market.'

'Okay, that's better.'

And they continued their way to the hotel on foot.

As soon as they entered the hotel lobby, the receptionist ran towards them.

'Madam … Mrs Niloofar, is that you?'

'Yes, that's correct. I am Niloofar.'

'What's the matter? What do you want from her?'

'Nothing, I just want to inform her that Mr Connor Moore, is waiting for your arrival. It was expected for him to arrive tomorrow, but luckily he came back today. I informed him of your arrival and he is very excited. He has been waiting for you for two hours now.'

'Where is he?'

'He is that slim Englishman sitting in the corner of the lobby, next to the last window, reading a book.'

Her uncle was a man with blond hair and mustache, somewhat thin, in his early forties, handsome, and wearing a brown suit.

She gave the child to Mansour and ran to him, standing in front of him.

He lifted his eyes from the book to see her, and his serious expression changed to a sad smile as he spoke in English.

'Niloofar … is it really you? You are definitely Niloofar …'

She didn't answer him, but her tears did.

He stood up and hugged her tightly.

'My dear daughter … my precious daughter … fifteen years we have been searching for you. Even my father passed away while waiting to see you or know anything about you … Oh my beloved, my daughter, let me see you clearly, my God … Oh holy mother, you are a copy of your father, a photographed image of Gerald …'

And he hugged her again.

'My God, how grateful I am to you for your grace and favor. My God, how happy my mother will be when she sees you.'

That scene was truly emotional. Everyone in the lobby turned to see this scene that not only affected Niloofar's and her uncle and husband's emotions, but also stirred the emotions of everyone else.

'We were missing my brother in this life, and now you have completed it. Let's travel together to our homeland, your father's homeland, to meet your grandmother and relatives.'

Then Mr Moore noticed Mansour and the child.

'Is this our son-in-law, Mansour?'

'Yes, Uncle, this is my husband Mansour, your son-in-law,' she replied in her broken English.

'And who is this beautiful child? Is he your son? You didn't tell me that you were expecting a child in your letter?'

'Sorry, I wasn't pregnant at the time.'

'Ah, yes, you wrote the letter in April of last year.'

Mr Moore warmly shook hands with Mansour and said: 'You are our son-in-law, Mansour. How are you, my son?'

'I'm fine, Praise be to Allah. I'm happy to meet you and be with you.'

'I'm happy too, my son. I see that you speak English very well, even better than Niloofar.'

'Yes, we have had British military rule in the region, and my direct superiors at work are English, and I have been a partner with three Englishmen in a commercial establishment for more than a year and a half, so we have learned English from them and they have learned Arabic from us.'

'That's good, my son. Wait until you see London, you will love it, as many Arabs have been seen there.'

'Yes, I have heard that too, but they must be wealthy.'

'Yes, maybe. Can I hold the child?'

'Of course.'

'My brother's little grandchild, a beautiful child. He is a mixture of three races: English, Indian, and Arab. He carries our white and red blood, doesn't he? This child will become a distinguished man in the future.'

And after they conferred for two hours, they agreed to go out early in the morning to the office of the British Embassy in Bombay to obtain visitor visas for Niloofar, her husband and the child to Britain, under the sponsorship of Mr Connor Moore, who had some contact with the most important men of the British Embassy in Bombay.

(59)

On the following day, the four of them left in the hotel's car that was under Uncle Connor's command to the embassy. After finishing their application for an urgent visa to visit Britain, which was expected to be obtained the next day, they went to the travel agency to book tickets to London, and all these expenses were voluntarily covered by Mr Connor Moore from the beginning.

They got travel tickets for April 3, on the coming Friday morning.

'We have two days in Mumbai, and I want to make the most of every hour to show you all the places I love.'

'That's right, Uncle. I'm eagerly looking forward to visiting beautiful places, but Mansour and I had planned to go to the photography shop to take a picture of the three of us for memory, and since you're with us, the four of us will go together to take a picture, in addition to Mansour's plan to visit the Indian spice market to buy goods for his company.'

'What a great idea! First, we'll go to the spice and herb market and buy all the goods you want. Then, I'll make sure myself that the goods reach your company in Dubai within the next ten days, and you can send a telegram to inform your partners about this shipment.'

'Yes, but the telegraph center is far away from us, and no one reads telegrams, at least not for personal or commercial use. I can write a letter to my partners and attach it to the shipment, and they will do the rest.'

'That makes things easier then. So, we'll go and drop Niloofar at the hotel, then we'll go together to the spice market and buy the quantities you want, and then we'll take them to the customs to send this shipment on one of the commercial ships heading to Dubai, and by the time we return, Niloofar and the child will have prepared to go out for the photo shoot, and then I will take you on a tour of Mumbai.'

'Thank you for your keenness and generous cooperation, you have made things easier for me.'

'Don't thank me, my son. This is some of the rights of my daughter that we couldn't give her.'

And it happened exactly as Uncle Connor had planned …

At the photoshoot location, Niloofar wore a tight, knee-length navy blue Indian Punjabi dress with sleeves that reached down to her elbows, and long, narrow navy-blue pants embroidered with colored threads. She also wore a transparent head cover embroidered with the same embroidery, which she had placed over her shoulders to cover her chest.

She adorned herself with golden jewelry, applied a little lipstick, lined her eyes with kohl, and let her golden hair loose, attaching it with the golden clips given to her by her mother-in-law. She looked like a princess from the Ottoman court in India. Mansour wore a white shirt with gray vertical stripes and tight gray pants. The child was wearing a red outfit with a short-sleeved shirt and shorts, and looked like a glass doll with his blonde hair, rosy cheeks, and lips. As for Uncle, he wore a gray suit and a black tie.

Four pictures were taken of them: one group photo of the four of them, one of Niloofar with Uncle Connor, one of Niloofar with Mansour and the child, and one of Niloofar and Mansour alone.

The photographer had promised to develop the photos and complete them the next day, after which Uncle Connor took them on a tour of his beloved Bombay. The first place he took them to was the beautiful Chowpatty Beach, where people from all walks of life and nationalities gathered. The beach was alive with activity and entertainment, such as horse, camel, and elephant rides, as well as beautiful carts pulled by donkeys. Various food carts were also scattered along the beach, offering grilled corn, sweet potatoes, fried snacks, sugarcane juice, lemon juice, and crushed ice mixed with concentrated and sweetened flavors, which was placed in a cup and served with a stick to be eaten like ice cream. Everyone enjoyed their time on that beach.

From there, they took a small boat to Alibag, a tourist island that was a huge park containing palaces, forts, and castles surrounding a large and clean lake. It also had entertainment and recreational facilities, and people mostly visited it to enjoy the various foods served in the many restaurants in the area. It was also a sanctuary for deer and peacocks that were abundant, and it is said to have belonged to kings and princes who used the island as a summer resort in ancient times. Some of the rooms in those forts and castles were also rented to tourists.

'This is my favorite place in Bombay.'

'That's clear, sir.'

'And during the day, this island looks even more beautiful. If we had enough time, we would rent two rooms and stay here tonight. But we can't do that now, as it's late and we have to return to the city to be able to go to the embassy early in the morning.'

After having dinner at one of the island's restaurants, they took the boat back to Chowpatty Beach and then boarded the car back to the hotel.

It was one of the most unforgettable days for the couple.

(60)

In the early morning, they got up and had breakfast at the hotel restaurant with Uncle Connor, and then they took the car to the British embassy. They waited for two hours until they got the visa that allowed them to visit Britain.

'Thank God, you got the visa. What are your plans now? What do you want to do and where do you intend to go?'

'I don't know, sir, whatever you prefer.'

'What about you, my daughter? Today is our last day in Bombay. Are you thinking of going somewhere?'

'I was thinking of visiting the place where my parents lived behind the temple in Kendala Mountain.'

'Oh, my daughter, I expected you to make this request. The place you want to visit is very far, it will take us five hours to get there by car.'

'Can we go and come back today?'

'Yes, we can do that. You will also see a surprise when you go there.'

'Does that mean you agree?'

'I totally agree. Let's go now. We'll arrive there at 4:00 pm. The car will stop for an hour to cool down and for the driver and his assistant to rest while you see the place. After that, we'll head back and arrive at the hotel after 10:00 pm. In the morning, we have to wake up early for our flight.'

Everyone agreed and got in the car to go to Kendala Mountain, which was a very long distance. The child cried, so she comforted him and breastfed him.

Then Mansour slept, followed by the child. After that, Uncle Connor slept, and Mansour carried the child. She also slept while the driver's assistant took over driving, and then the driver slept. Uncle Connor woke up, and so on.

Then they stopped to have lunch at one of the popular restaurants, and set off again to their destination, arriving after 4 o'clock.

'Come on, my daughter; let me show you the place. Come on, son, you too.'

The place was a ground-level plain among the mountains, where wooden, mud, and modern concrete buildings were built. The ancient temple was located at the forefront of the village, and its walls were painted with strong colors to distinguish this village, which was known as Mandhar Gao (Temple Village), from the rest of the villages.

'Look, my daughter, this is the temple that your late mother used to visit to ease her hunger and collect the value of the telegrams she sent to us.'

Without a second thought, Niloofar ran towards the temple, almost stopped by Mansour, but Uncle Connor stopped him. She entered the temple courtyard, which was empty except for the priest who was busy worshipping in front of the statue of Krishna. She walked down the stairs that led to the statue, to the place that her mother described to her in the letter. She stood there, imagining her mother waiting for someone to give her a morsel of food or some kindness, and tears streamed down her face, expressing her great sorrow for her mother's state of isolation, carrying her pain, loneliness, and humiliation inside her.

Niloofar almost lost her balance and sat on the sand, sensing the presence of her beloved mother. Suddenly, she felt two hands lifting her from the ground; it was Uncle Connor who wanted to bring her back to reality.

'Come on, my daughter, let's leave this place.'

With a heavy weight that she had never felt before on her body, as if the mountains of the earth had climbed onto her shoulders, she walked out of the temple, losing her senses.

Mansour rushed to her and wiped her tears.

'Don't cry, my dear, pray for her and ask for her mercy.'

'May Allah have mercy on you, Mother, may Allah have mercy on you.'

'Come my daughter, I want to show you something. Come with me.'

(61)

They walked behind the temple until they reached a building that looked like a school with a sign that read "Gerald and Nazia Orphanage".

'Look, my daughter, this is where your parents lived. When your grandparents and I arrived here, the place was burned down. Your grandfather bought the land and built this orphanage on it, hoping that he would one day find you here. Your grandfather used to spend half the year here and the other half in London, but his dream never came true. He never found you here or in any other orphanage in India. Come, let's go in. I want to show you around.'

They entered a high-walled compound with a large gate guarded by three armed men. Inside was a large courtyard where children gathered every morning for roll call. The courtyard was surrounded by trees, flowers, and greenery, and on one side stood a church where the orphaned children were converted to Christianity.

The main building had a reception room, administrative offices, and sixteen classrooms, each with a large room in the middle for activities such as sewing, drawing, music, carpentry, and mechanics. At the end of the building was a door that led to the back of the orphanage where there was a long two-story building. The top floor housed many rooms where the male and female students lived, and on the lower level was a dining hall for the students to eat their meals. There was also a long room that served as a nursery for infants, and facing it was a smaller building that housed the nuns.

'How many residents are in this orphanage, sir?'

'Now they are more than three hundred girls and boys, and every year the number of students increases. When our oldest students reach the age of nineteen, we provide them with a job, a house, and a marriage partner of their choice from the girls in this orphanage.'

'Are you the one who manages this orphanage?'

'My father used to manage it, and the Mother Superior has been in charge for fifteen years. I have been in charge since my father passed away, and after me, Niloofar, I want you to take over the management of this orphanage.'

'May Allah bless you with a long life, my uncle. I do not want to take over its management, as my heart aches at the thought that my parents lived on this land, and now after seeing all these young boys and girls who were orphaned like me when I was young, I feel a deep sadness.'

'It's okay, my dear. You are still young, and as you grow older, you will gain strength and focus your feelings more.'

'It is indeed a wonderful place, sir, and what you have done is a tremendous effort, but the idea of the church … I mean, if children were given the choice to choose their own religion, it would be better.'

'Oh, yes, I understand your point, Mansour. It was my father's idea to raise Christian men and women … Don't worry about these small matters; it's all God's will.'

'Could we go now, my uncle? I don't feel well.'

'Yes, let's go. We have a long journey ahead of us in the early morning.'

They all left the orphanage and the nuns bid them farewell with some of the children.

After a long and exhausting journey, they arrived at the hotel around eleven o'clock.

In the hotel lobby, the receptionist addressed them: 'Thank God you arrived safely.'

'Thank you.'

'Here is the envelope that the worker brought from the photo shop today.'

'Oh, thank you very much.'

He turned to Niloofar and gave her the envelope. Her sadness and tiredness changed to joy and happiness when she saw the pictures in the envelope, and she began to carefully examine each one.

'I want you do me a favor, my friend.'

'Anything you want, sir.'

'I want you to settle my bill, my son-in-law's bill, and my daughter's bill now. Then, we will send workers to carry our luggage early in the morning since we are leaving for London.'

'Of course, right away, sir.'

After Uncle Connor Moore paid his bill, he said: 'This is just my bill. Where is my son-in-law's bill?'

'Sorry, sir. Mr Mansour paid for his room bill day by day.'

'What a good man he is! See you in the morning then.'

'Yes, sir. By morning, my shift would have ended. I want to take this opportunity to say that we were honored to have you with us and I hope you enjoyed your stay and all the hotel's services.'

(62)

At Mumbai International Airport, Uncle Connor completed all the baggage shipment procedures and passport stamping, and after a long wait, they boarded the plane heading to London. The plane stopped at Delhi's airport for refueling, food and cleaning, and on the second time it stopped at Beirut International Airport, and on the third time it stopped at Geneva Airport in Switzerland, and finally the plane landed at Heathrow Airport in London.

Niloofar enjoyed the beautiful flight above the clouds, and the delicious food and excellent service, something she had not experienced before, and Mansour also enjoyed the flight very much.

Everyone disembarked from the plane, and the bags were cleared from the shipment, and they exited to find Bernard the driver waiting for them in the black Larkstead Baker car, a beautiful and spacious car with shiny leather seats, better than any car they had seen in India.

The weather in London at the beginning of April was very beautiful, it was spring season following the snowy and rainy winter season, and gentle rain drops fell.

Niloofar watched those drops on the car window saying: 'Uncle, London is very beautiful!'

'Yes my dear, it is as beautiful as you are. I told you that you will like London very much.'

'How far are we from home?'

'Not far, we will arrive at our home soon, maybe after another twenty minutes.'

And when they arrived in the area where the house was located, Niloofar said: 'This area is full of flowers, Uncle, it's like a garden.'

'This, my dear, is our area, Queens Mary Rose Garden.'

'It is a beautiful area.'

'It is, now we have arrived at our home.'

It was exactly as her mother had described in the letter "a large, tall house built of red bricks with long windows. It was surrounded by a low iron fence, and behind the fence were planted white gardenia trees, which bloomed all year round, even in winter and snow. From the gate to the main entrance, there was a large courtyard with a sandy granite stone floor, and the door was a strong, shiny wooden door made of cedar wood with a dragon-shaped doorknocker". She wished she could enter and see her mother and father.

When the car stopped in front of the main gate, the servant and the old maid Magdalena rushed out to greet them.

They welcomed Uncle Connor, who asked about his mother: 'Where is my mother, Magdalena?'

'She is in the living room, waiting for you. Is this the young lady, sir?'

'Yes, Magdalena, this is the young lady, and this is her husband and child.'

'Oh, my holy mother, she looks so much like my late master Gerald.'

'Of course, Magdalena. Let's go in now.'

As soon as they entered the door, they heard the voice of Grandma Betty calling out to her son: 'Connor … my son, have you come? Did you bring the little girl? Answer me …'

Connor whispered to Niloofar and Mansour: 'Mansour and I will stay here, Niloofar. You go see your grandmother, and we will watch you from here.'

Niloofar walked from the entrance to the living room, and the first thing she saw in the living room was a painting hanging above the fireplace. The painting was drawn in oil colors of her parents, the same picture she had. She felt a strange sense of belonging to this place she had never seen before, as if she had grown up there all her life.

Then she heard her grandmother's voice sitting on the wheelchair in front of the open window in the dim lights: 'You are Niloofar, aren't you?'

'Yes, grandma, it's me.'

'Come closer to me, my dear, so I can see you well.'

As Niloofar approached, her grandmother gasped and lost consciousness. Everyone rushed to her aid.

(63)

When the grandmother woke up, she was in her room and the nurse was sitting beside her.

'Cecilia, my dear, where did everyone go?'

'They are outside, ma'am, waiting for you to regain consciousness.'

'I want to see them, can you please call them for me?'

'Very well, ma'am.'

The nurse went out to inform Conmor, his wife Beatrice, who had just arrived from outside, and their sons Andy, who was nineteen years old, Michael, who was seventeen years old, and Niloofar and Mansour.

'Wait here, Niloofar, until I check on her health.'

'Okay, Uncle.'

Everyone except Niloofar, her husband, and their son entered the grandmother Betty's room.

Connor and his mother started talking.

'How are you feeling now, Mom?'

'I'm fine, Connor. I don't see my granddaughter among you?'

'And do you remember her, Mom?'

'How could I forget her? Don't tell me she's gone, I would be very sad.'

'No, no, don't worry, Mom. She hasn't gone anywhere, she's outside waiting for you to call her yourself.'

'Please call her now, Cecilia, would you help me sit down?'

Everyone moved away from the mother's bed, and Niloofar approached her grandmother.

'Come closer to me, my daughter, excuse my weakness, since the death of my son Gerald, who is your father, I have become weak, and I cannot withstand shocks. When I saw you, I saw my son's face, you resemble him a lot.'

And burst into tears.

'Don't cry, Mom, please. Niloofar, say something, try to calm her down.'

Niloofar couldn't say a word, but she kissed her grandmother's head and hands and cried with her.

Connor intervened, took Niloofar away as Mansoor hugged her, and he went to his mother to calm her down.

'Look, Mother, God has sent her to bring you happiness. You are luckier than my father who passed away before he could hear about her arrival. Isn't that right?'

'Yes, my son, you are correct.'

'Then why all this crying? Your granddaughter, whom you have waited for over sixteen years, is now in front of you. Live the beautiful moments with her and make it up for her for all the affection that she has been deprived of all these years.'

'You are right, my son. Come to my embrace, my daughter. I want to live the rest of my life close to you.'

Two days after their arrival in London, Uncle Connor obtained the necessary documents proving that Niloofar was the daughter of Gerald Moore. He also obtained a passport and a British identity card for her.

In the second week, Niloofar suffered from a severe fever due to the climate change. The family doctor advised her to stop breastfeeding the baby to prevent him from getting infected with the fever as well. She stopped breastfeeding him and replaced it with formula. His diapers, which consisted of cotton cloths and then a plastic diaper that were wrapped around him and washed every time he wet himself were replaced with healthy, cotton baby diapers that were thrown away after each use, which was the advice of Mrs Beatrice Moore, her uncle's wife.

Niloofar recovered after ten days and spent the happiest days of her life with her relatives. Granny Betty Moore also gradually regained her health and started to drop her wheelchair, thanks to her granddaughter and her little baby. However, Granny did not approve of Niloofar's marriage to Mansour because she believed that the age difference between them was unfair.

(64)

Niloofar learned from her English relatives the Western lifestyle and acquired from them the skills of etiquette in dealing with people, how to use the fork and knife, and how to wear simple, low-color clothes. Her English language also improved. Her grandmother, Mrs Betty, gave her half of her jewelry, which she had designated for her son Gerald's wife, but it became Niloofar's share.

Every evening, Niloofar went out with her husband, her uncle's wife Beatrice, and their children either to shop at Harrods or Old Bond Street. What she loved most in the market were women's lingerie that she had not seen before and high-end cosmetics. She also went on a stroll to Buckingham Palace, Big Ben Tower, Piccadilly Circus, Trafalgar Square, the British Museum, and the Wax Museum. She went on a boat trip on the Thames River, visited Hyde Park, and the cinema. She attended the opera performance of William Shakespeare's famous novel Hamlet at the Royal Opera House. She also went to beauty salons that she had not heard of before.

Every Saturday evening, she wore the most beautiful new clothes that her grandmother bought for her to welcome her relatives to dinner parties for socializing. Everyone admired her captivating beauty.

On one evening, Niloofar wore a long, silky blue dress with short sleeves and a long bouquet covering her entire neck. It was narrow at the chest and wide at the bottom. Her hair was tied back with a crystal clip in the middle of the back, and the rest of her hair flowed freely until the end. She applied cherry-colored lipstick and wore two dangling diamond earrings in her ears. She also wore a circular blue sapphire ring surrounded by small white diamond stones on one hand and a large white gold bracelet studded with small diamonds on the other hand.

She wore shiny silver high heels.

'Niloofar, come here, my dear, so that I can introduce you to my cousin's daughter, Mrs Sara Edmund.'

'Hello, madam.'

'Hello, Niloofar, how are you?'

'I'm doing well; I hope you are having a pleasant evening.'

'Yes, very much so, especially after seeing my cousin's daughter, Mrs Betty Moore, healed and no longer needing a wheelchair.'

'Thank God for healing my grandmother.'

'And this is also thanks to your presence with her.'

'I hope this is the motivation that brought her health.'

'The credit goes to you my dear, ever since I saw you and the child, my life has brightened again.'

'May God bless you with good health and wellbeing, my grandmother.'

'You are so beautiful, Niloofar. You resemble your father very much, but you are much more beautiful, your beauty is English mixed with the charm of the East.'

'Thank you for your praise, madam. And you also still possess beauty, elegance, and a slender figure.'

'Let's not talk about that, my dear. If you weren't married, I would have introduced you to my son, Mark. He is a handsome, intelligent, and successful young man, and you would have found happiness with him.'

'It would have made me happy, but I am happy with my husband and love him very much.'

'May God bless your marriage, my dear.'

And that evening passed, with everyone admiring Niloofar, she had drawn a lot of attention.

She spent a lot of time with her grandmother, gaining wisdom and sharpness of mind. She even attended church with her every Sunday at the Giray Feriars Rose Garden Church to earn her approval.

As for Mansour, he also enjoyed his time in London, often going out with his uncle Connor to play golf or polo, and with his sons Andy and Michael to watch football matches, as well as going on motorcycle rides and car tours.

Beautiful pictures were taken of Niloofar with her relatives, in which she appeared as a beautiful and sophisticated English lady.

One day, Niloofar woke up to the sound of knocking on the door, as Mansour had gone out with her uncle to visit some friends. She opened the door …

'Good morning, madam.'

'Good morning, Magdalena.'

'My lady of the house requests that you get ready, as she wishes to go out with you.'

'Today is not Sunday, is it?'

'No, madam. Today is Thursday.'

'Very well, please tell her I'll be down in fifteen minutes. But where is the child?'

'He's downstairs. Lady Betty was feeding him, and now he's with Ben.'

'Okay, thank you. I'll be down shortly.'

Niloofar quickly took a shower and put on a knee-length, pink georgette dress, along with linen stockings in the same color. She tied her long hair into a small ball at the back of her head, and secured it with a hairnet that matched her hair color.

She wore some of the jewelry her grandmother had given her: a white pearl necklace with small beads, pearl earrings, a lightweight diamond bracelet around her wrist, and two diamond rings made of white gold, one of which had three medium-sized diamonds in the center, and the other had a teardrop-shaped diamond in the center. She wore medium-heeled cream-colored shoes, applied a little light pink lipstick, and went downstairs to her grandmother, who was waiting for her in the dining room.

She kissed her cheek …

'Good morning, my beloved grandmother. How are you today?'

'I'm fine, the most beautiful woman in the world. How did you sleep last night?'

'I slept well, and how about you?'

'I slept well too, but I woke up worried.'

'Why, my grandmother, what's wrong?'

'I'll tell you later. Now I want you to have your breakfast quickly so we can go out.'

'Alright, but where to?'

'I'll tell you in the car.'

In the car, Niloofar asked her grandmother: 'Where are we going now, Grandmother?'

'We're going to the bank.'

'And why the bank?'

'I want to give you the value of the stocks that your grandfather Cedric Moore had saved for your father. When Gerald died and we found out about you, it became Gerald's heir when we found him. Before your grandfather's death, he allowed me to dispose of it, and now I want to give it to you. It's your right.'

'I don't want anything, grandmother. Your love and care for me are enough, and you have already given me so much.'

'You're humble, my dear, and you resemble your father even in his qualities. He never cared about money and collecting it. Listen to me, my daughter, you are Cedric Moore's granddaughter, and this is your right. Your grandfather will ask me about it when I meet him in heaven, and this is a trust I want to fulfill. You can do whatever you want with your money, but please don't tell your husband. You don't know men's hearts; they change quickly like the state of water.'

At the bank, Mrs Betty Moore converted the stock bonds into a cash amount in a check for 200,000 pounds and handed it to Niloofar, making her wealthy.

(65)

They have been staying in London for two months, and it's time to return.

On the last Sunday evening before leaving Britain, they were all gathered at the dining table waiting for Uncle Connor to join them for dinner.

As soon as Uncle Connor entered the dining room, he said: 'Good evening everyone.'

'Good evening.'

'I have brought your tickets to Bombay, and from there you will board the Tara ship to Dubai.'

'When is the trip, Uncle?'

'The day after tomorrow morning.'

'Are you leaving me, my dear granddaughter?'

'Yes, Grandma. Mansour has to return to work, and my mother-in-law is an elderly woman waiting to see her grandson. Also, I have missed several classes.'

'Why don't you all move here and you continue your education here?'

'We will try but it would be difficult.'

'I would have traveled with you to be near you but I would not be able to bear the difficulties of travelling.'

'Don't worry, Grandmother, I promise to visit you every year to stay here for two months. I will also complete my academic and university education in London as Uncle Connor had promised.'

The next day, Niloofar went out with Beatrice and Mansour to buy gifts for their loved ones in Dubai. She bought perfumes, bags, and beautiful clothes for her mother-in-law, sisters-in-law, and their children, as well as for Sanota, Moftah, and the child who were waiting for them. She also bought gifts for Dr Mohammad Ayoub, his wife, and their children, and for Dr Sarouj and the righteous nurse.

On the day of departure, everyone stood at the gate of the house to bid farewell, even Grandma Betty Moore, and their eyes were glistening with tears.

'Don't be late for your visit, Niloofar. I'll start counting the days from today, and you must return on the three hundred and sixty-sixth day.'

'I promise I will come back to see you, my dear grandmother.'

'Please take care of yourself, the baby, and the fetus you carry in your womb.'

'Yes, I promise, and you promise to take care of your health and wait for my return, please.'

'I promise, my dear.'

The car, driven by her cousin Andy, headed to the airport, with Uncle Connor sitting next to him, and Niloofar, her husband, their child, and her cousin Michael sitting in the back seat.

At the airport, Uncle Connor gave Niloofar an instructional letter for her teacher, Dr Mohammad Ayoub, in Dubai, from the Institute of Education (University of London), to teach her the basic sciences she would need when she would begin her studies in London after completing her studies with Dr Mohammad Ayoub.

He also gave her a deposit of five hundred pounds as a token of his love, bid her farewell with Mansour and the child.

'I have shipped boxes of baby formula that you will need in your husband's country, which are good for up to eighteen months. I have also shipped boxes of healthy baby diapers that you can use for a year, and I will send larger sizes when the child grows a little.'

'This is too much, Uncle, I don't know how to thank you.'

'Don't thank me, you are my dear daughter.'

She thanked him a lot, she kissed him on the forehead and left with her husband and child, along with all travelers while he stood there waving goodbye until she disappeared from his sight.

She was in the saddest state on the plane because of her separation from the people she loved and who loved her. She did not listen to any word that Mansour said. Rather, she was recalling all those happy moments that she spent with her relatives in her father's homeland. How much she loved that country more than her love for Dubai, the home of her husband and children, a love that she never felt before, not even in India where she was born and raised.

(66)

After a long flight, they arrived at Mumbai International Airport, cleared their luggage from customs, and took a taxi to the port of Mumbai to board the ship that would sail in four hours.

Mansour asked her: 'Where did you put the jewelry box?'

'I put it in that large black suitcase.'

'I'm afraid it might get searched and stolen.'

'It won't get searched, I sealed the suitcase with the Queen's seal, and no one is allowed to search it, neither in India nor even in Dubai.'

'Praise be to Allah, don't worry then.'

'I'm not worried about the jewelry box, Allah will keep it safe for me until I return home.'

'And where did you put your cloak and headscarf?'

'They are with me here in my handbag, my dear.'

'Okay, you'll have to wear them when we get to Dubai.'

'Yes, I know that.'

Upon their arrival at the port, a customs officer ran to them to facilitate the process of shipping their luggage and to receive the tip that tourists give for their help.

They boarded the ship after completing their visa procedures and shipping all their luggage, and spent sixty-eight hours on it until they arrived at the port of Dubai on the evening of Monday, June 15, 1964.

From the port, they took a transport car to their home.

When they arrived at the area, Mansour's Land Rover was parked in front of the house.

They knocked on the door and Mansour's young nephew, Rashed, opened it and shouted with joy: 'My Uncle Mansour … my Uncle Mansour …'

Everyone ran to the door …

'My dear son Mansour, I missed you all so much!'

Mansour kissed her on the forehead and hugged her, and then he kissed her hands.

'I missed you more, my dear mother … so much.'

'Praise be to Allah for your safety, my brother.'

'May Allah protect you from all harm, how are you all?'

'We're all fine. Praise be to Allah.'

They hugged Niloofar and the child and thanked them for their safety.

And Sanota came out with her big belly.

'Uncle Mansour … Aunt Niloofar … you have lightened up the house with your arrival.'

Niloofar hugged her tightly.

'How are you, my dear? Your belly has grown, and you look active.'

'I'm fine. Praise be to Allah, and my pregnancy is going well. But you have become more beautiful, madam, you have become a lady in every sense of the word!'

'Thank you, Sanota, and how is your husband?'

'My husband is fine, he just left a little while ago to attend the funeral of Mr Saif Al-Sunaidi.'

Mansour was shocked to hear that.

'What? The merchant Saif Al-Sunaidi passed away?'

'Yes, my uncle, his condition had deteriorated a lot two days ago, and when he went to the clinic, he had already passed away.'

'We belong to Allah and to Him we shall return …'

'May Allah grant you and all of us patience.'

'May Allah grant you and your family patience, my brother, they left first and we shall all follow them someday Insha'Allah.'

With a tone of sadness mixed with anger, Mansour began to blame himself.

'If only I had come a little earlier, I could have seen him.'

'Don't say that, my son, it was fate, inevitable, no one knows when or where the end will come.'

'I will change my clothes and go to them, where is the funeral being held, Sanota?'

'At his house, my uncle.'

'I'm going to them now.'

(67)

Mansour entered his room to change his clothes, and Niloofar addressed his mother saying: 'It seems that Mansour is very sad, Mother.'

'Yes, my dear, he was his companion, and he gave him the car as a gift before your trip. It's as if he felt his time was near, and he trusted him very much.'

'I'll go see him, maybe he needs me for something.'

'Leave him for now, my daughter, he's in a disturbed state and you won't be able to talk to him. Let him return to his normal state, and come sit next to me. I've missed you so much, and I missed the little one too. He's grown and I see that he has a tooth …'

'Yes, Aunt, he's completed his fifth month.'

'And he seems to be in good health. Are you feeding him?'

'Yes, he eats boiled and mashed food, and drinks the canned milk that my aunt's wife brought when I stopped breastfeeding.'

'Did you get sick there, my dear?'

'Yes, Mother, I caught a severe cold that drained my strength.'

'But Praise be to Allah, you and the child and Mansour all look wonderful and in good health, by the grace of Allah.'

'I'm also expecting my second child.'

'Is that right? May Allah bless you. How far along are you?'

'A month and a half, and the doctor there has scheduled my delivery date for January 20.'

'Praise be to Allah. Take care of yourself, my daughter, and don't worry about work. Sanota and I will take care of our duties.'

Then Mansour's sister intervened: 'No, Mother, you can't handle the household work. We'll bring another girl until Sanota recover her strength after childbirth.'

'Please, don't worry about me. Insha'Allah, I will do the household work with Sanota as much as I can handle.'

'Let's see what Allah provides. So, tell us what did you do there?'

Niloofar proceeded to recount to them everything that had happened to her since boarding the ship on her way to Mumbai, all the way until she disembarked in the port of Dubai. She showed them the pictures she had taken of them there, where they all looked like strangers. She also showed them the jewelry box that her grandmother had given her as a gift, which impressed them greatly. Umm Mansour requested that she keep it with her to prevent it from being stolen or lost, and Niloofar complied without hesitation. She also distributed the gifts she had brought for them, which made them very happy.

Afterwards, they ate the food that Moftah had brought from the House of Mourning, and then each of them went to their room to sleep. Niloofar slept like a dead person after preparing her baby's milk bottle, changing his diaper, and giving him to her grandmother, who asked to keep him for the night.

In the early morning, Niloofar woke up to the sound of the closet doors closing.

'Is that you, Mansour?'

'Did I wake you, my love?'

'No, not at all. I need to get up to pray and change the baby and prepare his bottle. I'll leave him with mother, then I want to go with Sanota to the clinic and then to my school.'

'Alright.'

'What's wrong, my dear? Are you alright?'

'I'm fine.'

'Are you still sad about losing your friend?'

He sighed the sigh of the troubled loser heavily.

'Yes, I am sad about losing him, and the responsibilities of the institution have increased on my shoulders. It has also burdened me with the responsibility of taking care of his children in case anything happens to him.'

'Why not? You can take care of them, my dear. They are orphans now. You can go to them from time to time to inquire about their well-being and see if they need anything. I can also visit his wife to check on them.'

'May Allah bless you. Can you believe that the English partners decided to sell their shares in the partnership to me and the heirs of the deceased? I don't know if I can buy their shares in the partnership, or if I have to sell my own share to the heirs of the deceased. This is already a loss that will break my back.'

'No, don't sell your share, my dear. How much money do you need to buy their shares?'

'I need a huge amount, as the company's business is expanding day by day, and its income is doubling every day.'

'I remember that when you entered this trade a year ago, you invested ten thousand rupees, right?'

'Yes, and I was a partner with four other partners, and that was more than a year ago, and the company was small and its profits were low.'

'How much do you think each partner's share would be now?'

'I don't know. I have to leave for work now. I don't want to be late. See you in the evening.'

He was really upset because he did not like to look at her face and explain the situation to her. She was also upset because he left in a bad mood after her questions.

(68)

Niloofar wondered to herself:

What should I do? Should I help him with the money that my grandmother gave me? Should I give him the jewelry to sell? Or should I stay quiet and not get involved? No, that would be a really shameful thing to do. Does he make me feel like I'm obligated to help him, since he asked me when my grandmother gave me these jewels?

'These are valuable jewels, Niloo. How much do you think they are worth now?'

'My grandmother says they are worth a fortune, as she inherited them from her mother. They are delicate and finely crafted jewels that cannot be matched in quality nowadays.'

'Hmm … I think they are somewhat old-fashioned, maybe you could replace them someday or sell them and buy something new.'

'I will never give him my grandmother's jewels. She gave them to me with love and tenderness, and I will never give up her jewels or her love. I will endure his displeasure with this matter and wait for a week to make sure he really needs the money to buy the partners' shares. Then I will tell him about the cheque from my grandmother, which is worth two hundred thousand pounds sterling, my share of the shares that my grandfather left me. He is, after all, my husband who saved me from the clutches of evil and misery that I was stuck in, and he loves me, trusts me, treats me well, and is the father of my children. I will never betray him as long as I live.'

After having breakfast, she and Sanota went to the clinic to greet Dr Sarouj and to give her the gifts she brought from London, a beautifully crafted luxury handbag and a box of chocolates. Then she went to the school and greeted Dr Mohammed Ayoub and his family, giving them the commemorative gifts, she brought from London, a brass Big Ben clock figurine, a luxury handbag for the doctor's wife, and clothes for the doctor's daughters and sons, impressing everyone with the gifts and souvenirs she brought for them. She then gave the doctor the educational guidance letter from the Institute of Education (University of London) that her uncle Connor Moore gave her, so he could teach her the sciences she would need in no more than two years, after which she could enroll in the institute to complete her academic education.

The doctor was impressed and asked her: 'Tell me, my dear, have you taken any placement tests at this institute?'

'My uncle Connor Moore took me there one day, and I took the placement tests and passed with good grades, but there are still some sciences I need to learn, and once I succeed in them, I can enroll in the institute.'

'I am ready to dedicate a whole semester just for you, so you can learn in a special and fast way, and then join that academic institute. I am sure that you will pass this stage with ease, as you are intelligent and a fast learner. May Allah bless your efforts.'

'Thank you, my teacher. Can I start learning today?'

'No, my dear, excuse me. I am going to the British Air Force base in Sharjah to perform medical examinations for some soldiers, and I will be back late in the evening. Come tomorrow at 7:30 in the morning.'

'I will see you tomorrow, Insha'Allah. Thank you very much, my teacher.'

'May Allah bless you, my daughter.'

On their way home, she noticed that Sanota was walking with difficulty and sweating.

'Are you okay, my dear Sanota?'

'Yes, my aunt, I'm fine.'

'Does walking like this tire you out?'

'A little, but it helps to facilitate childbirth.'

'Yes, it does, but if you can't walk all that distance, don't force yourself to bear what you can't handle. It won't be helpful. What do you think if I get Moftah to walk to school every day?'

'That's a good idea, my aunt.'

At home, she unpacked the bags and put her and the baby's belongings and Mansour's belongings in the closet. She remembered the stone she had received as compensation from that creature that had caused her and her babies harm.

She closed the door, lifted the iron panel from the bottom of the cupboard, and inserted her hand to search for the package. She took it out, unwrapped it, and the stone's brilliance shone, reflecting its light on the room's walls.

How beautiful this stone is! How can I dispose of it and sell it? I will find a way someday, even if I have to take it with me on my next trip to London.

(69)

Niloofar resumed her education. Every morning, she left her child with her mother-in-law and went to school to attend classes that Dr Mohammed Ayoub had assigned to her according to the guidance letter from the Institute of Education (University of London). She would return home in the afternoon. Mansour, on the other hand, left every morning to go to work and returned home for lunch. Afterwards, he would change his clothes and go to the institution, not returning until everyone was asleep. Niloofar felt he was either upset with his situation or perhaps with her.

That week went by, and Niloofar only saw her husband at lunchtime when he was in a hurry. His frustration increased day after day. She decided to give him the value of the English partners' shares. She waited for him to come in the evening, and as soon as the door opened, she felt it was him.

'Mansour, is that you?'

'Yes … what's wrong? Are you okay?'

'I'm fine, my love.'

'How's your pregnancy?'

'It's fine, don't worry.'

'Why haven't you slept yet? Won't you go to school tomorrow?'

'I will, but I missed talking to you.'

'About what?'

'About everything.'

'Leave me alone, Niloofar. I'm tired and busy.'

'I know, but I wanted to give you something to take your mind off all those thoughts.'

'Nothing takes away my worries and thoughts except the money that will save the institution from falling apart.'

'I will relieve you of your worries and thoughts, Insha'Allah.'

'How? Will you give me your jewelry box to sell and save the institution?'

'No, I won't sell my jewelry box. It's my grandmother's trust with me.'

'How is it a trust when she gave you the jewelry?'

'She did give me the jewelry, but she expected me to wear it from time to time.'

'Then why did you say that you would relieve me of my worries and thoughts? Are you playing with my feelings?'

'I'm not playing with your feelings. I'm telling you the truth. I will give you the money you need.'

'Where did you get the money from?'

'My grandmother gave me my share of my grandfather's inheritance.'

'Why are you only telling now? Don't you trust me?'

'No, that's not it. I was waiting for the right time, and I think it's time to use it to solve our problem.'

'How much did she give you?'

'Tell me first how much you need to buy out your partners' shares?'

'I need a large sum.'

'How much is that?'

'100,000 rupees each, which is 200,000 rupees in total. It's a lot of money, isn't it?'

'Yes, it is, and there's no easy way to get it. The annual income of the business is twice that amount. However, they are in a hurry to return to their home country before the end of the coming year, within the next five months.'

'Can you take me to the bank tomorrow morning to cash the cheque?'

'Yes, but you didn't tell me how much the cheque is worth.'

'It's a large sum, don't worry.'

'What's the amount of the cheque?'

'200,000 pounds sterling.'

'Are you sure?'

'Yes.'

'If the exchange rate is around 400,000 rupees per pound, I can use it to buy out the partners' shares, make some expansions in the business, and add a food refrigerator. I can also finish building the house and furnishing it, right?'

'Yes.'

She said it while feeling sad inside. She wished she could spend this amount of money on setting up her own clinic as a doctor after she graduated from university.

'What's wrong, why are you sad? I promise to pay you back this amount at the end of next year. What do you think?'

She became very happy.

'Really, are you sure?'

'Yes, trust me.'

'I trust you completely, my husband, and I know you won't let me down.'

She rejoiced at his words, and he took off his clothes and got into bed with her in his arms.

(70)

Niloofar emerged from the bathroom after taking a hot shower the next morning. Mansour had already showered and dressed and was in the courtyard having breakfast. Niloofar put on her clothes and retrieved the bank cheque from the large envelope she had hidden under her clothes in the closet, putting it in her bag before heading out to join Mansour.

'Did you bring all of your identification documents, stock exchange papers, and cheque issuance papers from London Bank?'

'Yes, I brought everything.'

'Okay then, my dear, let's quickly have breakfast. We need to hurry to finish at the bank and I'll take you to school before heading to the center to request permission for today and tomorrow.'

'Alright.'

Before Mansour's mother and the child got up, they left the house and got into the Land Rover, driving to the British Bank of the Middle East, which was located on the banks of Dubai Creek.

In the bank, a customer service representative approached them and asked: 'How may I assist you, sir?'

'I want to cash a cheque for my wife.'

'May I see the cheque, please?'

Mansour showed him the cheque.

'Yes, sir, for an amount as large as this, you need to meet the bank manager to approve the cheque's cashing. Please wait for me here.'

The representative left for a few minutes and then returned.

'Please come with me, both of you.'

They walked with him to the end of the corridor, and then climbed the stairs to the second floor; where there were many offices adjoining each other, including a large, single office with a glass I.

'Please come with me, sir. This is the bank manager's office, Mr Steve Baker.'

Mr Steve Baker greeted them in his broken Arabic, saying: 'Peace be upon you, welcome. Please have a seat.'

The two sat across from him, and Mr Baker said: 'I have reviewed the cheque, Mr … I'm sorry, what is your name, sir?'

'My name is Mansour Mohammed Ahmed.'

'Yes, sir, Mansour, the cheque is issued in the name of Niloofar Gerald Gabriel Moore, who is English, is she not?'

Niloofar signaled her husband to allow her to speak, and he granted her permission.

'Yes, sir, I am half English. My father, Gerald Gabriel Moore, was a first soldier in the British Indian Army in Andhra Pradesh, and my mother is Indian from India.'

'Did you live in India and Britain?'

'Actually, I was born and lived my entire childhood in India until I married Mr Mansour and came to live with him here in Dubai. And just two months ago, I visited my relatives in London for the first time.'

'Did you like the country?'

'I did not like the country as much as I liked London.'

'Excellent, then. You are a mix of English and Indian, and your husband is Arab. It is remarkable. You should make a name for yourself in history and do something to elevate yourself and those around you.'

'That's what I am determined to achieve.'

'Let's get back to the topic. Do you want to cash this check now?'

'Yes, sir. I need the money for an urgent matter.'

'Why don't you cash half the amount and leave the rest as a deposit to earn monthly profits until you receive it? You can use it here or in London or even India since our branches are in most countries in Dubai, Europe, and the Middle East.'

She looked at Mansour, who seemed to reject the idea from his facial expression.

'The truth is, I'm in a hurry. I want to cash the entire amount, if I didn't need the money, I would have left the amount with you as a deposit.'

'There's no harm in that since you're originally British. Why don't you open a savings account with us and deposit small monthly amounts so that you can use the amount after it earns bank interest here or in London or even in India? Our branches are in most countries in Dubai, Europe, and the Middle East.'

'I truly appreciate your suggestion, and I will consider it, but for now, may I have the check amount, please?'

'Do you want the amount in the local currency?'

'Yes, sir, please.'

'Then, with the exchange rate of pounds to rupees, the amount will be three hundred and eighty-five thousand rupees. I will inform the employees to prepare the amount for you. In the meantime, could you give me your identification papers so that I can review them and record the information in the register?'

'Sure, here you go.'

She gave him all her documents, and he proceeded to record all the important information. After about an hour, a bank employee entered carrying a large envelope.

'The amount is complete now. If you'd like, you can go over it.'

'Yes, please. We want to make sure the amount is correct.'

'Certainly. I'll step out for a moment and be back shortly. Take your time and count the cash.'

The manager, Steve Baker, stepped away from them, and Mansour took one envelope and gave the other to Niloofar. They each counted the cash in their respective envelopes.

When they finished counting, Steve Baker returned to them. They thanked him and left the bank.

'I'll take you to school and then go to work.'

'Okay. Will you come to pick me up after school?'

'Yes, I will because I'm leaving early today. Thank you, my dear. You saved the company and me.'

'No need to thank me. You're my husband and the father of my children. If you carry me when I fall, then I carry you when you fall. This is marital life.'

'Truly, you're a wonderful woman. Allah has blessed you with beauty inside and out.'

'And you're the best of men, my dear husband. I won't forget the moments you've shared with me since we got married. If it were another man, he wouldn't have agreed to marry me from the beginning. And if he did, he wouldn't have allowed me to travel to faraway lands to meet my relatives. Also, you spent a lot of money to make me happy and fulfill my desire to travel.'

'May Allah bless you, and may He never deprive me of you.'
'And may He never deprive me of you, my love.'

(71)

Mansour spent six months preoccupied with his work at the institution and in commerce, and how to increase profits to provide his family and wife with the comfortable life he had always wanted for them. He also visited the children of the merchant Saif to check on them and see what they lacked. Even Sultan, the youngest son of the merchant, had a strong attachment to Mansour, calling him "father" out of his love for him. Sometimes, he even stayed at Mansour's house overnight or traveled with him to Iran, India, Bahrain, and Sri Lanka for trade. This did not bother Niloofar or make her upset; rather, she was compassionate and empathetic towards the child and his siblings.

As for her, she ended each school year with excellence and success, gaining more knowledge and confidence. On the other hand, Sanota gave birth to a girl she named Aoushah, five months ago. Niloofar gifted her a small golden necklace in the shape of a heart. Her due date was still a month and a half away.

One morning, Sanota asked her husband: 'Can you stay with the baby, please? I'm going to visit my aunt to give her breakfast if she's awake.'

'Okay, but don't be late. This is the time when my aunt Noura, leaves for school.'

'What's bothering you? You seem upset.'

'I really am upset.'

'Why?'

'What should I say to you, my dear Sanota? I heard rumors from people and I got tired, and when I confirmed it, I got even more tired. What if my aunt Noura knew?'

'Knew what? What happened? You are scaring me?'

'Listen, but don't tell anyone, do you understand? No one … I heard that there's some sort of relationship between my uncle Mansour and the widow of the merchant Saif, whose name is Sheikha. The neighbors say they see him leaving their house at night'

'That's true, even my Aunt Noura knows about it. He's just taking care of his friend's children and nothing else.'

'Yes, but when he goes in, he goes in normally with her children, and when he comes out, he comes out alone and secretly before dawn, and he puts a veil on his face so that no one recognizes him in the dark.'

'What are you saying, Moftah? You scared me. Don't believe what people say, man.'

'I wouldn't have believed what people say, but I saw it with my own eyes.'

'Keep it to yourself, man, and keep it hidden. It's none of our business. May Allah guide him.'

One night, Niloofar woke up to the sound of water falling in the bathroom, so she approached the door and said: 'Mansour, is that you inside?'

'Yes, my love.'

'What are you doing now?'

'I'm taking a shower.'

'Why now? You don't shower at night.'

'I sweat a lot today and I smell bad.'

'Okay, come to bed when you're done.'

'I will, I'll be there soon.'

And the days passed, and Mansour's relationship with the widow of the merchant Saif became stronger, and Niloofar didn't feel anything or care except for the approaching delivery.

(72)

One day, she received a letter from her relatives in London, in which they inquired about her and her pregnancy and mentioned her upcoming travel plans to visit them on vacation. She waited until Mansour came in.

'Good evening.'

'Hello, good evening.'

'How are you and the pregnancy?'

'I'm fine; I want to tell you something.'

'What is it?'

'We received a letter from my grandmother and uncle in London reminding us that we need to visit them in June when the school closes for summer vacation (as Dr Mohammed Ayoub began following the semester system in the academic year).'

'What should I do?'

'Book tickets for us and give me some money that we will need for the trip.'

'Book tickets now and we haven't even entered January yet … from now, Niloofar?'

'Alright, then give me some money. I want to start saving and buying some necessities for the upcoming baby.'

'I'll give you whatever you want, but I want you to know that I may not be able to travel with you to London, as I have many responsibilities, and I cannot leave them without a provider.'

'You can at least come with us and then return after a few days to deliver me, and then return after three months to take us back.'

'I don't know if I can do this too, but I will try.'

'Mansour, I will have two children, how can I carry them alone?'

'This is not a problem, my dear. There are many helpers for hire on the ship, and you will spend the first three days alone in your cabin with your children. In the port of Bombay, you will meet your uncle and his children, isn't that right?'

'Yes, that's true, but I am a woman with two children. Is your business more important to you than us?'

'No, of course not, but I am busy, and I have complete confidence in you.'

And he said to himself … *(I will not be able to stay away from Sheikha, that seductive and lethal female who tortured me with her love and the magic of her body. I will not stay away from her for even one day, and when you travel, I will marry her).*

And then he noticed what she was saying … 'Mansour, why have you changed like this?'

'I have changed! What do you mean?'

'I mean that I didn't expect this from you. You used to love me very much, and whatever I asked of you was answered. When you refused, you would convince me of the reason for your refusal. But now, I don't even see you, and if I see you, I see a different man. You can't even stand my touch, or look me in the eye, or approach me …'

'That's because you're pregnant.'

'I'm sorry, but you didn't convince me. This isn't my first pregnancy, and I am not used to you being like this.'

He couldn't respond or comment on what she said, and he felt remorseful about her. However, his obsession with Sheikha had turned his world upside down, as he had become like an animal driven by his instincts, forgetting his family, wife, children, and even his business.

The next day, Niloofar wrote a letter to her grandmother in London, reassuring her about her and her child's condition and pregnancy, and confirming that she would travel to see her in June. The days passed slowly and miserably for Niloofar as Mansour stayed away from her until the day of her delivery.

On a rainy night, Niloofar woke up screaming from labor pains, and Mansour was not by her side. Her mother-in-law and Sanota rushed to her, and Sanota woke Moftah up.

'Moftah, Uncle Mansour is not at home, what do we do now, Aunt Noura?'

'What's wrong?'

'She's giving birth!'

Angrily …

'I will go and call him from that whore's house!'

'Don't say that, Moftah, and don't do that. I fear he will get angry with you or something like that.'

'This is Haram. His wife and children are here, in a difficult situation, and that whore is enjoying his closeness and love, warming her bed! I'm sure he's there now!'

'We don't want him and we don't want him here. I hate him after all the respect and admiration I had for him. Never mind him now. Come on, let's take her to the clinic.'

'And how do we take her? On a bicycle in this cold, rainy weather?'

'Yes, on the bicycle. She will sit on the bicycle, I will hold her, and you will push the bicycle. And I'll carry some blankets so we don't all get sick from the rain.'

'Okay then …'

'Let me take Aoushah to older Aunt and we'll get ready to go.'

She found Mansour's mother at the door of the room, and Sanota was very afraid.

The mother carried the baby, Aoushah, saying: 'I heard the whole conversation, don't be afraid, I won't mention your names.'

And they carried Niloofar on the bike, with her heavy weight, and took great care to keep her stable on the bike, with the rapid labor pains, the heavy rain pouring down, the wet, unpaved and muddy ground, they finally reached the clinic with all kinds of hardship.

As soon as they arrived at the clinic, they took her straight to the delivery room, and sent for Doctor Sarouj who had told them to call her in case Niloofar was brought to the clinic in labor.

(73)

After two hours, Mansour returned home carrying shame and disgrace on his shoulders. He entered the house to see his mother and his son and Sanota's daughter sleeping in the courtyard.

'Mother, Mother, why are you sleeping here?'

She woke up from her sleep to pour on him a torrent of reprimand and rebuke.

'Don't you feel ashamed? Don't you fear Allah in yourself, your wife, your children, and in me?'

'What happened now, Mother?'

'Don't you know what happened, you shameful person? Who is that fallen woman that you associate with? The merchant's widow, isn't she? I wish I was dead and didn't know about this. I wish I died with your father, you despicable!'

'Mother, please stop scolding me. Lower your voice, people will hear. Niloofar will hear you.'

'Don't you feel ashamed saying this to me? Niloofar is not here. The poor thing is suffering from labor pains and went to the clinic. And you are absent in the arms of that fallen woman. May Allah take revenge on her.'

Angrily and loudly, he screamed: 'I forbid you. She will soon become my wife. Don't say this about her.'

'You are crazy. Get away from me. I don't want to see you!'

He left the house and went to the clinic, where Moftah and Sanota were standing in the corridor leading to the delivery room. When they saw him coming from afar, Moftah became angry.

And when he reached them, he did not seem to regret or even be embarrassed.

'Good evening.'

'Good evening.'

'Is your Aunt Niloofar inside?'

'Yes, she is inside, my uncle. It seems her delivery is difficult.'

'May Allah help her.'

'Amen, my uncle.'

'I will lie down there in the waiting room on the waiting chairs, and as soon as she gives birth, wake me up, Moftah.'

And he went cold heartedly, as if he was another person.

'Moftah, look at his actions, could he be under a spell?'

'I don't know, but when a man is infatuated with a woman, he becomes senseless like this one who was just spoke to us!'

After half an hour, Dr Sarouj came out, overjoyed.

'Hello.'

'Assure me, Doctor.'

'All is well, Sanota. A blessing came to her, a baby girl who looks just like her and both are in good health, Praise be to Allah. But where is her husband? Where is Mansour?'

'He's here, Doctor. I'll go call him immediately.'

Sanota ran to tell Mansour the good news because Moftah refused to go to him.

Mansour came in to see the baby, picked her up, and kissed her.

'She's beautiful and looks so much like you.'

'Where were you? Why did you take so long to come?'

'I had a lot of work at the office, and it was raining heavily.'

'We faced a great difficulty getting here with all that rain on the bike.'

'I was busy with work. What can I do?'

'You know that I was about to give birth , right?'

He got angry … and shouted: 'You're always like this, blaming me for everything and reprimanding me … I don't hear a word of thanks or kindness from you. I'm a busy man with a lot of work, why don't you try to understand the situation and adapt to it?'

And he slammed the door behind him. Mansour's behavior was different from usual; he had never treated her like this before. What was wrong with him? She burst into tears, and Sanota ran to comfort her.

Mansour's change greatly frustrated Niloofar and plunged her into a vortex of despair with no solution. She remained in the hospital for two days until she regained her health and Mansour came after she sent him Moftah to sign the necessary papers for the clinic. Throughout the journey, he did not utter a single word, and she remained silent as well.

Her husband was no longer her husband, and she began to say to herself:

He has changed a lot since money came into his hands, just as my grandmother said, men change when they see their wealth increase, and what I can do now is that I have lost the love of the only person who loved me and whom I loved. Now I have the love of my children, the love of my relatives in London, and the love of my husband's kind mother. I have their love, all except for his love. He didn't even turn to look at me as if I had become a monster).

He dropped her off at home and drove away in his car.

Mansour's mother received her and took the baby from her.

'Praise be to Allah you're safe, my dear.'

'Thank you, Mother. How are you? And how is little Mohammad? I missed you all so much.'

'We're fine when you're with us, my dear.'

'I'm with you, Mother, and Allah is with us.'

'Come, my daughter, come to your bed, and I'll bring you hot soup.'

Niloofar fell asleep exhausted from grief and woke up to the sound of the baby's crying, who was in pain from hunger. Her mother-in-law came running.

'My dear, get up and breastfeed her. The poor thing is hungry.'

'Yes, Mother, I'll breastfeed her.'

'You haven't told me her name yet.'

'I haven't named her yet, and Mansour hasn't thought of a name as well?'

'As her mother and the one who endured the hardship of giving birth to her, not Mansour, name her yourself, and don't be afraid.'

'As you mentioned, he won't care about this matter, for we have become his last concern.'

'What do you want to name her?'

'I want to name her after you, Mother, Hessa.'

'My dear, may Allah bless you. Little Hessa, it honors me that you named this child after me. This is a great pride for me.'

'No, you are our pride and honor, dear Mother.'

(74)

After a few days, Mansour announced his marriage to Sheikha, the widow of the merchant Saif Al-Sunaidi. Sheikha was known as a provocative woman whose fame for her femininity, arrogance, and beauty extended beyond the region.

It was said that her low reputation and excessive greed was what made Saif Al-Sunaidi ill and eventually killed him.

When Niloofar first learned the truth, she wept bitterly for a week and was overcome with sorrow, which weakened her and diminished her desire for life and trust in those around her. But then, she realized that her marriage had collapsed and her husband had left forever, and that she had to regain the responsibilities and trust that she had entrusted to him, whether they were material or moral. He may withhold his hand from spending on her and her children, and they would go hungry on some days with nothing to cook.

He also stopped funding the construction of the house, which was in the second building phase. His respect for his mother diminished day after day, and every time she reminded him of Niloofar's and her children's rights towards him, he would get angry and behave badly towards her. Until she sent to her daughters to ask to return with them to Fujairah, and returned the jewelry box to Niloofar.

'Will you leave me and my children alone, Mother?'

'I don't want to leave you, my daughter, but I have no choice. I am an old woman, and my health has deteriorated. I can't bear mistreatment anymore. Mansour is no longer my son. He has been consumed by the daughter of Satan, and he no longer distinguishes between right and wrong.'

'And is it easy for you to abandon us like this?'

'I haven't abandoned you, my dear, neither you nor your children. Only Allah knows how much I want to take you with me, so you don't have to go back to living in this hell.'

'I can't go anywhere. I am still his wife and the mother of his children. Perhaps he will come to his senses one day, and my studies at school are still ongoing.'

'May Allah help and strengthen you. Don't worry my daughter. I will send you money from time to time to spend on the house and to feed Moftah and his family. As for their wages, we will pay them when we have the means.'

Sanota who was heavily crying intervened: 'Don't worry, my aunt, we only want to and to be with my aunt Noura and her children, and what happens to them happens to us.'

'How well-raised you are, Sanota.'

'I was raised at your house, Aunt.'

The mother bid farewell to the children and Niloofar when her eldest daughter's husband, Adhijah, came with a transport car to take her to his house in Fujairah.

She advised her: 'I don't want to tell you my daughter, don't think about selling any piece of this box or neglecting it, as it is your asset for the future. Don't let go of it, keep it safe …'

'Yes, Mother, don't worry.'

The mother left to her eldest daughter's house, Adhijah, to get away from Mansour and his harm, while Niloofar remained alone to endure the loneliness, need, and bitterness of patience. The situation remained the same, and she returned to studying after her daughter completed her forty-day period.

After spending all her inheritance on his personal desires and business, Mansour stopped spending on her and her children, and refrained from sharing his emotions. She started spending on the house from the 500 pounds sterling that her uncle, Connor Moore, gifted her, which she had deposited in the bank for 950 rupees and bought tickets for herself and her children on the Tara ship to Bombay on June 10 of the same year.

With what was left, she bought a sewing machine and some fabrics, and sent a message to the women of the district to inform them of her readiness to receive requests for women's clothing weaving for small amounts, and the requests poured in.

She spent half her day sewing and the other half studying, sleeping, and taking care of her children. And with what she earned, she spent it on the house and saved for the expenses of traveling to London, and what her mother-in-law sent her, she gave Moftah and Sanota their wages, as the luxurious life she once enjoyed was no longer present.

(75)

On the verge of summer, Niloofar finished her academic year with excellence, as she was preparing to travel in a week.

Sanota entered the room and calmed her crying daughter, who was sobbing due to hunger.

'Why don't you calm her down, Moftah?'
'How can I do that? You are her mother … breastfeed her.'
'You could have distracted her with anything until I came back.'
'Please, Sanota, take your daughter and go away, as I am not doing well.'
'Why? What's wrong with you? How do you feel?'
'I am hungry, Sanota, and broke.'
'Broke? I understand that we don't have any money, but how are you hungry?'
'I mean that I eat only half a meal a day to save food for you, and as a result, I am starving. Do you understand?'
'Yes, I understand, but what can I do, my husband? I can't do anything.'
'You can, actually.'
'What can I do?'
'We can escape from this country and go to Qatar to live there and trade, and become wealthy. Nobody will recognize us there.'
'But what about my aunt Noura and her children? How can we leave them and go away?'
'I haven't forgotten about them, but your aunt Noura, will travel in a few days to her wealthy relatives in London, and she doesn't need to stay in this misery and suffer alone.'
'Yes, but …'
'Listen to me, Sanota. Bring her jewelry box, and we will escape to Qatar and trade it there to become rich. We will consider it a loan that we will repay once we have enough money. She doesn't need this jewelry box, and she doesn't

wear its contents. She has also confirmed on several occasions that she will not sell these jewels even if she and her children starve to death. Do you remember?'

'Yes, I remember, but what is our desperate need that would force us to steal her beloved jewelry and sell it to traders for its value? And what do you know about trade, Moftah?'

'Did you forget that I was the one who managed the business during the days of my late uncle, the merchant Saif?'

'Oh, right …'

'Believe me, ten or fifteen years from now, we will return to this country as masters, not slaves.'

'I'm afraid for my aunt Noura, her heart will be more broken than it already is.'

'Don't worry, your Aunt will travel to her family in London and maybe stay there. Perhaps she will come back with another jewelry box. Don't worry, how long will we remain slaves? And when Aoushah grows up, do you want her to serve the masters?'

'No, I don't want that!'

'Then go and find out where your aunt is hiding her jewelry.'

'I know where the jewelry box is.'

'Okay, then I will prepare for the trip the day after tomorrow, and you get ready and prepare food and clothes for us, as we will travel by one of the transport trucks. Do you understand?'

'Yes, I understand.'

'I don't want you to open your mouth and tell anyone about this. Do you understand?'

'Yes, I understand.'

(76)

The day before her trip, Niloofar sent Moftah to go and inform Mansour of her and the children's travel schedule to London.

And to take the necessary papers for the child Hessa to be able to travel. She then went to knit the rest of the clothes for her neighbors.

After she finished, she called out to Sanota: 'Sanota … I want to take a cold bath, please fill the bath tub for me. I feel very hot.'

'Of course, Aunt, right away.'

Then Moftah returned from Mansour's place.

'Aunt Noura … Aunt Noura.'

'Yes, Moftah. Please come in.'

'I went to see my uncle Mansour and informed him that you and the children will be traveling tomorrow on the Tara ship to Bombay, and he gave me the child's passport.'

'And what did he say?'

'He didn't say much, Aunt.'

'Tell me exactly what he said?'

'He said, "May they travel safely", Aunt.'

'Thank you, Moftah.'

'You're welcome, Aunt. Excuse me.'

Moftah had already prepared all their necessities and put them in the small shipping car parked outside the house. So that Sanota would bring the box to him when she had the chance.

Niloofar entered her room and saw Sanota sitting with the three children, Niloofar's children and her daughter …

'Sanota, please take this dress to our neighbor Umm Ibrahim. I just finished knitting it, and tell her that when I come back from the trip, I will finish the remaining clothes I have.'

'Right away, Aunt.'

'And don't forget to take payment from them, as I am in dire need of it. Go and I will sit with the children until you return, and then I will take a bath and you can stay with the children.'

'Alright, Aunt.'

Sanota left with the new dress in her hand to the neighbor, Um Ibrahim, and she Moftah outside the house.

'What are you doing here?'

'My aunt Noura sent me to take this dress to her neighbor now, and she wants her payment.'

'Is this the right time for it now?'

'Don't worry, I'll go and come back quickly.'

'As fast as lightning.'

'Don't worry, I'll be back right away.'

And Sanota went to the neighbor's house, and returned quickly with the knitting payment.

'Now come in and bring the baby, and before the baby, bring the box, do you understand?'

'Yes, I understand.'

She went in and gave her payment and waited for her to go take a shower. Niloofar carried her clothes and went into the bathroom.

As soon as Sanota heard the sound of water, she hurried to the clothes cabinet and pulled out the hidden jewelry box under the clothes, and took out a long golden necklace adorned with colorful precious stones and left it for her, saying to herself: 'I'll leave this for you, Aunt Noura, to wear on your trip.'

And she took a piece of cloth to empty the contents of the box and closed it tightly like a box, and put the necklace back into the box, and returned it to its place in the closet.

She spread a large sheet on the floor and put Niloofar's babies on it, and carried her daughter …

While she was leaving, she called out to Niloofar: 'Forgive me, Aunt Noura.'

Niloofar heard the sentence and wasn't sure if what she heard was true or a hallucination.

'What are you saying, Sanota? What did you say? I didn't hear you well, Sanota, what did you say? Sanota?'

And she didn't expect such a catastrophe to happen.

(77)

When she came out after taking a shower and saw her children on a mattress on the floor, she got scared and called out to Sanota, but there was no answer.

She picked up her daughter and held the little one's hand as she left the room to find that the house was silent.

She knocked on the wall separating her house from Sanota's and called out many times, but there was no response.

She was very afraid, so she put on her headscarf and went out the door to enter her neighbor's house. The road was crowded with people, and when she entered their house, whose door was wide open, she saw that the room was in disarray, with things scattered all over the place, as if they were moving out of this house. The cupboards were empty, and some of the boxes were empty, and the worthless items were thrown here and there.

Tears gathered in her eyes.

Could this be true?

Could they have escaped?

They could have told her they wanted to leave and quit their work, and she would have simply allowed them to look for another job. But they fled like cowards after she gave them her complete trust and affection.

She could not control her tears, which continued to flow nonstop. She left Sanota's house and locked the big door behind her and entered her own house and locked the door behind her.

'If Mansour hadn't left us and married another woman, I wouldn't have seen this day … it's just my bad luck that Mansour left me, then my mother-in-law, and now Sanota … everyone leaves me and abandons me except my sorrows and misery; they are my faithful companions who will accompany me as long as I am alive.'

She remembered her jewelry box and wished she would find it in the place where she had hidden it. She searched the closet and was happy when she found it. Yet she was greatly shocked when she opened it and found only the precious stone necklace.

She trembled and screamed loudly from the shock and disappointment with Sanota … until she collapsed, crying between her two frightened children.

The three of them slept from crying so much until the next day.

The next morning, the child woke up hungry, and she woke her mother and brother up. Niloofar got up with all her weight and sadness, heated the water to prepare milk for little Mohammed, then sat down to breastfeed her daughter while thoughts swirled in her mind from all directions.

After feeding her children, she prepared boiled rice with dried fish powder, for her to eat. Then she put on her cloak and headscarf, carried her children, and left the house to stand on the roadside corner.

She stood there until she found a driver who expressed his willingness to take them to the port the next morning, as everyone else refused because she was a woman with children, fearing that she might not be able to pay them.

She returned home to prepare her travel bag, a large bag for her and her children, and put everything they would need there. She remembered the stone her midget friend had left her. Had it also been stolen?

She lifted the side of the iron board from the bottom of the closet, put her hand in, and pulled out the roll in which she had placed it. She opened it, and the shine of the stone reflected in all corners of the room.

If she had hidden her jewelry in this place, it would not have been stolen, but what was the use now?

She wrapped the stone in a black cotton cloth to prevent it from showing up in X-ray machines used to check the contents of the bag. She placed on it the clothes and gifts that her mother-in-law had brought her before she left, men's cotton fabrics, silk and embroidered women's fabrics. In a small bag, she put long-term food, sweet water, a milk box, a feeding bottle, some baby diapers, and some clothes that she and her children would need on the ship, along with their identification papers.

(78)

The driver arrived early on the morning of the next day and carried her suitcase to the car. She had locked all the doors with the locks, and she and her children got into the car, heading to the port. After the driver was paid, the worker took her suitcase to her cabin, where she stayed for three days without leaving. She ate the bacon sandwiches she had prepared, breastfed her baby, and made the milk bottle from the drinking water she had brought from home.

On the third day, when the ship docked in Bombay, she remembered the first time Mansour was with her and the baby, and she wasn't worried about anything because he took care of everything.

The worker brought her suitcase down, and she gave him a tip. The porter came to take her suitcase outside, and as soon as she reached the arrival hall, she heard the voice of her cousin Michael calling her name. Mr Connor Moore and his children had traveled to Bombay to receive Niloofar and take her to London.

They headed from the port to the Taj Mahal Hotel, where she stayed with Mansour the last time. The places were the same, and the people were the same, except for Mansour, who was the only one missing.

'من لي أغلى منك ، فأنت ابنة الغالي وأطفالك هم أعز ما لدي.'

On the next morning, they went to Mumbai International Airport and boarded a plane traveling to the British capital, London.

There, her relatives welcomed her and her children with love, respect, and appreciation, and they asked about Mansour's absence, and she explained that he is currently very busy with work, and he only comes home for a little while.

She concealed all her distress and troubles from her family, but her wise old grandmother, Mrs Betty Moore, understood that there was something wrong.

One morning, Grandma Betty sent the maid, Magdalena, to wake Niloofar up and ask her to get ready to go out.

After she got ready and went down the stairs, Magdalena told her that everyone was waiting for her in the car to go out.

The driver was Bernard, and next to him the sat the servant was carrying the child Mohammed, and in the back seats was the grandmother Betty holding the child Hessa.

Niloofar rode with them and they set off to Hyde Park.

'The sun is beautiful today and it will benefit me and the children, right?'

'Yes, my dear grandmother, it is. Have you had your breakfast or not yet?'

'No, I haven't had it yet.'

'Neither have I, but what about the medicine?'

'Don't worry; I brought the medicine with me. We'll have our breakfast today at a cafe next to the river in the park, where children play on the grass. What do you think?'

'It's a great idea, my dear thoughtful grandmother.'

'There is no one more precious to me than you, you are my precious granddaughter and your children are the dearest to my heart.'

(79)

They sat in the garden having breakfast while the servant took the children for a walk in the double stroller.

'You look relaxed and at ease today, my dear.'

'Yes, Grandma, I feel comfortable and safe with you.'

'Do you know, my dear, that when you come to stay in London, you regain your glamour, your energy, and your happiness?'

'Really? Does it show on me?'

'Of course, it does. Why don't you stay here? This is your father's home. Stay with us, settle down and live here.'

'I can't, Grandma. Mansour is alone and he wants us.'

'Don't lie to me, Niloofar. Don't lie to me.'

Niloofar trembled, and her eyes welled up with tears.

'You are my flesh and blood, my dear. I feel you as I felt my son Gerald. You always fail to hide the things that bother me, and each time I reveal them. What's wrong, my dear? Why has happiness left your life? I saw the sadness and its traces around your eyes when you arrived, and I haven't seen you wear your jewelry since you came.'

'I'm fine, Grandma. Why are you worried like this?'

And in a harsh, angry tone: 'Didn't I tell you not to lie? Lying is what I hate the most in this world, and I hate to see it coming from someone I love so much.'

Niloofar lowered her head and burst into tears.

'Please, Grandma, my heart is swollen with the wounds of the whole world. I need you as a balm for my wounds. I have no one to complain to except you and God.'

The grandmother approached her, hugged her, and kissed her.

'I am a balm, but this balm will not heal wounds other than your wounds, my daughter. Take out what's in your bag. I intended to leave the house today so that no one except me could hear you. Everything you say is a hidden secret.'

Niloofar told her grandmother everything that had happened to her since the day she arrived in Dubai.

When her grandmother heard everything that had happened, she said: 'Do you know that I have the power to keep you here and prevent you from seeing that wicked man again?'

And tears streamed down her face.

'Please, Grandma, don't do this. His children need him, and I need him too. I still love him, and I will always love him. Even if he pushed me out of his heart today, there will come a day when he takes me back into his heart again, asks for forgiveness, and I'm sure of that, Grandma.'

'Do you mean that you are like a piece of tissue paper that he uses when he needs you and then throws you away when he is done with you?'

'No, Grandma, I am his wife and the mother of his children.'

'And what will you do if he divorces you?'

'Please don't say that, Grandma.'

'Let's assume, just for argument's sake, that everything that happened to you was not anticipated, is that right?'

'That's right.'

'And if he divorces you, what will you do?'

'I'll come here to live.'

'Then you should divorce him yourself; file a lawsuit demanding a divorce.'

'No, Grandma, I won't do that. I don't want my children to grow up far from their father, as I did.'

'Your children are now far away from him, my dear.'

'I'm confident that it's just a phase, and life will return to normal with him.'

'I don't know what to say to you?'

'Don't say anything, Grandma, just wish me luck.'

'I always wish you luck, but how can my life be happy when I see you returning to that hell again?'

'I will stay with you for another three months, and then I will return to Dubai to stay there for only nine months because it is the last year of my studies there. Then I will come back here to join the British Institute, and when I finish the Institute, I will specialize in medicine at one of your strongest universities. This means that when I return from Dubai next year, I will stay with you for seven or eight years until our situation stabilizes, and maybe forever.'

'Yes, that's true, but promise me that you will take enough money with you for the next nine months so that you don't have to weave people's clothes.'

'I cannot take the money, Grandma, because if I took it, I would be without work, and my free time would increase, and bad ideas would play in my head that would lead me to ruin. Let me work and eat and feed my children from my daily bread. It is only nine months, and then I will be close to you and spend on you as you wish.'

'How simple and pure you are, my dear. God will give you everything you ask for and deserve.'

(80)

Niloofar spent three months in Britain during the summer, one month of which was in London and two months she spent in Scotland at her rural family's house with relatives and some friends. It was truly a relaxing vacation where she collected herself and gained strength to support her personality. After that, she returned to Dubai as planned, took care of her children, and took them to school with her before returning home to knit people's clothes. She didn't cook much because her neighbors sympathized with her situation and the fact that she was alone with her young children, so they would send her food most of the time. The nine months almost passed without any news about Mansour.

On Eid al-Fitr, Niloofar wore a beautiful, colorful dress that she had knitted herself and another one for her daughter, and she dressed her son in a white outfit that her uncle Connor Moore had given her as a gift.

She made the milk and vermicelli drink with nuts that people in India make during the holiday to offer to visitors. Her neighbors, who had started visiting her to get to know her since she began knitting their clothes and giving their children private lessons in science, drank the drink, and the children greeted her with small coins called "ana" (a small coin that was insignificant in value, but it was enough for the children to buy sweets and nuts).

On that day, her mothers-in-law, sisters-in-law, and their children came to visit her.

She learned from them that Mansour had become a frequent traveler for business affairs, and that the four children of the merchant had been taken by their uncle to Qatar to live with him after their mother married Mansour. Niloofar was very sad because with this news, it seemed that Mansour's bond with his wife had become stronger, and there was no hope for him to return to her and their children.

Niloofar completed her education and was awarded a certificate by Dr Mohammad Ayoub, which was authenticated at one of the academic centers in the British region.

On June 20, 1966, Niloofar traveled with her children to Bombay, and from there, her uncle and his children accompanied her to Britain, this time to stay for a very long period.

Niloofar joined the diploma classes in the Medical Sciences Department at the British Institute (University of London) and devoted all her attention to her education, forgetting all her sorrows and pains. Her children were taken care of by their grandmother, who looked after their food and drink and their schools.

In university life, Niloofar met many Arab and even English youth who approached her with romantic gestures, but she did not pay attention to anyone who showed her affection, as that part of her heart was only for Mansoor, who had become among the dead due to his prolonged absence.

After completing her two-year diploma, she joined St George's University, affiliated with the University of London's medical school.

(81)

On December 23, 1968, on the night before Christmas Eve, Bernard Niloofar left home and returned with Mrs Beatrice Moore, the wife of Mr Connor Moore.

Niloofar entered the living room to see her grandmother and the two children, Mohammed, aged five, and Hessa, aged three, decorating the Christmas tree with their grandmother.

As soon as she saw Niloofar, her grandmother addressed her, saying: 'You came back early today, my dear?'

'Yes, grandmother … Ah, what a beautiful tree this is!'

'It is the little ones' decoration, my dear. I hate to say it, but you must read the telegram. You'll find it on the table.'

'And who is this telegram from, grandmother?'

'It's from Dubai, from Dr Sarouj.'

'Ah, yes, that's my friend. I miss her so much.'

Niloofar read the telegram:

"Dear Niloofar,

I have missed you so much. I hope you and the children are well and happy, and that you have the most enjoyable time with your relatives during the Christmas holidays. I hope you will visit Dubai as soon as possible to see how your husband is doing.

Yours truly and lovingly, Dr Sarouj Deepak."

'What is this, grandmother? What's wrong with Mansour?'

'I don't know, and I don't care enough to know.'

'I am going travel to him.'

'And how would you travel now, Niloofar, during the holidays?'

'I'm sorry, but I have to travel. I'll travel as soon as possible.'

Niloofar agreed with her cousin Michael Moore to travel to Dubai as soon as possible.

They traveled on a British plane from London to Bahrain and then took a sea plane that arrived in Dubai Creek on Friday, December 30, 1968.

As soon as they set foot on the ground, Niloofar ran to the nearby clinic with her cousin following her, after asking the airline official to send their belongings to the clinic.

In the clinic, she spoke eagerly and urgently: 'Hello, peace be upon you.'

'And peace be upon you.'

'May I see Dr Sarouj?'

'Yes, but she's on a medical visit outside the clinic. You can wait for her; she will be back soon.'

They waited in the waiting room for about an hour until Dr Sarouj entered. Niloofar ran to her.

'Niloofar, is that you?'

'Yes, Dr Sarouj, how are you?'

She embracing her tightly.

'I'm fine, my dear. Thank you for coming. You look very beautiful in your European clothes. You're really European.'

'Oh, I forgot to introduce you to my cousin Michael Moore.'

'Welcome, Michael. I'm honored to meet you.'

'The honor is all mine, madam.'

'Tell me, Dr Sarouj, what did you mean in the telegram?'

'Oh, Niloofar, thank God you're here.'

(82)

Doctor Sarouj spoke to the nurse at the reception desk and said: 'Please tell the clinic driver to take us to Al Maktoum Hospital, and then I will go home as my shift for today has ended.'

'Okay, Doctor.'

While the nurse went to find the driver, the doctor waited with Niloofar and Michael at the clinic entrance.

At Al Maktoum Hospital, the doctor led them to the men's ward where the patients were lying on beds on either side of a long room. Niloofar was afraid of the sight of the suffering men, each one in pain from a different part of his body.

The doctor took Niloofar by the hand and led her to the second to last bed on the right side of the room, the one Mansour was occupying. He was in a terrible state, unconscious, with his body tightly bandaged, and stitches visible on his chin, forehead, and nose, with black bruises around his left eye and lips.

Niloofar's body shook with fear and tears flowed from her eyes as if they were recording every second, minute, hour of the pain she had endured for days, weeks, months, and years of separation.

'Hold yourself together, Niloofar, as Mansour is in a lot of pain, heavily sedated most of the day … and his condition is unstable, with no significant improvement in the past fifteen days.'

'What happened to him, Doctor? Please, tell me what happened?'

'Calm down, cousin, please.'

'Tell us doctor, what happened?'

'Please, follow me.'

Then the doctor led them out of the patient's room to the corridor.

'Please sit down, it is a more suitable here than inside the ward.'

And they both sat there, eagerly waiting to hear her speak while staring at her facial expressions …

'Two weeks ago, I was in the clinic about to finish my shift, when suddenly an ambulance and a police car caused a commotion in the clinic's courtyard. I and the other doctors went outside to see the emergency situation; a car had fallen from the Al Maktoum Bridge, causing significant damage to the bridge, the street, and the cars that were damaged along with their owners. There were three people involved, and one of them was Mansour, who was in critical condition, while the other two suffered moderate injuries ranging from fractures to severe wounds.'

Niloofar gasped and blushed intensely, and tears started to roll down her face …

Michael held her close to his shoulder and said: 'Please, my dear, try to keep yourself together. Please, continue speaking, doctor.'

'Yes, Mansour was in a severe state of exhaustion, and the four of us doctors were at a loss as to where to begin. Should we revive his heart? Should we stop the bleeding caused by the large wound in his chest? Or should we deal with the seventy percent of his shattered bones? The situation was truly a nightmare, and I have to admit that death was more merciful to him than living in such excruciating pain for the rest of his life. When he was brought to the treatment room, he looked like a pile of meat, not a human being …'

Niloofar wanted to interrupt the doctor, but Michael stopped her.

'After a resuscitation process that took longer than usual for any heart, and an effort that I cannot describe to you, his heart began to beat again, but it was weak. We then started to remove the dust, dirt, clotted blood, and shattered glass debris intertwined in his flesh and skin. We cleaned the wounds and stitched them to stop the bleeding, thank God. However, the most difficult task was his shattered bones that no one here could begin to set. The challenge was that if one part of a bone like the hip was set correctly, then the leg bone would inevitably be set incorrectly, and the bone structure was already distorted.

'When he woke up the next day, he was unable to speak or even open his eyes for more than five seconds, and all he could do was make moaning sounds.

'We sent a letter to the Al-Maktoum Hospital to consult if they could admit him because they had the most advanced medical facilities and equipment.

'They agreed immediately, and we transferred him to the Al-Maktoum Hospital. A visiting orthopedic surgeon from Germany, Schzelinger, treated him for a week and then requested to send him to Germany, India, or the UK as soon as possible. Such a treatment journey would cost millions of rupees. I remembered that you are a resident in the UK and forgot all recent disputes between you, as he is still your husband and the father of your children. Isn't that right?'

(83)

When Niloofar heard the doctor's words, she cried a lot.

'What do you think his recovery chances are, doctor?'

'I cannot answer that question, you are a medical student, tell me from your point of view what do you think his recovery chances are?'

'Very weak …'

And she burst into bitter tears. After they left the hospital, they went to the clinic to take their belongings and necessities, and from the clinic, they took a taxi to the nearest hotel and booked two separate rooms for each of them.

In the lobby of the Ambassador Hotel, Niloofar was standing with her eyes swollen from crying.

'Tell me, my cousin, what do you intend to do?'

'I don't know, Michael, I am confused. This is my husband and the father of my children, the man I loved and still love, and I will always love him until I die. How can I leave him? And I remember before I traveled here, my grandmother told me: "Be careful, Niloofar, not to let me see or deal with Mansour as long as I live." Meaning, she won't stand by me in the matter of his treatment …'

She bowed her head and when she looked up, she saw in the darkness of her eyelids, at that moment, her midget friend approaching her. She was surprised to see this awakening and looked back for a second to see him approaching her, a third time he reached out his hands to her, and in the fourth he was holding the shiny stone she found in her clothes.

And she stood still.

'What's wrong, why did you stop? Are you okay?'

'Yes, I want to make an international call!'

'Who are you going to call?'

'I'm going to call my uncle Connor … your father …'

She told her uncle about the issue and asked him to help her with the transportation of Mansour on a plane to Hemer Smith Hospital in London.

Then, she went back to Michael …

'What did you tell my father?'

'I told him everything that happened with Mansour, and that I want to transport him to London on a plane equipped with medical equipment to ensure his safe travel and arrival. I also asked him not to tell my grandmother. He said he will inquire with the hospital tomorrow morning, and I will call him back tomorrow evening.'

'Do you know, my dear cousin, that this issue will be very expensive, more than you think?'

'I know, and I am willing to bear all the consequences.'

'Do you think your grandmother will help with Mansour's hospital expenses?'

'I don't think so, but things will work out, trust me. I won't need money from anyone.'

He kept silent, as he didn't know how to respond.

(84)

On the following day, after returning to the hotel from visiting Mansour, Niloofar said to Michael: 'Wait for me here, I'll call my uncle.'

She called her uncle and got all the necessary information to transfer him to the Hamersmith Hospital in London. She was informed that the hospital would provide the patient's designated section on the plane with oxygen devices, strong painkillers, and a skilled nurse to take care of the patient until they arrived at the hospital, all of which were part of the paid treatment plan, which would cost a lot of money.

The next morning, Niloofar requested medical reports from Al Maktoum Hospital for Mansour's condition, and she also obtained medical documents requiring his urgent travel for treatment. She got his passport and identification papers, which the police had deposited with the hospital authorities when they were extracted from the wreckage of his Land Rover.

Moreover, her uncle sent a telegram to an important person in the British diplomatic corps in Dubai, who in turn sent a telegram to the Hammersmith Hospital, which sent oxygen devices, some strong painkillers, and a skilled nurse on a naval plane that landed in Dubai Creek specifically to transport Mansour, Niloofar, and Michael to Turkey's port, then to Turkey's international airport, and finally to London Heathrow Airport on January 9, 1969.

Mansour was immediately admitted to the hospital.

After ensuring his condition at the hospital, Niloofar returned home and kissed her children, hugged them, and cried a lot …

'Where did you go, Mom?'

'I traveled far away and came back to you.'

'Why are you crying, then?'

'I am very sad, my dear, because your father is very sick.'

'Does he love us?'

'He loves us very much.'

'Then I want to see him.'

'I will take you and your sister to visit him when he recovers, so let us pray to God to heal him.'

As the grandmother intervened: 'Welcome back, my dear, how is he now?'

'He is as good as dead … he poses no danger, Grandma.'

'His share of the world.'

'But it's my share too.'

'What do you mean?'

'I mean that my fate and that of my children are tied to it.'

'Nonsense …'

'Please, Grandma, not in front of his children. You asked me not to involve you in anything related to him, didn't you? And I will keep my word and not bother you with anything related to him.'

'I don't understand what you mean?'

'I just want some space; please let me try to fix what time has ruined.'

'As you wish.'

(85)

She quickly changed her clothes and asked the driver, Bernard, to take her to her uncle's office, Connor Moore.

When she arrived at Mr Connor Moore's office, she greeted her uncle: 'Good evening, Uncle.'

'Ah, good evening, my beloved daughter. When did you arrive in London?'

'We arrived three hours ago, me, Michael, and Mansour. We took him to the hospital, and then I went home to put away my things and change my clothes, and came to see you immediately.'

They both were quiet and an eerie and unsettling silence descend upon them.

'Are you okay, Uncle?'

'I'm fine, my dear.'

'You seem preoccupied. What's wrong?'

'Well, Niloofar, I agreed to let Mansour come to London for treatment, and as you know, the cost of his treatment will be a fortune. Yet, you assured me that you would cover all the expenses.'

'And I stand by my word. I knew you were worried about this, so I want to show you something.'

She pulled out a red package from her bag and retrieved the shiny stone from it.

'What is this, Niloofar?'

'I believe it's a gemstone.'

'Where did you get it?'

'It's a long story that I can't tell you, but rest assured it's a gift. I didn't steal it from anyone or anywhere.'

'What do you want me to do?'

'I want you to find me a precious stone dealer who will buy this stone from me at a good price, and keep the sale and purchase confidential, even from your closest associates.'

'That's a great idea, Niloofar. Let me think about it first, and then I'll find a precious stone dealer, contact them, and summon you afterwards.'

'Take your time, uncle, but keep in mind that I'll pay for travel expenses, as well as the cost of tests and scans next week.'

'Don't worry, we'll find a solution quickly.'

After a week, she returned from university to change her clothes before going out to visit Mansour, who had regained consciousness, but his mind was still in a deep sleep. As she prepared to leave, Magdalena knocked on the door.

'Please come in, Magdalena.'

'Miss, Mr Connor called and urgently requested that you come to his office to meet Mr John Ferguson.'

'Really? I am leaving now. Did you inform Bernard, please?'

'Yes, ma'am.'

Forty-five minutes later, Niloofar knocked on her uncle's office door, and he allowed her to enter.

'Welcome, my daughter. Let me introduce you to Mr John Ferguson, the diamond expert and trader. This is Niloofar Moore, my deceased brother Gerald's daughter.'

'Hello, sir. It is a pleasure to meet you.'

'Likewise, madam. I am pleased to meet you.'

After exchanging greetings and questions, Connor asked Niloofar to show the trader the stone. After examining it, he confirmed that it was a raw diamond of high purity, and that no human hands had intervened in it yet.

'Really, Mr John? And how much do you think the stone will be worth if we sell it?'

'Let me think for a moment. I can cut this stone into five hundred pieces that are ready for retail. Each piece can be sold for 1,000 pounds sterling.'

'What are you saying, sir? I know that raw diamonds are expensive. My niece and I will not accept less than 4,000 pounds sterling for each piece of this stone.'

'No, that's too much.'

'As you wish, Mr John. I can look for a French or Italian diamond trader. They pay without negotiation.'

'Don't say that, Mr Connor. Let's come to an agreement. What do you think of 2,500 pounds sterling?'

'No, I will not accept less than 4,000 pounds per piece of this stone.'

The trader, John Ferguson, agreed, knowing that he was still a winner in this deal, since the stone was worth twice that amount. The deal was concluded, and a few days later, the trader purchased the stone for two million pounds sterling. Niloofar paid the initial costs of the project …

(86)

Half of the remaining amount was allocated to Mansour's treatment, while she requested from her uncle to use the other half to purchase a property for her and her children to live in for the rest of her life.

She remembered her midget friend's words when he told her in a dream, 'Please forgive me. I will leave you the most precious thing I have to compensate you for all the pain. Just as you killed the dearest person to you, I will save the dearest person to you.'

She looked up at the sky and said: 'Thank you so much, my friend. You have saved my husband. I will never forget your kindness, and I want to let you know that I have forgotten all the harm you have caused me and my children.'

Days passed, and Niloofar was busy with her studies, her children, and the hospital where her husband was recovering. His heartbeat had become regular, his blood pressure had stabilized, the wounds on his chin, forehead, and chest were healing and new tissues were forming, announcing the beginning of the healing process.

A month later, when she got into the car with Bernard after leaving the university, she greeted him by saying: 'Hello, Bernard.'

'Hello, madam. Excuse me, Madalina told me before I left the house to inform you that the hospital called and asked for you urgently.'

'I hope everything is alright. What happened?'

'Don't worry, madam. We'll go there now, with your permission.'

'Yes, please.'

At the hospital, Niloofar headed towards the room of the doctor in charge of Mansour's case.

'Good evening, Dr Taylor.'

'Good evening, Mrs Moore. Please come in.'

Niloofar entered and sat in the chair opposite him.

'I was informed that you called me to come to the hospital?'

'Yes, ma'am. We called to let you know that Mansour has fully regained consciousness. He is now fully aware of his physical and mental condition, and he has requested to see you more than once.'

'He asked for me by name?'

'That's correct. He said he wants to see his wife, Niloofar.'

'Can I see him now?'

'Yes, please. But don't pressure him with words or actions. Let his mind recover his memories on its own.'

Niloofar walked to Mansour's room, feeling both happy and scared.

How would she face this situation? How would she confront the years of separation? Did she really forgive him for the pain he caused her and her children? Could she confront him now to ease the burden of pain on herself?

She arrived at the room, feeling confused. Where should she start the conversation with him?

(87)

She knocked on the door and waited for his response.

'Please come in.'

She entered, dragging her feet and feeling the increasing pull of gravity. She stood before his bed.

'Niloofar … You've finally come. I've been waiting for you for so long!'

Tears streamed down his face without pause.

She stood silently, staring at him as if trying to absorb his pain. But her heart was breaking for him, and her body wanted to succumb to the pull of gravity.

'Are you still angry with me, Niloo?'

What should she say? Yes, to make matters worse? Or no, to lie to him?

'I know you're still angry with me, and that's your right. I won't blame you. Could you sit in front of me? I want to look at you. You've become even more beautiful and feminine. You seem to have grown taller and stronger.'

'Yes, I've grown a few centimeters taller.'

'How old are you now?'

'I've just turned twenty.'

'Masha'Allah, you've become a mature and successful woman, with the whole world ahead of you. As for me, I've just turned thirty-one, and I've lost everything. I've lost my wife and children, my money, my business. And now, I may lose my health and my job.'

'Please, spare yourself and don't talk too much.'

'Let me finish. I've been holding back for almost two years, and now it's time to let it all out and free myself from the internal torment.'

'There's no need to tell me now. You can tell me later.'

'Listen to me now, please. You know that after the merchant Saif Al-Sunaidi passed away, I took on the responsibility of taking care of his children. I would send them food and money and visit them personally, standing outside the house to check on their well-being without entering, knowing that there was no man in the house. One day, their mother sent for me because one of the children was suffering from a fever, and I went to check on him or take him to the clinic.

'When I arrived at their house at noon, the door was open, and I knocked but got no answer. I gathered my courage and went into the courtyard to see the children sleeping in the room opposite the door. One of them was vomiting in the courtyard by the palm tree, and their mother was standing by him, supporting him. She was wearing a transparent black dress that showed off the best of her body, and her hair was flowing down to her waist. Her heavily kohl-lined eyes and her overpowering perfume made me fall for her, with a love filled with excitement and adventure. My love for you, the quiet, clean, pure love for my house and children was overtaken by this black, impure love for her. I was caught in the whirlwind of this thrilling experience, away from your safe embrace.

'I indulged in her and her pleasures, forgetting the world and everything in it. When my skin touched hers, it was as if I was in an endless ecstasy, an overwhelming desire without limits. I even put all my money and trade under her command to prove my love and loyalty to her.

'When the Qatari uncle of the children found out about our marriage, he sought a court order to regain custody of the four children, who were his brother's sons, and as soon as the ruling was issued, he took the children and traveled with them. There was no one left in the house except me and her. In the morning, I would go to work, and she would go to the institution to manage it, and in the evening, I would take her place at the institution, and she would return home.

'On that horrible day, I went to the institution and stayed there even after the Maghrib prayer. I was signing on some transactions and I needed the institution's stamp but I could not find it. The worker told me that the lady might have taken it home with her. I drove the car home and another car was standing by the back of the house in the dark, and the view was suspicious ...

'I tried to open the door of the house, but it was tightly closed from the inside, and I was filled with suspicion when an old lady, one of the neighbors, came out and looked at me with sympathy, shaking her head as if a tragedy had occurred. At that moment, I couldn't bear it and started throwing a wooden box and some scattered stones here and there. I climbed the wall of the house to listen to those moans that I was familiar with. The devil possessed me, and I became like a raging bull. I opened the door of the room to find the traitor stripped of her clothes and modesty, with the egg merchant, that young boy. Unconsciously, I began to hit them with my hands and feet while they screamed and tried to cover themselves. Then they pushed me to the ground and threw the wardrobe on me. I went to free myself from under the heavy wardrobe, using all my strength to remove the weight from my body until I was completely exhausted. By then, they had already got into the car parked behind the house and fled. I ran outside to catch up with them when I saw a crowd of people gathered and showing sympathy for me and condemning them. One of them pointed out that they had fled in that direction. I started my car to catch up with them, but I lost control of the car and collided with a column, sending me flying in the air and crashing down on the asphalt. I didn't realize what had happened after that, but I knew that I was dead for sure as I fell.

'I wish I had died and not experienced this moment of weakness. I wish I had died before causing harm to you, the children, and my beloved mother, whom I hurt so much with my words. I don't deserve your compassion or your money or your efforts to keep me alive and restore my health. I took away your money and happiness and gave it to that fallen woman who robbed me of my money, reputation, honor, and health. Please forgive me, Niloofar, forgive me …'

The pillow on his side was soaked with tears.

She approached him and held his hand.

'I forgave you when I saw you fighting for your life, and I forgave you when I saw you in the faces of my children, and I forgave you because I am still your wife, and I still love you.'

(88)

The first two years of treatment passed, during which Mansour received bone-setting treatment in the hospital and his bones were set multiple times because there was always some malfunction in the setting process due to the severity of the accident. Each time, the doctors had to break the bone and reset it, causing Mansour a lot of pain, and he considered it a punishment from Allah for his wrongdoing, in addition to losing everything, until his entire body was properly set. In the third and fourth years of treatment, Mansour underwent two more years of physical therapy to prepare him for using his body parts and moving correctly.

In the same year, Niloofar graduated with honors from the St George's University of London's medical school and had the opportunity to train at the Royal London Hospital for a year before practicing medicine independently. With everyone's efforts and Niloofar's persistence, Granny Betty finally agreed to allow Mansour to come and stay at the house after he completed his four-year treatment period. Mansour came to the house, and Granny Betty forgot what he had done to Niloofar. They lived a happy life, and after more than eight years of separation, the couple reunited.

Two days after Niloofar completed her training at the Royal London Hospital, she gave birth to her third child, a beautiful baby with European features, blond hair, and blue eyes, whom they named Hamdan.

They spent another year in London before returning to Dubai, where Niloofar sold the property that had tripled in value and shared the money with her grandmother Betty and her uncle Connor, despite their strong refusal to accept it. She had converted her money into a bank check, in addition to the amount she had saved from her medical training job, giving her a total of 1.02 million pounds sterling.

Niloofar boarded a plane with her recovered husband Mansour and their children, Mohammed, Hessa, and Hamdan, from London Heathrow Airport to

Beirut International Airport. From there, they took another plane to Dubai International Airport on March 3, 1975.

When they returned to Dubai, the state of the country had greatly and noticeably improved. The country had been liberated from British colonialism, and the reconciled Emirates had united to become one country under the presidency of His Highness Sheikh Zayed bin Sultan Al Nahyan, the ruler of Abu Dhabi, and his brother, His Highness Sheikh Rashid bin Saeed Al Maktoum, the ruler of Dubai.

The streets were adorned, the buildings had risen, private cars and taxis had multiplied, some of the main streets were planted with flowers, large electric lamps lit up the streets, and advertising signs and traffic signals were put up … The country was undergoing major development.

When they arrived at the house they had lived in, all the buildings had been replaced with new ones behind the Gold Souk and the area was called "Souk Murshid". They then rented a room at the Astoria Dubai Hotel until they found a house to rent and Mansour bought a Datsun car to drive.

Their house, which Mansour was about to finish building, had parts of it demolished and the children vandalized it. Mansour renewed his old ownership papers from the Land Department and requested a new design from an engineer to start building the house after obtaining approval from the municipality.

As for Niloofar, she submitted her papers and certificates to the Dubai Health Department to work at Rashid Hospital as an obstetrician and gynecologist, and Mansour gifted an electronic tools store in Bur Dubai area to sell washing machines, refrigerators, and electrical tools.

With time, Mansour's trade flourished, and he had a large electronics showroom in Dubai. The number of their children increased to become eight: four males – Mohammed, born in 1963, who studied engineering and worked as an engineer in one of the oil fields in Abu Dhabi, Hamdan, born in 1974, who studied law and opened a law firm in Dubai, Ahmed, born in 1978, who studied medicine like his mother and specialized in cardiology, and Hamed, born in 1982, who joined the Air Force Academy to become a fighter pilot.

And four daughters: Hassa born in 1965, who studied natural sciences to become a biology expert, Maryam, born in 1976, studied dentistry. Alia, born in 1980, had artistic inclinations and studied fine arts, and Khawla, born in 1984, joined the media industry to become a TV presenter.

Niloofar excelled in the field of medicine, where she worked at Rashid Hospital for ten years before opening her own clinic in the Qarhood area. She became a consultant at Rashid Hospital, Dubai Hospital, and Al Wasl Hospital.

As the children grew up and each went their own way, Niloofar did not spare any effort in raising them and taking care of her husband and their beautiful large house, where she hired four maids of different nationalities, an Asian driver, and a farmer.

Her relationship with Mansour's mother and family returned to the way it was before, and they purchased land in Fujairah where they established a large farm with a big house, a swimming pool, and farms for roses, tomatoes, and palm trees. They also purchased land in London and built a private house for themselves to stay in during vacations.

(89)

One day, Niloofar gave a lecture in the university lecture hall that lasted for two hours, which included the lecture itself and answering students' questions. After feeling exhausted, she walked heavily out of the university campus where her driver was waiting for her. Along the way, she thought about how to retire from her job to dedicate herself to her husband, children, and grandchildren, as she was almost sixty years old now.

In the living room, she slumped heavily on the couch and rested her head on the back of the couch. Her maid brought her a glass of water and asked if she needed anything.

'No, thank you. I'll go wash up and pray, and you can prepare the table for all of us to have dinner. Who's at home now?'

'Everyone except your daughter Khawla.'

'Right, she said she's going shopping with her cousin Amal, and they might have dinner together.'

'Yes.'

'It's okay. Prepare the table and save her share of dinner, and if she comes back hungry, serve it to her.'

'Yes, madam.'

She walked slowly and wearily, taking the elevator to the top floor and entering her dark room to find Mansour deep in sleep.

'Mansour ... Abu Mohammed, how long have you been sleeping? Didn't you go to pray Maghrib? What's wrong, my dear? You didn't call me all day. You know, my dear, I liked your idea and decided to retire from my job and work only one or two days a week at the clinic. What do you think?'

He didn't respond, still asleep.

She bathed and dressed, then returned to him again to wake him up.

'Mansour ... Mansour ... Abu Mohammed ... What's wrong? Why won't you get up?'

She shook him a little, but he didn't stir. Her heart raced with fear, so she sat next to him and took his pulse, realizing it was slow. She screamed …

'Mansour, my beloved, answer me, please!'

She turned on the lamp next to him to see his face bluish, realizing he may have had a heart attack. She ran to the phone and called for help, then called for her children and the servants.

Mansour was taken to the intensive care unit, and the whole family waited for him in the waiting room, except for Niloofar, who stayed with him as a licensed doctor. From time to time, she went out to reassure her children about Mansour's condition.

The resuscitation process took two hours, and Niloofar prayed to Allah to lift the affliction from her husband, grant him health and wellness, and keep him her companion until the end of her days. He was the source, the one who made her a human being in the first place, and who planted life in her after her misery. She wouldn't be able to live without him.

(90)

After the first resuscitation process, Niloofar received a report from the responsible doctor regarding her husband's condition. The report stated that Mansour's blood pressure had risen significantly, which caused him to have a stroke while he was asleep, and that happened five hours ago, making it beyond control. If it had happened while he was awake, the medical staff would have been able to control it. The stroke led to partial paralysis in his right limbs, and due to his advanced age, the chances of his recovery are slim.

She entered the room quietly, and he was still asleep, affected by the stroke and the sedative dose he was given to sleep for the next 24 hours to regulate his blood circulation and pressure. She did not want to see him sick after that treatment period in London, and burst into tears. After a moment and upon hearing the machines connected to him, she tried to control her emotions and decided to be the strong person who controls things now until Mansour regains his health and life returns to normal. However, her tears refused to obey her, so she wiped her hands, recited the Fatiha chapter of the Quran seven times, blew on his face, prayed for his recovery, and left the room quietly to the responsible doctor's room.

'Excuse me, doctor. Can I talk to you a little about my husband?'

'Of course, please sit. Your husband's name is Mansour Mohammed, isn't it?'

'Yes, he is my husband. I want to ask you some questions and consult with you on some matters.'

'As it is clear that Mansour has suffered a partial paralysis on the right side of his limbs, and that it is difficult for him to recover and return to normal, being a doctor, I know that one should not give up seeking treatment and recovery in the hands of Allah, isn't that right?'

'Yes, definitely.'

'So, I thought about suggesting the idea of taking my husband to the United States to continue his treatment. I know that the country has provided all modern medical means, but I prefer to take him to a hospital in the United States, which is one of the best centers for treating strokes.'

'Yes, why not, but as a doctor here, I advise you not to rush. Treatment here is just as effective as treatment abroad.'

'Yes, but I don't want to spare any effort or waste time. Do you understand me, doctor?'

'Yes, you are a doctor yourself and you know what needs to be done. Start the procedures when he wakes up from anesthesia so we can decide what to do.'

'Yes, if he wakes up from anesthesia and his condition stabilizes, we will start the travel procedures and how to transport him.'

'Before that, you should send the report to the hospital so that you receive a quick response.'

'Yes, I will send it immediately. Thank you very much, doctor.'

'You're welcome. I wish your husband a speedy recovery.'

In the waiting room, everyone asked her: 'How is my father now?'

Niloofar told them everything contained in the report, and what was discussed between her and the doctor, and the idea of taking him on a treatment trip to the United States, specifically to the best medical center in Nebraska for treating strokes. She would prepare all the necessary documents, submit a retirement request, and apply for an unpaid leave until retirement was completed.

Her eight children agreed to her proposal, and her eldest son, Mohammad, suggested that he take care of all the necessary procedures and travel with his father. However, Niloofar refused his suggestion and preferred to stay by her husband's side during his treatment trip. The children could take turns accompanying her on this treatment journey.

(91)

After a long treatment journey, Mansour and Niloofar returned from a trip that lasted more than nine months, after he had fully recovered and stabilized his health.

On their first Friday after returning from America, they gathered in the farm's lounge after the noon prayer, as usual on every Friday, but this Friday was different from its predecessors. On this Friday, the couple returned completely healthy after an absence that lasted more than nine months, and they returned to see that new members had joined the family tree. Their youngest daughter, Alia, gave birth to twin boys named after her father, Mansour, and their grandfather, Mohammed. Their eldest son, Mohammed, had become a grandfather as well, as his son Ali's wife had given birth to a girl named Marwa. Hamdan's foreign wife, Susan, was also present. He married her fifteen years ago during his bachelor's degree studies at Harvard University in the United States, and she gave birth to his son and daughter, whom he kept hidden from his family for many years and only visited four times a year. He finally introduced them to his wife and children after being fed up with her continuous complaints about staying away from him. Even though, she was his first wife, the other wife enjoyed his closeness and the position of the main wife, and officially the mother of his children. They all blended in well with his wife and children, and the entire family.

This family gathering was like a beautiful family party, where the sounds of laughter, beautiful conversations, classical music, bright colors of clothes, and varieties of food and drinks that captivate the hearts were heard. Relatives and congratulating kin attended the party to celebrate Mansour's safe and healthy return.

Although there were breaks for prayer, the party continued until the stars twinkled in the sky.

(92)

Mansour stood alone in a distant corner, atop a pile of dirt that had been placed on the side of the farm for some agricultural work. He gazed up at the sky, but his little grandson, Suhail, saw him and crept up behind him to surprise him. Mansour felt him coming and turned around just as the child climbed up behind him and stood behind his back.

Suhail boomed out in a loud voice: 'Ha ha ha! I found you!'

'Oh my God, you scared me! Who are you?'

'I am the monster.'

'What do you want from me, oh monster?'

'I want to eat you.'

'Why do you want to eat me? I'm old and my taste won't please you.'

'Nope! I'll still eat you.'

Then he turned to the little one and hugged him tightly while tickling and kissing him until his laughter filled the sky and added joy and happiness to that night.

On top of that pile of dirt, Mansour spoke to his grandson saying: 'Do you see this dirt my child? We were created from it and we will return to it.'

'Yes, Grandpa I know but I can't imagine how we were made from this dirt. I mean how we were made until now?'

'You'll know when you grow up, my son. Don't rush it.'

He then raised his head towards the sky and said: 'And do you see that Al-Yaah up there?'

'What is Al-Yaah, Grandpa?'

Mansour pointed with his finger towards it saying: 'That big bright northern star. The brightest star. Do you see it?'

The little one pointed at it with his tiny finger and asked: 'Is that it?'

'Yes, my son, that's it.'

'It is truly beautiful and radiant, my grandfather.'

'Indeed, it is also very useful, as it has always guided us and our ancestors on long sea voyages during difficult times. It was the beacon of light that led us, and without it and Allah's guidance, we would not have reached the farthest lands and benefited from them.'

'Really? Then it is like a compass, isn't it?'

'Yes, my child, it is. Its importance in navigation remains significant to this day. And I want to tell you something.'

'Allah has created for every person in life their own special Al-Yaah star.'

'Where is my star, grandfather?'

'You will find it someday, my child.'

'When? Perhaps now or in the future, I do not know exactly. But you will find your star someday.'

'And where is your star, Grandfather?'

'It's here with me, living with me in the house.'

'In the house! Where?'

'It's with me.'

'Can we see it too?'

'Yes, all of us can see it.'

'How and when, Grandfather? And what does it look like?'

Mansour took out his wallet from his pocket and opened it up to show Suhail the picture inside.

The child exclaimed: 'This is a picture of my grandmother Niloofar when she was young and beautiful!'

'And she still is beautiful today.'

'Did you name her as your star?'

'Yes, she is the one I named as my star, she is the one I named my Al-Yaah.'

(The End)

Al-Yaah

Al-Yaah, the North Star, has long been a crucial navigational tool for sailors in the Arabian Gulf and neighboring countries. The origin of the word is "Itijah" meaning direction, from which it was shortened to "al-jah" and then further abbreviated to "jah". Over time, it transformed into "yaah" like other letters that that went through historical shifts in pronunciation.

The North Star, also known as the star of Capricorn, being the brightest star near one of the Earth's poles, it is almost always visible and appears stationary in the sky due to its proximity to the celestial axis. Since it is a little close to the horizon, directions can be determined using it, except in areas close to one of the poles of the earth where the North Star is high in the sky. Therefore, the importance of this star has been recognized since ancient times and it remains one of the most famous stars in the sky today.